THE BROOD

OTHER TITLES BY REBECCA BAUM

Lifelike Creatures

THE BROOD

a Novel

REBECCA BAUM

Published by Thomas & Mercer, Seattle
www.apub.com

EU product safety contact:
Amazon Media EU S. à r.l.
38, avenue John F. Kennedy, L-1855 Luxembourg
amazonpublishing-gpsr@amazon.com

ISBN-13: 9781662530562 (paperback)
ISBN-13: 9781662530555 (digital)

Cover design by Caroline Teagle Johnson
Cover image: © photo_iget, © Thang Tat Nguyen, © wenpu wang, ©McKinneMike / Getty

Printed in the United States of America

For my dear cousin Perch.

Chapter 1

May 2013

A funeral dirge thundered from the pipe organ of Saint Catherine the Divine. From her pew, Mary Whelton contemplated the passing casket, a slow-moving missile piloted by pallbearers. Decades ago, she'd kissed the lips of the body ensconced within, swooned in the gaze of the eyes now sewn shut, entwined her bare flesh with limbs destined for the worms.

But she felt nothing.

The casket came to rest on the funerary platform, and the congregation awaited the priest's invitation to be seated. The church was packed despite the remote location, a hamlet ninety minutes from Syracuse. The front pews swelled with the ranks of one of the oldest families in the Northeast. Mary's section was next, filled with other high-ranking attorneys and the partners from Bell, Pruett, Dreiser & Carrington, the law firm founded by today's guest of honor, Theodore "Teddy" Bell III, dead at eighty.

The nation's business and social aristocracy occupied the rest of the church, discreetly texting or else surveying the who's who of mourners, including Mary. At fifty-seven, she cut an imposing figure. Her dark tailored suit emphasized her elegant height and lean physique, her broad shoulders holding the world at bay. A single silver streak shot through her dark curls. Hazel eyes blazed above the mild puffiness of a recent cosmetic uplift. Strong cheekbones tapered to an angular chin broken by a slight cleft.

Mary and her partners had barely managed cursory nods of greeting as each filed into the pew. Once a certain camaraderie had existed between them. But that ended when Teddy retired from the firm twenty years ago. She was grateful that the hard wooden pew was spacious enough to allow several inches between their expensively clad bodies. But as the opening prayer began, Mary's assistant, Michael, slunk past her and squeezed in, packing the pew tighter. "Sorry," he whispered. She shot him a withering glance, then dropped her eyes to her lap.

An emerald-cut diamond smoldered on her middle finger, a gift to herself years ago after her first six-figure bonus, not long after she'd ended the affair with Teddy. They'd met the summer before her final year of law school, when she'd defied the odds as an unconnected nobody and landed a highly competitive internship at his firm. She'd spotted Teddy's disease right away—the desperate need for validation, the mothlike gravitation to pleasure of all kinds. She'd welcomed his advances, though she hadn't consummated their affair until the following year, after she'd been offered an associate position with his firm in New York City.

It helped that back then, Teddy was gorgeous and debonair, with oceanic eyes and a smile that melted the clothes right off her. During the nine-year affair, they'd met regularly in the firm's pied-à-terre overlooking Central Park. He'd also mentored her professionally and socially until New York's power elite accepted her as one of their own. By her midthirties, she'd become a killer corporate lawyer with a special focus on sensitive investigations such as sexual harassment in the workplace, ironically informed by the various personal and professional pitfalls she'd encountered during her affair with Teddy.

After her position and value were firmly cemented, she'd ended the affair. Despite six months or so of Teddy buzzing her apartment at all hours in embarrassing displays of raw, wounded male ego, they'd eventually found equilibrium as friends and professional allies—even as his dalliances continued at the firm and elsewhere. She'd helped clean up at least a dozen of his messy affairs, drawing up paperwork and acting as intermediary with the angry, victimized, or opportunistic women.

Her gaze slid left, to the pew nearest the altar, where Teddy's widow, Claire, clutched a tissue in her gloved fist, their son on one side, daughter on the other. Teddy had hardly spoken of his wife during his affair with Mary and only a handful of times afterward, during rare moments of remorse. Each time he sang her praises, swearing she knew nothing of his cheating and whining about how he didn't deserve her. Mary had always remained silent on these occasions. Who knew what and who deserved whom—these matters were between the two of them.

More than thirty years later, Mary was still with Teddy's firm. She'd passed on multiple offers to become a senior partner, eschewing title and bureaucracy for the thrill and power of the legal battlefield. Now she was by far the firm's biggest rainmaker. As soon as optics allowed, the partners would phase their founder "Bell" out of the firm's name, along with all traces of the man.

Of course, Teddy had been loved and admired by many, both personally and professionally. Even after he retired, politicians and business leaders frequently tapped him for advice. And he'd continued advising the firm in an "of counsel" capacity until last year. But the rumors that had circulated for decades—that he was an inveterate womanizer, at times a sleaze—were a growing liability. The cultural winds had shifted, and it was unlikely Teddy's reputation would survive intact. He might surface as a minor or major character in a tell-all memoir or a salacious docuseries. Best to put distance between him and the firm to minimize any potential collateral damage.

Mary's fingers slipped beneath her dense coils of hair to probe a scaly patch behind her ear. After three miraculous months of clear skin, her psoriasis had reappeared. Dozens of inflamed splotches on her arms were sure to follow. Fortunately, she was heading to her Cape Cod home immediately after the funeral. Alone on her private island, she'd be free to wear short sleeves. Despite having spent her entire career at the same firm, only her assistant knew of her condition. Humans, especially her cutthroat colleagues, were always scanning for weaknesses. She could not reveal even a hint of bodily compromise in her work environment.

A pair of solemn altar boys lit a row of large candles, casting an amber glow over the sanctuary. The mourners rose, sat, knelt, and rose again. Teddy's coffin seemed dense and immutable, a tide of Catholic ritual swirling around it. The air grew heavy with incense and grief, both real and manufactured. As Mary stood from kneeling after an especially long prayer, dizziness overtook her, and her legs almost gave way. She'd been practicing intermittent fasting and hadn't eaten since the night before. Gripping the pew in front of her, she locked eyes with Christ, impaled on a great, gilded crucifix above the altar. In the flickering candlelight, the wound in his side became a gaping mouth, and she was transported back to Saint Agnes's. Despite years of mental discipline to avoid morbid excursions into the past, her mind crept toward the childhood she'd barely survived, like a dumb animal sniffing its own excrement.

The summer sky, vast and blue, beckoned to Mary as she waded through the field of waist-high grass surrounding the orphanage. She knew her eyes should be down, following the other children. At eight, she was the oldest. The rules said the older ones kept the younger ones from harm, away from the raging creek and sagging barbed wire fence.

But alien sensations had possessed her—wonder, openness, joy—uncoiling her tense muscles and lulling her into a mild trance. Her vigilant gaze softened, and rainbow refractions danced in her peripheral vision. Her clenched jaw melted into a smile. She allowed herself to be invaded by pleasure, swaying in a warming sun that, after a while, seemed to shine from within her.

Wham! A sudden blow to her skull split her vision in two. She cried out. Her knees buckled, and the ground rushed toward her. As she lay in the grass, a metallic hum throbbed in her head. A familiar silhouette loomed above her. "Selfish! Staring at clouds when you're meant to mind the children." The nun's coif and veil eclipsed the sun. Grass bowed against her black robes. "If it's only you you're thinking of, then it's you you'll keep company with."

Later, locked in a small lightless closet at the foot of the basement stairs, Mary mortified her flesh with a stolen tack, leaving a row of small punctures on her inner thigh. "Remember that feeling," she hissed to herself as metal penetrated tear-streaked flesh. Unbidden, a warmth arose, a remembered comfort in her own skin beneath a welcoming sky. She twisted the tack deeper. "Don't go near it," she panted. "You hear? Never again."

"You okay?" Michael whispered, rescuing Mary from her reverie. She rebuffed him with a stern look. Of course she was okay. Her blood sugar was out of whack from the fasting, nothing more. This also explained the dredging up of an old memory that was both useless and distracting.

The communion line began to form. A matronly woman in a beige skirt suit shuffled past Mary's pew. After accepting the wafer, the woman returned, this time facing Mary. She seemed familiar. Mary followed her progress until she was reseated, hand resting on the arm of a well-known congressman. It dawned on Mary that she was one of Teddy's ex-lovers, though twenty years older and sixty pounds heavier.

Mary frowned. The woman had once been beautiful. How had she let herself descend to such a state? At least she'd landed a congressman. Teddy's hush money must have opened a few doors before she'd let herself go.

But hadn't there been a stay at an institution? Perhaps a suicide attempt? Mary remembered hearing something in the years following the secret settlement, which she had helped to engineer. Why attend Teddy's funeral, then? But Mary knew why. The husband wouldn't miss the opportunity to rub shoulders with New York's political and social luminaries, no matter what the deceased had done to his wife.

Deep within, Mary felt a stirring of emotion. Could she be grieving Teddy despite having disconnected from him years ago? The feeling expanded, leaching into her chest like poison from a dart. This wasn't grief. It was guilt—or rather some slippery, embryonic version of guilt—for the fate of the congressman's wife.

The organ blasted through the church again, but Mary barely noticed, instead raging against the unwanted feeling. She was not at fault for how the woman's life had turned out. Survival meant every person for themselves, and some were too weak to hack it. Not Mary. Had anyone ever offered her protection at any point in her life? Much of her childhood was a blur, but there were plenty of choice snapshots to sift through if she were so inclined.

And what of the boardrooms of leering men she'd endured for decades? The old boys' clubs? Or early in her career, when her own clients indulged in obnoxious innuendo even as she reviewed their cases? Today's young female hires at the firm seemed eager to sprint to HR for every slight, real or imagined. The list of "inappropriate" behaviors had expanded to fill volumes. But Mary had navigated her humiliations on her own, forging each into the thick skin, cool rationality, and steely demeanor for which her clients now paid considerable sums. Mary's gaze again found the congressman's wife. She silently projected her verdict: *I owe you nothing.*

After the service, she fell in behind the rest of the funeral attendees exiting the church. Through the bright marble archway, a faint noise, like chanting, drifted from outside. She planned to beeline for her car, avoiding conversation, so she could hit the road and reach Cape Cod by nightfall. There she'd begin the ritual she employed with all her difficult cases. For three weeks, she would map out every second of her upcoming trial, designing a strategy that would blindside the opposing legal team. The case was especially thorny. Her client, MaxFauna, a multinational corporation, was accused of fostering a misogynist culture that led to the alleged rape of an employee.

She was fiercely protective of her island retreat. It had become her secret weapon, a space of pure creativity where the full force of her intellect came online as she kept company with the only person in the world she trusted completely—herself. While she was there, everyone at the firm was under strict orders to withhold communication unless she initiated. Her few friends knew the same.

While descending the church steps, she caught sight of a crowd of protestors and realized they were the source of the chanting. Many carried signs: **DEATH CAN'T SAVE YOU** and **RIP: WOMEN'S LIVES DESTROYED BY THEODORE BELL**. A dozen press vans darkened the road in front of the church, cameras trained on the funeral procession. The mourners either fled or stood their ground to express outrage at the intrusion. Mary slipped through the throng to her Mercedes in the church's crowded parking lot.

She steered toward a side entrance, narrowly avoiding a Lexus and its panicked driver, and glanced at the chaos on the church lawn. One of the protestors locked eyes with her, yelling, "It's Bell's fixer! Mary Whelton!"

Mary shot from the parking lot as three press vans revved their engines and accelerated onto the road. She sped through a yellow light and headed for the wooded outskirts of town. Moments later, she checked the rearview mirror. The lead van was far enough that footage of her would be hazy at best. Normally she would have stayed to confront them. But the mere mention of her name in relation to this protest could trigger a storm of nasty press that might affect the MaxFauna trial. The firm might even ask her to surrender her role as lead attorney.

She left the village behind and began making random turns onto back roads, gradually ascending a worn mountain range. Every few minutes she caught sight of one of the press vans, still far behind but clearly in pursuit. Her irritation grew, overriding her caution. She was on the verge of slamming the brakes to either threaten them with a lawsuit or cajole them with the promise of an exclusive when she spied a dirt road nearly obscured by the surrounding forest. She braked, threw the car into reverse, and tucked into the shadows.

From her hiding place, she watched the three vans zip past. She waited another few minutes, then barked at Siri to activate Waze. The digital voice directed her through a series of turns onto a narrow, winding road. The landscape shifted from fallow fields to patches of forestland and back again. When Waze offered to navigate a faster route, she accepted. Trees fell away, revealing the washed-out remnants of a town, houses pressed against the road, every other structure abandoned.

A derelict gas station with one working pump marked the end of the town. The woods reappeared, only denser, gray trunks hemming the road. "Dammit," she hissed, as Waze once again offered a faster route. She peered at the console. The network connection wavered. Somehow, she was off course by almost sixty miles on a barely paved backcountry road. She lit a cigarette, the one a day she allowed herself, and released a plume of smoke. She knew the game with the press piranhas. She might be lost and behind schedule, but at least she was out of their chum-filled waters for the next three weeks.

As she accelerated through a winding curve, something exploded against the windshield, obscuring the glass with yellow ooze. Scattered in the viscous smear were tiny ovoid heads, shattered wings, and segmented insect bodies. Jerking the wheel, she veered onto the bumpy, unpaved shoulder. An embankment flashed into view. She swerved to stay on level ground but slammed into a tree, the car halting with a sudden violence she wasn't prepared for. The steering wheel slammed her forehead. She fumbled with the seat belt and wrenched open the door, fighting to remain conscious. After staggering forward, she fell to her knees. Darkness descended.

She surfaced once more, briefly. A pair of scarred work boots appeared near her face. Then she blacked out completely.

Chapter 2

Mary lay on a rickety pallet beneath a worn quilt, fighting her way back to consciousness. Her head pounded. Her body ached. She resisted the weight of her eyelids, focusing on the hazy movements at the far end of the long, narrow room.

When her eyes adjusted, she made out a hulking figure standing naked before a metal washtub. Short, coarse hair, like wax-clotted honey, capped the skull. Planes of flesh flowed across belly and back, gathered in hummocks of hips and thighs.

The great body turned toward Mary and raised a dripping, wadded cloth from tub to skin. The glow of a hanging kerosene lamp revealed mountainous breasts that cast a shadow over much of the lower torso. The thickset legs tapered into bare feet.

Fighting grogginess, Mary dragged her gaze elsewhere, to a window just beyond the figure. The warped glass panes distorted the landscape, a forested mountain range rose-tinted with either dawn or dusk.

Beneath the quilt, Mary's fingers brushed against her skin. She flinched, feeling bruising and tenderness. Her eyes flew open.

Teddy's funeral.

The car wreck.

Why was she in what appeared to be a decrepit cabin? And why hadn't this backwoods person called 911 instead of taking a sponge bath? She raised her arm to summon the woman, but the world tilted and nausea overcame her. An image arose of her forehead slamming into the steering wheel. She fell back on the pallet, panting.

When equilibrium returned, she propped herself on her elbows, taking care not to move too quickly, and took in the rest of the cabin—the raw-wood ceiling and floor, the rustic windows punched into each of the four walls, the screen door that was the single point of entry. Wooden shelves bore neat piles of mismatched plates and bowls. A hand pump perched above a second washbasin adjacent to the stove. A wide bench occupied the rear wall, between a battered TV and a simple wooden trunk. Light came from several kerosene lamps placed throughout the cabin.

A vague unease arose in Mary as she studied the crude surroundings. Where the hell was she? Perhaps only a short time had passed and the ambulance was en route. She patted her suit pockets, searching for her phone and the key fob to her car. Finding neither, she scanned the room in vain for her Fendi handbag.

She pushed her aching body to a seated position. An object thumped from the pallet to the floor. She leaned forward, hoping to find her phone. Instead, she discovered a carved wooden figure with exaggerated breasts and a protruding behind. The feet tapered to a sharp point.

A soft cry sounded from across the room.

Mary started, triggering another wave of dizziness, though less intense than the last. When Mary's head cleared, the woman was staring at her. A timid smile softened the rugged countenance. Cupping one enormous breast, the woman hurriedly toweled the moist skin beneath. An abscess clung to the side of her torso. Mary shuddered. Probably a boil from lack of hygiene. Today's sponge bath must be a rare occurrence.

"Where am I?" Mary asked.

The woman donned a short-sleeved flannel shirt and corduroys, then approached the pallet. Her eyes flicked from Mary's face to the floor and back again. She looked to be fortyish but displayed a bashfulness more suited to a young girl. Something was definitely off. A familiar dread settled around Mary, of unknown quantities and loss of control. She decided to take a firm tack. The woman mustn't be indulged into thinking Mary was going to sit around and chat.

"Who else is here?" Mary asked.

The woman mumbled something.

"Excuse me?" Mary asked.

The woman cleared her throat and tried again. When she spoke, her voice was a rusty spring, as if seldom used. "No one comes by here. It's just me. And you."

"Understood. Well, thank you for helping me. I'm feeling better now. I'll take my purse and be on my way."

Mary rose from the pallet, swayed, then plopped down again. Darkness danced at the edges of her vision. The gash on her forehead shrieked, seeming to split open anew.

The woman was suddenly on her knees next to the pallet, holding a mug to Mary's lips. Mary drank deeply of the chill water, then accepted the cold compress the woman placed on her forehead. She slumped against the wall behind the bed, focusing on the coolness of the cloth until the world came back into focus.

The woman remained kneeling. "You said you'd come back. With the Brood." She shook her great head. "Mostly believed you. But"—her eyes shone—"sometimes I didn't."

Mary tossed the wet compress aside. So the poor ding-dong thought she was someone else. That would explain the hangdog stare of affection. She sat up and straightened her blazer. "Ma'am, I think there's some confusion."

The woman chuckled and swatted her knee. "I ain't no ma'am. Just Girl. Like always."

"Girl," Mary repeated. Possibly the most unimaginative nickname ever adopted. She extended her hand. "I'm Mary."

"I've got something to show you!" Girl leaped up with surprising ease. Something in her voice, a childish pleasure, set Mary's teeth on edge.

Girl moved toward one of the cabin's few nonutilitarian items, a small painting on the far wall. Mary peered through a window at the rear of the room. A wall of trees bordered the yard, entry point to the dark wood that ascended the mountain range. There was no sign of the road where she'd left the Mercedes.

"My car. I assume it's outside?" Mary asked. The impact had been violent, but she had no memory of the airbags deploying. Perhaps the car was still drivable.

The woman seemed not to hear the question. "Been a long time. Brood's come twice," she said, removing the painting from the wall. She returned to the pallet, head bowed, and presented it to Mary for inspection.

Up close, the painting was more like a tapestry, a muddy swirl of rust and brown at the center of the thin cloth. In a few places, the paint had hardened into clumps. "But I shoulda kept faith," the woman continued. "You always said I had ants in my pants."

"You can put away your craftwork." Mary glanced briefly at the tapestry. "I'm not whoever you think I am. I need my phone. Please. And my car. Now." Her pumps were tucked alongside the pallet. She slipped them on and moved to stand.

"Craftwork?" Girl pressed the tapestry closer, forcing Mary to remain seated. Her face flushed and the timid smile returned. "My first blood, Mama. Saved it for you."

Mary recoiled. Her gaze dropped to the tapestry. Like a gruesome Rorschach, the outline of a moldering pair of underwear, stained and crusted with old blood, sharpened into focus. Girl traced a finger along the edge of the frayed cotton. "Them men you used to bring here. You said after I got my first blood, I didn't have to do that no more. But you left. Before the blood came."

"Get that away from me!" Mary snapped, repulsed by the underwear, but more by the bottomless yearning that burned in the woman's dark eyes. She stood, rising to her full height, inhaling deeply to stave off dizziness. She was almost as tall as Girl. Her shoulders were just as broad, even with the woman's girth. She fixed Girl with a chilly stare. "I'm not your mother. I'm Mary Whelton, an attorney from New York City. I have no children."

Girl stumbled backward, as if blown by the force of Mary's words. Her face crumbled. Her dark eyes flooded.

"I appreciate everything you've done to help me," Mary said, softening her voice. No need to be unduly cruel. "But it's getting late, and I'm expected. People, my staff, will be looking for me."

As she spoke, Mary tested the truth of this statement, running through the people who normally populated her universe. In fact, no one would be looking for her. By now, she should have been alone on her private island, organizing her office overlooking an ocean awash in the setting sun. Everyone in her life knew her time in isolation was inviolable.

"Now please. Take me to my car," Mary said. She strode past Girl and pushed open the screen door leading to the front porch. The evening air was bracing after the cabin's close confines. Unseen insects thrummed a steady beat from the forest depths, a pulsing, high-pitched buzz. A battered, decades-old Ford pickup was parked a few feet away beneath an elm tree. A cluster of small amber husks, perhaps dried leaves, gathered near the front tires. "Or just give me a ride to town, if that's easier," Mary called to the woman.

Still wobbly, Mary paused to clutch one of the wooden poles supporting the porch's overhang. Again, she scanned the landscape, searching for the road she'd followed into this godforsaken nowhere. The chances of a hospital in less than a hundred-mile radius were slim. But within what she imagined was a region riddled with opioid users, a walk-in clinic was likely.

A footpath wound past the truck and continued for a hundred yards to the edge of a quarry, a huge bowl with blasted rock walls gouged thirty feet into the earth. Rain and mineral runoff had collected at the lowest point, forming a cloudy, aqua lake. The footpath continued along the lip of the quarry, then ascended abruptly to a dark, cave-like opening in the mountain. Just above the cave, supported by a thin crust of earth, an ancient oak tree pressed lush branches against the purpling sky.

A plump black insect landed on Mary's sleeve as she stepped from the porch. Six jointed legs sprang from the dark thorax. Its iridescent wings were flecked with orange. The eyes, bulbous red orbs, smoldered in the light of the setting sun. She recognized the bug, a cicada, from her days at the orphanage. A bright-green variety had frequented the old maple trees surrounding the yard. She glanced back at the truck tires, realizing that the amber husks were in fact molted cicada shells.

Mary cocked her thumb to flick the bug from her arm. Pain exploded in her shoulder joint as her arm was yanked backward. "What the fuck!" she shrieked. The force spun her around, her body rebounding against Girl's breasts.

"No children," Girl hissed. Her mottled face swam into view, streaked with snot and tears. "Like you told them men that I was your sister." The woman pounded her own skull, her roars echoing up the forested slopes. "Wouldn't claim your one and only daughter." From the forest, the chorus of insects grew louder, as if sympathetic to Girl's anguished rage.

"I'm not your mother!" Mary gasped. Powerful fingers dug into her biceps. Her knees buckled.

"All I did was wait! And wait!" Girl said, each word weighted with anguish. "Who kept this ground safe while you was gone? Who made ready for the Brood?" Girl gripped Mary's lapels and hauled her down the porch steps.

Mary stumbled, blindly punching at Girl's flesh. Her designer pumps skimmed the ground, plowing through cicada shells and catching in the moist earth. She strained to see the space in front of her. Girl seemed to be heading for a mound of earth with a hobbit-like door.

"You get the root cellar, Mama! Like you used to do me," Girl sobbed. She flung open the small door.

The doorframe scraped Mary's face as she was tossed into the shadowy interior. Shelves of dusty mason jars flashed past as she tumbled to her hands and knees. She knelt in the dirt, struggling to regain her breath. The door slammed, followed by the creak of a rusty lock.

"Padlock still works, Mama! After twenty-seven years. How 'bout that?"

At first Mary was glad for the quiet. Girl's tortured keening had gone on for some time, just outside the root cellar door, before she'd wandered off. But soon the silence revealed different sounds, the skittering of tiny claws and other mysterious susurrations. The pounding of her own heart. A faint fungal odor arose from the hard-packed floor. The last dregs of daylight filtered through a tiny, dirt-smeared slit of a window, reinforced with layers of chicken wire. She climbed to her feet and violently shook the door handle. The ancient wood rattled and bowed, but the padlock held. "Girl!" she cried, pounding the door. "You are holding me against my will. That's a felony. Understand? A crime." She pressed her ear against the rough wood. "You could lose your home!" she yelled. "Not to mention your freedom. Let me out now, and I'll consider not pressing charges."

She held her breath, listening for a heavy footfall or a plaintive sob. Her fingers curled into icy fists. A map unfolded in her mind; the day's journey traced over 250 miles from Manhattan to this wretched place. The distance felt more like light years than miles. She backed up and rushed at the door, throwing all her weight against it. "Goddamn it," she gasped, clutching her shoulder.

She massaged her temples, wheeling between fear, outrage, and disbelief. How had she stumbled into a B-grade horror film? Her day had started in the glittering marble lobby of Bell, Pruett, Dreiser & Carrington, where she'd hosted a press conference to prime the court of public opinion on behalf of MaxFauna; then the long drive to Teddy's funeral, where she'd averaged ninety-five miles per hour so as not to arrive late; and now the climax—entombment by a feral mountain woman.

And all because of the press. Her spinning emotions halted at anger. Reporters—whose fickle hungers she normally exploited with ease—had caused this. She searched her blazer pocket for her phone, prepared to record the name of every journalist she'd recognized at the funeral so she could sue them into oblivion. But her fingers closed on empty air.

The last rays of sunlight retreated. Soon the root cellar was shrouded in total darkness. The walls of earth seemed to press closer, the ceiling to dip lower. The heavy fungal odors of the lightless space triggered visions of drowning in wet mud or being buried alive.

She jumped to her feet and rattled the door handle. "Hey!" she yelled, fist hammering the door. "Is anyone out there?" Her voice, normally a precision instrument, trembled and caught. She pounded the door until her breath was ragged. Exhausted, she slumped against the door. She was acting like a fool. Instead of thrashing about, as unhinged as the cretin who'd imprisoned her, she needed to examine her surroundings, to formulate a plan. How secure could a hole dug into a hill for turnip storage be?

She tested the door handle once more, then felt for hinges. Perhaps the cellar contained a tool or some other object that could bust the frame or break open the door. She traced the contours of the screws, the point where wood met metal, the gap between door and frame. Then she examined the tiny window, pressing her fingers against the rigid chicken wire covering the glass. Four, maybe five, layers of heavy gauge mesh were fastened to the frame with a multitude of nails and industrial staples. And then she paused, struck by a grim realization.

What was it the woman had been yelling before she'd thrown Mary in here? The multiple layers of wire had been installed not to secure chickens, but a young girl.

A faint clicking, like tiny mandibles opening and closing, stirred in the darkness behind her. Or was it coming from above? Her pulse raced.

"Get it together, bitch," she muttered.

She'd faced off against stone-faced juries and coldhearted judges, gone toe-to-toe with sociopathic CEOs, battled fire-and-brimstone DAs who'd staked their political futures on a guilty verdict against her clients. She succeeded in every instance because of her preternatural cool. Her male peers called her "ice queen," "ball crusher," "the emasculator." She earned every misogynistic moniker in the book, fair and square.

And bugs were going to bring her down?

But it was more than the hidden insects. The darkness and the dirt, the confinement, her inability to see her own body. For the second time today, she felt herself being nudged in a direction she'd forbidden herself to go. The past.

She sank her nails into her thighs, letting the pain anchor her in the present. Her breathing slowed. Her thoughts settled. This situation was bizarre, yes. But ultimately it stemmed from a misunderstanding. She could fix this. Her lawyer's mind, rational, calm, solution oriented, would command the situation, as it always did.

The snot-glazed face flashed across Mary's mind. The woman was clearly insane—she called herself "Girl" after all. And she was capable of violence. Mary's shoulder throbbed as if to support the assertion. But Girl had seemed happy, even gentle, before Mary had burst her bubble. Was it possible she wasn't inherently violent? Judging by the disgusting menstrual souvenir, her love for her monstrous mother was genuine and enduring. She shuddered, remembering Girl's fragmented childhood recollection in the cabin. From the sound of it, the mother had prostituted her young daughter to strange men. Horrifying. Perhaps Girl's mind was merely warped from years of abuse followed by years of isolation.

And yet . . . Mary paused, poking at her own assumptions. Even if Girl truly loved her mother, that didn't negate the possibility that she was dangerous. Or even a killer. She thought of that desperate yearning in the woman's eyes. Mary had seen it before. Many of the women with whom she'd negotiated settlements for Teddy had reeked of the same need. More than once, the women had turned to Mary, representative of their supposed victimizer, for advice on how to invest the settlement, or start their lives anew, or for a shoulder to cry on. Mary came to see it as a kind of Stockholm syndrome, with a maternal twist.

In her youth, Mary had spotted this need for female nurturing in herself. She'd been terrified by how vulnerable it made her. With time and discipline, she buried it so completely that she'd forgotten about it. Until now. But Girl seemed firmly in its grip. Could Mary somehow exploit this?

It was also possible that she was surmising too much from a limited set of facts. The woman could be manic. Or an addict. In a few hours, she might come down from her high or break through her mania. She'd notice Mary's tailored suit and diamond ring, not to mention the stark differences in their physiques. If needed, Mary would point out additional inconsistencies: her ownership of a luxury car, her expensive dental work, her manner of speaking. Mary was clearly not this poor, rural, uneducated person's mother. The woman would realize her mistake and let Mary go. Or at least, that's what Mary hoped. She felt her mind tugging the threads of darker scenarios and decided to tackle a task she'd been avoiding. She had to pee.

She shuffled toward the back of the cellar, cursing as a thick cobweb tickled her face, then unbuttoned her slacks and squatted. Urine splashed her ankles, and she rebalanced, tenting her fingers on the cold dirt. A small, soft body scurried over her thumb. She gritted her teeth and finished.

She found her way back to the door. The sun set after 8:00 p.m. in May, so it must be 9:00 or 9:30. Maybe the woman had cried herself dry by now. Perhaps her exhaustion would soften her defenses and offer Mary an opening.

"Hey!" she called through the door. "I understand why you're upset. It must have been terrible to be left alone like that."

The drone of a faraway jet drifted from the heavens. She cursed, rocking back on her heels, then froze. Had she heard a faint creak? She pressed her ear against the rough wood and detected a swishing sound, like someone striding through dew-soaked grass.

"Girl!" Mary belted out the non-name. She paused to listen. Footsteps in the grass. She was sure of it. "Let's talk! I'm confident we can reach an understanding."

The footsteps approached the door. Mary rose to her feet, her adrenaline surging. She planned to bolt past Girl as soon as the door opened. But the swishing continued past. She beat her fists on the door and yelled. What could the woman be doing? Killing dinner? Maybe caring for this precious brood she kept mentioning.

Brood. Wasn't that the name for a group of birds? Or their offspring? She hadn't noticed any chickens or turkeys. But her survey of the area had been far from complete. Whatever these birds were, Girl seemed to have a powerful connection to them. They somehow bound her with her mother, another detail Mary might leverage.

Unable to stomach lying in the moist dirt, she sat cross-legged, her back against the door. Her throbbing head had quieted; her shoulder resettled into the socket. But she felt weak. She considered breaking into the mason jars but dismissed the idea. She wasn't desperate enough to risk botulism. Instead, she huddled into herself and tried to sleep. It was crucial to keep her brain and body rested and balanced.

She'd just nodded off when something jolted her awake. Hearing nothing, she readjusted her position against the door and again tried to doze. But the totality of the silence infused her with dread. The woods outside, and even the minuscule creatures within the root cellar, seemed to be waiting and watching. Her body responded with an animal vigilance that made sleep impossible.

She shifted and turned, trying every possible arrangement of her limbs against the door. The hours passed and the silence thickened, flowing around her like chill waters blending present with past, submerging her in long-buried memories. A time of dirt and squalor. Of the absence of anything sacred. A time when nothing about her was valued. When all the world screamed that she did not matter.

Her consciousness blurred, collapsing into the powerless confines of her infant self. A vision of meth-rotted teeth and jaundiced lips swam across her mind. Her mother's stinking mouth, a spigot of black curses and threats, drew closer. A spoon knocked past her two new teeth, forcing rancid beef gel onto her tongue.

The memory dissolved, replaced by the voice of her foster father. "You are stupid as they come," he railed at her four-year-old self. A broken egg shimmered between her bare feet, dropped while she collected from the chicken coop. "No wonder your mama gave you away." He'd forced her to her knees in the dirt, pushing her head until she'd lapped up the viscous pool, a blood speck gleaming in the golden yolk.

And her earliest days at the orphanage, just turned five, when her skin had ached not with the psoriasis that would arrive with puberty but with the hunger for human touch. During a group photo for the diocese newspaper, she was singled out by the photographer to pose on the lap of a white-gloved benefactress. The woman's sweet smell was dizzying. Mary leaned into her lovely softness. The photographer repeatedly barked, "Sit up straight!" But Mary's yearning was so overpowering that her body disobeyed, slumping into the warm chest behind her. The woman's arm briefly encircled Mary, almost a hug, as she tried to right her for the photo. The contact flooded Mary's parched nervous system. She shuddered and her bladder released. The woman leaped up, shrieking, and Mary slid to the floor. She was shaken by one of the sisters and ordered from the room. The last thing she saw was the look of pure disgust on the woman's face. The ache returned with greater force.

"But I won," Mary yelled, testifying to the darkness. "I beat them all. On my own." The sound of her own strong voice dispelled the ugly reverie. But the effort resurrected the pounding in her skull. She'd been in a car accident. She'd gone hours without food and water. She dropped her head between her knees, fingers gripping her hair.

Gradually, light crept beneath the door. The small, filthy window grew leprous with daybreak. She could make out the dark stain in the corner where she'd relieved herself and the markings of her movements on the dirt floor.

A key creaked in the padlock. She forced herself to rise, ignoring her pounding head. When the door swung open to reveal Girl, Mary lurched forward, then gripped the doorframe to steady herself. She squinted against the daylight, questioning her eyesight, questioning her sanity.

Girl's work shirt now seemed several sizes too large, the front slackened into empty folds. Beneath the fabric, her enormous breasts, the great masthead of her body, had somehow disappeared.

Chapter 3

Mary screwed her eyes shut, hoping to clear her vision. But when she reopened them, the impossible sight remained—Girl's once massive breasts now sagged like empty wineskins. Had Mary been so concussed and delirious yesterday that the woman had only seemed excessively endowed? Or was she delirious now? Whatever the case, the look in Girl's eyes remained unchanged. A starved devotion that made Mary's skin crawl.

The tang of urine wafted from the root cellar. With a hound dog sniff, Girl traced the scent into the darkness. Her face creased with distress.

"Just so we're crystal clear," Mary said, "I suffered a concussion in the car wreck. Without treatment, I could die. You will be held responsible." She was only mildly exaggerating. She felt woozy. Her vision was blurred. Her knees buckled, and she slid down the doorframe, splinters shredding the sleeve of her blazer. Girl shot forward and scooped Mary into her arms. Mary's five-foot-eleven frame was lean but dense with muscle, a product of a militant fitness regime maintained for decades. Yet Girl carried her as if she were featherlight.

"Jesus! Put me down," Mary gasped. She pushed weakly against the deflated chest, then jerked her head away, recoiling. A syrupy-sweet odor oozed from Girl's skin.

Cradling Mary in her arms, Girl made her way from the backyard to the front of the cabin. To one side, the forest loomed, a black-and-green wall that ran the length of the property. The cabin itself seemed a wind's breath from collapsing. The weathered wood buckled; the small back porch slanted like an unhinged jaw. Girl increased her pace, her breath leaving a treacly residue on Mary's neck. Mary's stomach heaved, and she couldn't contain it. Girl waited out the bout of vomiting, then continued across the yard with Mary in tow.

"Get me to the hospital now," Mary said, twisting in Girl's unyielding embrace. "Before you have a death on your hands."

"I know what you need, Mama." Girl thudded up the porch steps. Mary's heart sank. For the second time, she was crossing the cabin's threshold in the arms of the strange behemoth. She kicked and punched as Girl lowered her onto the pallet. But the dizziness returned with a vicious torque that left her immobilized.

The woman tut-tutted and moved toward the hand pump. "Making yourself sick. You got to keep still." She returned with a cool compress and chipped mug. Her eyes were the shade of ocher mud; her short, wavy hair, a bird's nest overturned. A tear tracked through her rough complexion. "You're back. The Brood too," she breathed. She threw her arms wide, then lowered herself onto one of the small metal chairs. "We're all home. Together."

Mary's stomach knotted. Clearly the woman still clung to the delusion that Mary was her mother. She waited for the room to stop spinning, then cleared her throat. "Girl. We both know I'm not your mother."

Girl's great cheek twitched, as if resisting a fly.

"Think about it," Mary continued. "Would your mother wear a business suit? Would she drive a Mercedes-Benz? And, I mean no disrespect, but would your mother . . . speak as if she had a formal education? I think you know the answer." Mary paused, torn between wanting to castigate the woman for her stupidity and beg for her release.

She settled on a middle way. Bribery. "That said, if you're looking for her, there are ways I can help you achieve your goal."

Girl cocked her head, eyes planted on her outsize work boots.

"And perhaps that's been your plan all along." Mary continued, adjusting her strategy to allow the woman to save face. "You're no fool. You pegged me for a wealthy woman. And you're right. Imagine what kind of investigatory work $100,000 could buy. You could locate whoever you wanted to by the end of the year. Even someone who might not want to be found."

Mary's eyes slid to the open door. The pickup truck hadn't budged from its spot near the porch. "And we wouldn't have to involve the police," she continued, pushing herself to an upright position. The dizziness seemed to be fading. "Forget about the kidnapping, use of force, failure to offer life-saving assistance—all punishable crimes that could result in the loss of your cabin. And of course, the Brood."

Girl's spine snapped straight. Her huge hands gripped her knees. Her muddy eyes sharpened. Mary continued probing for Girl's pain points. "Not to mention the potential for an expensive civil suit." She scanned the wall near the front door for a hook or shelf that might hold car keys. Finding none, she forced a smile. "And of course, I'd be willing to sign paperwork as a promise to never press charges or sue. What's called a nondisclosure agreement."

Girl leaned forward on the little chair. The cheek twitched again.

Mary prepared to deliver her final argument. Restrained. Precise. "This could be a game changer for you, Girl. If I *were* your mother . . ." She paused to let her words penetrate. "I would advise you to take the offer."

The woman plucked a tab of skin from her coarse knuckles, then spoke in a low voice. "I'm sorry. For locking you up all night. Had to do your business in the dirt. I'm ashamed."

"Well. It certainly wasn't pleasant." Mary's nostrils flared. She swallowed a few choice words and leaned forward, placing one foot on the floor. Her pulse felt stronger, more regular. She brushed dirt from her slacks. "But that's behind us. We've got a plan. Let's make it happen."

Girl extended her hand.

"Excellent," Mary said, reaching out to seal the deal with a handshake. Instead, she found her upper arm crushed in Girl's iron grip. She slid from the bed and fell to her knees, screaming as her hair was yanked and twisted by thick fingers.

Girl's lips drew back from saliva-slicked teeth. "I'm gonna help you, Mama." She jerked Mary to her feet. "You got the wandering spirit. Strong. Who wouldn't, after twenty-seven years?"

Mary sunk her fingernails into Girl's wrist, but it had no effect. Writhing and twisting, she was dragged toward the metal washtub. It was filled with the same water Girl had used to sponge bathe the day before. And then her face dangled above the oily, foam-flecked, gray water.

"We're gonna purge it, Mama. That wandering spirit. For good, this time."

Mary's scream was silenced as Girl forced her head and shoulders into the dirty water. She pushed frantically against Girl's body, an immovable wall of flesh. The rusted edges of the washtub sliced into her palms.

Girl ripped Mary's head from the water. Mary gagged, vomiting streams of filthy liquid.

"That's right, Mama. Get it out. So you can stop messin' with my head."

"Crazy bitch," Mary spat. Again, her head was plunged into the tub.

"No more driving fancy cars, Mama."

And again.

"Wearing fancy clothes."

Again. Again.

"No more tricks."

Girl continued the methodical dunking. Darkness clouded Mary's mind. Her body grew limp; her struggles ceased. Her existence collapsed to a sole function: gulping oxygen each time Girl ripped her from the water. When her legs gave out, Girl slung an arm around her waist and continued the unholy ritual. Darkness expanded in Mary's brain until she lost consciousness.

Light and sound dragged Mary from the blackout. She was belly-down on Girl's lap. Girl cooed encouragement as bitter water streamed from Mary's mouth. Afterward, Girl wiped the mess from

Mary's face, then carried her, a lank rag doll, to the pallet. She kissed Mary's forehead and tucked the quilt beneath her chin.

◆ ◆ ◆

A chill draft pulled Mary from her exhausted slumber. She cracked her eyes open to the vision of her bare breasts, fully exposed, the quilt folded at her ribcage. Beneath the coarse blanket, her bare legs were cool. Her pants had been removed, leaving only her underwear. Girl was bedside, Mary's satin La Perla bra dangling from her fingers. Mary jerked the quilt to her neck and tucked herself into a ball. She shook violently, drawing Girl's attention.

"You cold?" The woman's broad face broke into a tender smile. Tucking in a loose corner of the quilt, she nodded toward the woodburning stove, where a cast-iron pot steamed. The smell of boiling grains filled the cabin. "Porridge'll warm you." She rose, shoving Mary's bra into the back pocket of her worn corduroys, where it dangled like a child's slingshot. She swirled the wooden ladle, increased the flame, then returned to Mary's bedside.

Mary tensed as the woman withdrew the bra and fingered the lacy material. Was she a sexual deviant as well as a kidnapper? Images of the filthy tub of water flashed through Mary's mind. She gripped the quilt, pulling it tighter around her body. As panic threatened, she ordered herself to remain calm, to notice her surroundings, to stay awake and aware. She glanced around the room, reacquainting herself with the cobwebbed ceiling, the four windows, the metal table and chairs, the shelves of chipped crockery.

"Prettiest thing I ever seen," the woman muttered.

Mary's eyes returned to the face of her captor. The bra was engulfed by the wide, calloused hands.

"Fine as a cicada wing. Never had one," said Girl, biting her lip. "Can I try it?"

Mary studied the woman's sheepish expression. Rather than a sexual perversion, she might be witnessing more of the odd, guileless behavior of this unsocialized creature.

"You'll destroy it," Mary blurted before she could stop herself. The thought of the oaf pouring her body into Mary's intimates was too much. Girl's face melted into dejection, and Mary hastened to add, "I mean, it's rather old. The material is frail. Of course you can try. You'll just have to be careful."

Girl nodded, regarding the bra reverentially before removing her shirt. Mary was treated to another unwanted viewing of Girl's breasts. The dark, pebbly areolas were the size of saucers. The skin strained along the chest, as if the breasts longed to break free of Girl's body.

Mary frowned. Had the breasts regained some of their volume since this morning? And now there were three welts on the side of Girl's body. Had she failed to notice the other two before? She touched the gash on her forehead. She must still be compromised from the car wreck.

Girl approached Mary, head bowed, cheeks aflame. Her breasts bulged along the edges of the fabric, but the bra managed to contain most of the flesh.

"Very nice." Mary nodded, offering a stiff smile. "While we're playing dress-up, I'd love my shirt. Any idea where it is?"

Girl retrieved Mary's suit jacket from an upturned crate at the foot of the bed. "Shirt's drying on the porch."

Mary shoved her arms into dust-caked sleeves. The quilt slipped, exposing her own breasts, perfect orbs, beneficiaries of cosmetic refreshes totaling $40,000. She quickly buttoned the blazer.

"Yours are the same," Girl paused, her eyes on Mary's chest. "Like sisters. Not mine. It's like they're from different mothers. How come?" She reached for Mary's breast.

Mary knocked Girl's hand away. "Keep your damn mitts to yourself!"

Girl's face collapsed. "I'm sorry, Mama. I'm bad. I won't do that again." She gently removed the bra and laid it on the pallet, donned her flannel shirt, and slunk over to the simmering porridge.

Mary pressed her lips together, resisting the urge to yell that she was not the inbred's twelve-toed mother. She might not survive another dunking. She swung her bare legs to the ground, relieved to feel no dizziness. Her pedicured toes were bright against the rough floorboards. She prayed Girl wouldn't feel inspired to reveal her own bedraggled hooves or any other part of her anatomy.

The front door was open, as it had been when Mary first awoke in the cabin. Did Girl ever close it? Maybe the property was so secluded that trespassers were rare. Did such remote areas still exist in upstate New York? Was she even in New York? She suddenly felt cold. "How long was I asleep?" she asked.

"Since yesterday," Girl's voice was low and contrite. "Missed the Brood. But we can check 'em again today. After we eat." Her eyes flicked to the washtub. "I mean. If you feel ready."

"Absolutely," Mary replied.

While Girl ladled the bubbling porridge into wooden bowls, Mary examined her palms. Her wounds were still bleeding, leaving scarlet smears on the quilt. She needed a tetanus shot. And stitches. And probably an MRI. She glanced up from her ravaged hands to see Girl carefully bearing the steaming bowls, metal spoons upright, toward the pallet.

"I'll be good from now on, Mama. Focus on the Brood. Nothing else." As Mary took the porridge, Girl caught sight of her sliced palms. "Lord, lord. What have I done to you?" She raised her face to the cobwebbed ceiling. Tears leaked from one eye.

Mary blew on a hot spoonful, vapor purling along her cheeks. She swallowed, then pitched the bowl of scalding mush into Girl's upturned face.

Girl shrieked and fell to her knees. Her bowl went spinning, flinging porridge across the floor. Mary leaped up, sprinting across the room, through the open front door, and down the porch steps. She raced to the pickup truck, Girl's screams resounding from the cabin. She threw open the driver's side door and tumbled inside, bare legs sticking to the sun-warmed seat. "Goddamn it," she whimpered, as her fingers gripped the keyless ignition.

Girl's howls intensified. Sounds erupted—crockery shattering and furniture being overturned. Mary locked the car doors and grimaced in pain as her wounded hand worked the window cranks up. Desperately, she searched for a hidden key, tearing open the glove box and trawling the dusty dashboard. She ripped up the floor mats and poked under the seat. But there was no key.

Mary slid back to the steering wheel. Girl exploded onto the porch, hands covering her eyes. She stumbled down the steps, lurched toward the truck, and bounced off the hood. The porridge had blinded Girl. Mary was flooded with relief. Then Girl dropped her hands. A mask of melted skin surrounded lightless eyes that now bored into Mary.

Girl roared and darted forward. She tried the locked door, then began pounding on the metal and glass. Mary scrambled across the seat, unlocked and flung open the passenger door, then bolted. Her long legs devoured the ground, adrenaline numbing her bare feet to rocks and twigs. When she reached the far edge of the grassless parking area, the footpath appeared. She quickly assessed the trail, her eyes tracing the short distance to the quarry, veering up the mountainside, then coming to rest at the cave high above. She considered escaping to the quarry. But the walls were sheer on all sides, save a single faint path. If Girl discovered her, she would be trapped. Climbing to the cave seemed ill-advised as well. She had no idea of its depth or extent. Whereas Girl likely knew every nook and cranny. While she looked at the cave, a flash of orange gold lit up the dark recess. Was she hallucinating?

"Stop! Please!" Girl's voice boomed. Her footsteps beat the ground. "She'll make me hurt you!"

Turning from the footpath, Mary charged down the rocky single track that served as Girl's driveway. At the base, a narrow dirt road continued for a half mile, then curved from view. She decided to ignore the road and head for the woods. On the road, Girl's pickup could easily catch up to Mary. But in the woods, Mary would have a shot. She was fast. Her personal trainer was a flatterer, but his compliments regarding her speed were sincere. And Girl's weight would slow her down, increasing Mary's advantage. Eventually Mary was sure to run into a highway or even a town. This was the Northeast, after all. Contiguous forests extended only so far.

She plunged into the trees, disappearing into the chill, dappled understory. She leaped over lichenous stones, wild-armed ferns, and decaying stumps. When Girl's elephantine crashing sounded behind her, Mary reassured herself. It was to be a footrace now, and even with her battered body and empty belly, Mary would win.

She urged herself onward. Branches sliced her bare legs and tore the hair from her head. Granite boulders seemed to spring into her path, forcing her to reverse course or else squeeze her body through rough, narrow openings. At one point, a deer burst from the shadows. Every so often, she'd pause and listen to the forest. Each time, the sounds of Girl's pursuit were fainter. Until finally, she heard nothing but birdsong and her own labored breathing. Still she forged on, fueled by animal terror. She estimated it had been one hour, then two. As the forest ate away at her body, her run slowed to a walk. The forest canopy pressed down. The sunlight cooled and turned murky.

All at once, the forest fell away, and the ground dropped steeply. At the base of the slope, a narrow paved road stretched in both directions. She quickened her pace, sliding along on her bottom, her underwear catching on gravel and scree. She followed the deserted road, searching for her car and listening for a pickup truck. Gnats clouded her face. Her feet shrieked with every step, the soles scraped and bleeding. A droning sound in the woods gradually grew louder. At first she hurried toward it, thinking the sound might indicate a construction site, perhaps a cabin or country home in progress. But as the sound grew louder, she decided it was most likely an insect, or many insects.

The drone shifted into a pulsing trill.

Oweee-oooo. Oweee-oooo.

The insectile chant sent a chill through her. She quickened her pace. Up ahead, a metallic glint caught her eye, where the road curved back into the trees. She urged herself to run, ignoring her tortured feet. Suddenly, her Mercedes came into view, the silver body dazzling in the afternoon sun. She clenched her fists and charged forward. If that insane redneck dared emerge from the woods, Mary would relish crushing her beneath the tires—assuming the car still worked. Blackened skid marks streaked the cracked backcountry road. The front left section of the hood and part of the bumper were crumpled against a tall pine. The driver's side door was ajar.

Mary hurried toward the car. The buzzing in the forest blasted forth, as if a jet engine were revving in the trees. Covering her ears, she staggered forward. The shrieking grew louder, the pitch higher, battering her eardrums. She fell to her knees. Locking her eyes on the car, she willed herself to stand, even as the wave of sound crashed down on her. She felt a rush of air. Darkness fell and a great weight flattened her to the ground. She struggled to throw off what felt like a heavy net, but it began to shift and move. Horrified, she realized that the weight was a swarm of plump, red-eyed cicadas. More of the creatures landed, flowing around her like a squirming blanket. Light flickered off their iridescent bodies. A cloying sweetness choked her. Thousands of chitinous legs crawled along her face, beneath her jacket, and along her bare legs.

She wrenched herself to her feet, flailing her limbs and flinging cicadas from her body. An angry roar erupted from her chest. She scooped the wriggling beasts off her skin and tore them from her hair. Staggering to the car, she threw herself inside and slammed and locked the doors. Dozens of cicadas roamed across her thighs and chest. Grunting, she ground them with her fists, then collapsed against the seat, letting her racing heart subside.

With shaking hands, she reached for the wipes in the center console, cleaning bug guts from her palms. When she finally brought herself to glance outside, the swarm had mostly disappeared. A few stragglers crept across the dented car hood. She smashed the ignition button, praying the smart-key fob was somewhere in the car. A gleeful cry escaped her as the powerful engine roared to life. She threw the car into gear and punched the accelerator.

The motor sputtered, emitting a sound like whole fruit dropped in a blender. She locked her knee, pressing harder on the pedal. With a final wet thunk, the engine died.

Chapter 4

Mary pressed the ignition button. Again, the engine growled and hiccuped before falling silent. She cursed aloud, her voice dampened by the luxury interior, then surveyed the hood and the area around the car. The cicadas had disappeared as quickly as they had arrived. Even the few stragglers were gone. She glanced through the sunroof at the cloudless sky. Perhaps high noon was when they fled to their hive. Or took naps. She shivered, remembering the skittering across her skin. Did cicadas attack humans? She'd never heard of such a thing. But maybe this was some kind of invasive species, like killer bees.

Her gaze fell to the floorboard. A tube of lipstick, a notepad, and the keys to the Cape Cod house were scattered among mutilated bodies of cicadas. She spun around to find her Fendi bag upended in a corner of the back seat. She plunged her hand inside, searching for her cell phone. She found the key fob, a bottle of Advil, and a package of floss picks, but no phone. She searched between the seats and inside the car's storage compartments—nothing. Was it possible the ignoramus had swiped the phone? More likely the phone had been in Mary's suit pocket when she was carried, unconscious, into the cabin. It may have fallen out and was now lost on the forest floor. Or the woman may have discovered it and squirreled it away.

A faint crack sounded. She froze, breath suspended, while regarding the trees. Shafts of noonday sun pierced the swaying canopy. The forest floor winked with orange-gold light, breaking through shadows before again sinking into cool darkness. How long before the woman came crashing from the trees to the most obvious destination for Mary's escape? She peered through the rear window at the trunk, where her luggage was stored. Her laptop and mobile hot spot were cached in the exterior sleeve of her valise. Assuming the equipment had survived the crash, she might be able to Skype her assistant, Michael.

Craning forward, she reassessed her surroundings. The road sloped upward for about two hundred yards before curving into the forest and out of sight. To her right, a narrow band of trees edged a steep descent down the mountain. Should she retrieve the laptop from the trunk, communicate with her office, then wait for rescue in the locked car? It might be better to immediately commence her escape by foot. She imagined trekking down the mountainside and her bare feet convulsed with pain. She folded one foot into her lap. The sole was sliced and scored. Several cuts oozed blood. Without shoes, escape on foot would be impossible. Her eyes returned to the trunk. The luggage also contained a new pair of Nikes. And a fresh set of clothes.

She reached down to pop the trunk, then paused. A frisson shot through her as she recalled thousands of tiny legs on her body. Must she leave the safety of the car to access the trunk? She vaguely remembered Michael bungling some errand with her car, locking the keys in the trunk, then accessing it through the back seat. She spun around to study the rear of the car. The daylight dimmed dramatically. She glanced up at the sunroof, fearful that a search party might be hindered by a storm.

A scream burst from her throat.

A wave of dark green lapped against the exterior of the sunroof. Diaphanous wings flashed. Thousands of tiny legs chattered against the smooth surface. The darkness deepened.

Outside, the air was thick with cicadas. The creatures looped lazily around the car, then clotted together on the silver hood. They swarmed across the windshield, a seething curtain. The light dimmed further. She spun around to find cicadas converging on the back and side windows. A cloying, treacly odor drifted through the air conditioning vents.

She shook uncontrollably. Her breath came in staccato gasps. Again she tried the ignition button. Again the sputter and the strange wet thunk. She shrieked, slammed by the realization that the creatures must have infiltrated the motor, even before her first attempt to start the car.

She caught sight of her eyes in the rearview mirror, glazed and wild. And something else: her forehead, which yesterday had been a Botox-smooth expanse, now bore three ocher dots in the shape of an inverted triangle. Filtered through Mary's panic-warped mind, the sight resurrected a long buried memory.

The spring after her twelfth birthday, Mary was almost happy. Or at least not miserable. Saint Agnes had been cited for neglect. The state had mandated that the orphanage no longer care for children under the age of six. This meant Mary's babysitting duties were lightened considerably, allowing her to wander the grounds when not in class or at meals.

As well, her psoriasis felt less oppressive. She was much more skilled at hiding it than when it was first diagnosed a year ago. Sister Helen had explained that while it wasn't contagious, people might treat her as if it were. An angry patch on her forehead, shaped like an inverted triangle, was hidden by the neat bangs she'd trimmed herself. Her blouse covered another patch on her belly, about the size of her hand, and a third on her inner forearm.

On a day of wandering, just after lunch, she paused to watch a baseball game underway on the crude diamond that served as Saint Agnes's playing field. Equipment was always in short supply, and she was surprised that over half the outfielders had gloves. She found herself silently cheering for the pitcher, Seth Gready, a boy she'd hardly been aware of until a week ago. His small, scrawny body had suddenly morphed into a tall, gangly frame with broad shoulders. His voice had deepened and gained authority, if only around other kids.

While Seth was on the mound, the ball veered into foul territory and rolled toward Mary. She scooped it up, smoothed her bangs into place, and trotted to the mound. As she ran, she tried to ignore the discomfort caused by the changes in her own body, heavier by the day, fueled by the sweet things she craved, and often stole, from the larder. When she reached Seth, he extended his glove, a smile gathering in his blue eyes.

After the game, she watched, one hand shielding her eyes from the sun, while he clapped his winning teammates on the back, the center of an exuberant, dusty swarm. Suddenly, he swung toward her and shouted, "Stop your staring! Leper girl." Most of the kids had dispersed to wash before dinner. But a dozen remained, mostly boys. They whooped with laughter.

She noticed her blouse had crept up, too tight on her expanding belly, revealing a crusted red blotch on a pale bulge of flesh. She'd also exposed the patch on her forehead when shading her eyes. She met Seth's gaze, feeling her insides ice over. He tugged his cap low and turned to leave. But another boy, a recent arrival, composed his own original taunt. "Dragon lady! Fat and scaly," he yelled, spurring on the others.

Soon Mary was encircled by chants of *Dragon lady! Fat and scaly!* Shame blazed through her as she gaped at the boys with their sharp, yelling faces. Her body felt enormous and diseased. An unwanted thing in the world. Monstrous and disgusting.

Seth was dragged back by the new boy, who pushed him into Mary. When Seth regained his balance, his face was contorted, as if he'd eaten a bitter herb. Her shame morphed into rage. She lowered her head and plowed into Seth's midsection, tackling him to the ground. Pinning him with all the force of her weight, she lifted his shirt, offering the shrieking spectators full view while she ground her forearm into his bare belly. Her inflamed skin cracked and bled, leaving a crimson smear on his stomach. She then anointed his smooth, suntanned forehead, maneuvering her forearm to stamp a crude upside-down triangle, like hers.

She pressed her mouth to his ear, whispering, "Now you got it too."

More cicadas swarmed the Mercedes. A ghastly green light bathed the car's interior. The air was heavy and sweet, as if misted with maple syrup. Mary slammed her palms against the windows, screaming until she was hoarse, hoping to dislodge the bugs. Unperturbed, the cicadas streamed across the vehicle, layer upon layer, until the car groaned beneath the weight. The horn produced only a tired bleat. Despairing, she dropped her head to the steering wheel. The skin of her right foot tingled, and she yelped, jerking her legs onto the seat.

A stream of insects crawled from the floor vents.

And the dash vents.

And beneath the back seat.

In seconds, the car's interior was crowded with flickering, fluttering movement. A chorus of thousands blasted the small space with an eerie cry, a breathy, grating, almost metallic sound.

Oweee-oooo. Oweee-oooo.

Weeping, she clutched her ears. She threw open the door, but a dense throng of cicadas forced it shut again. "No," she whimpered, tugging the handle. The door held firm. Sharp pinpricks sunk into her skin. She tried to scream, but tiny legs darted between her lips and probed her tongue. The sweet stench filled the car, a suffocating fug that choked her airway and strained her lungs. She felt herself giving up and thought she was going to die.

The pulsing chorus deepened. The tempo slowed, punctuated by longer silences. As the hypnotic repetition continued, her terror waned, as if she were caught in a lulling sonic embrace. A kind of trance stole over her. She wasn't asleep. She was fully aware of her confinement beneath the shifting creatures, even picturing herself upright in the driver's seat, a person-shaped mass of dark, plump bugs.

But her thoughts, her emotions, her beating heart seemed no longer her own, now tuned to the collective pulse of the cicadas. Slowly, a strange sensation, not unlike pleasure, began to invade her body, warming her skin and spiraling up her spine. The pinpricks continued, lighting up nerve endings that seemed to reach beyond her body, through each of the thousands of cicadas, into the forest and the root system of the trees, and outward into the web of all living things. Some part of her knew this was impossible. *You are Mary Whelton,* her brain messaged. She struggled to hold on to her own significance. But the harried panic to survive at all costs drifted from her like expanding clouds of cosmic dust. She felt a whispered invitation to let go, to allow herself to disperse into the cicadas stacked thickly upon her body and into the proliferating life beyond.

Suddenly, the cicadas froze and fell silent, jarring her from her fugue state. She had no idea how much time had passed. The car door opened, and her cicada-covered body tumbled out. With a whir, like Lilliputian airplane motors, the darkness lifted, and they were gone. Her bare legs were cold and exposed. She squeezed her lids shut against the fading sunlight. She knew she needed to get up, to run. Or return to the car. But her body would not cooperate. Instead her mind flitted, mothlike, back to the glowing warmth that had just overwhelmed her.

A gust swept through the treetops, and the forest groaned. Footsteps sounded. Shadows flitted across Mary's eyelids. She forced her eyes open. A large, broad-shouldered silhouette eclipsed the sun. Mary lifted her scratched and bitten arm. "They were all over me," she whispered, dazed.

"Yup. That's how they do." A sugary dew drifted from above, dusting Mary's cheek. "Let's get you back home, Mama."

Mary's eyes fluttered open to the darkening sky, the green-black forest, the decrepit cabin. Her throat was bone dry, her body a sand-filled sack cradled in Girl's arms. With each of Girl's lumbering steps, the landscape shook, and the cabin drew closer.

"What the fuck do you want from me?" Mary's scream came out a whimper. The honeyed heaviness brought on by the cicada attack had not left her body.

"Hmm?" Girl lowered her mammoth ear to Mary's lips.

"I don't want to be here," Mary whispered as the road angled upward. The quarry came into view, then the cave perched above, a black egg nested in the roots of the venom-green oak tree. "Please," Mary added. Starbursts spiraled across her vision.

Girl's words seemed to reach Mary from across the quarry, borne on wings from the depths of the cave. "You had your time, Mama. It's done. No more running."

"I never ran," Mary breathed, prying her thousand-pound tongue from her jaw. Images from her childhood bled together like watercolor paint. "I hated them too much." She slipped from consciousness. Sleep devoured hours, maybe days. Mary spun through dreams of her young self, body heavy and immovable, sheathed in inflamed, scaled armor, a solitary dragon guarding her hoard. Between the dreams, she was dimly aware of Girl feeding her, bathing her, holding her steady while she used the bathroom. Each time she tried to awaken fully, a lulling, syrupy warmth would drag her back down.

When Mary finally resurfaced, it was to the sight of a cicada molting on a branch outside the window nearest the pallet. The creature convulsed and shuddered, moment by moment, worming its alabaster thorax from the shell of its former self. Mary shrunk from the blood-blister eyes that seemed to fix on her. Dozens of the cicada's newly molted siblings crawled drunkenly along the branch, weaving through the rubble of their own cast-off skins.

Mary gripped the bedclothes and turned away, remembering the whirring cumulus of prehistoric-looking bugs that descended upon her, the initial terror and disgust. And then the strange pleasure. There had been a handful of times in her adult life when she'd drunk too much and dropped her rigorous self-control for a few hours. She'd always regretted it, feeling exposed, that she'd endangered herself by letting go, that the world now had something on her. She felt that same nakedness and vulnerability now. Thank God there were no witnesses.

But why had the creatures attacked her in the first place? Did they have the same defensive mechanism as bees, to swarm then sting?

Maybe they'd injected some kind of poison, or venom, that numbed and intoxicated her, inducing those strange sensations. In fact, weren't most intoxicants nonlethal doses of poison? She tried to scratch her thigh but found she couldn't. Both wrists were bound by thick strips of leather fastened to the pallet. A chill shot through her. She pedaled her legs and discovered they were bound as well.

"Mama?" The greeting was delivered on a gust of overripe fruit. Girl's full-moon face hovered above Mary, her smiling eyes framed by seared skin. Girl leaned closer, her breath spuming along Mary's cheeks.

"Back." Mary turned her face away. "I need air."

Girl withdrew, humming as she tidied the room. She wore the same patched corduroys and work shirt. A small leather pouch dangled from one of her belt loops. Her breasts had regained their turgidity, at least fifteen pounds of added weight, by Mary's estimation. Had Mary been asleep, or drugged, for days? Surely her law firm would have alerted the police by now.

At least she was still alive. Girl could have murdered her several times over, disposing of her corpse in the quarry's cloudy water or the bowels of the cave. But she had not. Deranged as the woman was, it would seem murder wasn't her ultimate goal. But what did the half-wit want from her? They'd been together long enough that Girl should have realized her mistake, that Mary was not her mother. But then again, she knew from her experience as a trial lawyer that denial, fed by desire, had the power to distort reality in profound ways.

"How long was I asleep?" Mary asked.

"Three days," Girl chirped. "And look at you. Fit as a fiddle."

It was true. Mary felt incredibly well rested and refreshed. All traces of the drug-like trance the cicadas had induced were gone. And she felt strong. When Girl's broad back was turned, Mary tested the leather straps. Given enough time, she might be able to work her wrists free.

She gazed at the front of the cabin and through the screen door. Outside, the rock walls of the quarry gleamed in the sunshine. The little cave seemed ready to disgorge a cheerful company of gnomes. Birdsong drifted through the cabin's open windows. The bucolic beauty, reminder of an outside world marching forward without her, reawakened her panic.

How the fuck was she still here?

And what drove her to leave the city and her colleagues to work in solitude in the first place, like some kind of goddamn curmudgeon monk? She ran through scenarios that might prompt her office to interrupt her island retreat. She found herself hoping for a subway bombing. Or another Hurricane Sandy. Or for one of the senior attorneys to keel over.

Mary raised herself to her elbows, straining against the leather straps. "Would you please untie me?"

"Can't do that, Mama. You still got a hot foot. I can tell." Girl's lower lip slid forward, the unseemly pout of a giant woman-child. "But watch." She marched over to the pallet and fiddled with the underside. The wood creaked and groaned. Suddenly, the upper half sprang forward and Mary lurched to a seated position. The quilt slipped from her legs onto the floor.

"I rigged it like one of them lawn chairs." Girl fixed her starved gaze on Mary.

The upright position felt marvelous on Mary's spine. And her vantage of the cabin and the surrounding landscape was vastly improved. "Well done, Girl. Thank you," Mary said.

As Mary delivered the compliment, she was struck by the unfamiliar feel of the experience. She seldom voiced praise or appreciation for her colleagues or underlings. She expressed her gratitude with absence: of tongue lashings, of belittlement, of job termination.

The effect of the bird's dropping of praise on Girl was staggering. Her face blazed with gaudy joy. She tugged the cowlick that crowned her sandy hair, then wrapped her thick arms around her body, as if her delight were in danger of spilling out.

For a moment Mary thought the woman might hit her knees and kiss the hem of Mary's garment. Except there was no hem to kiss. Mary was still without pants.

"Can I get dressed?" Mary asked.

Girl sprang into action, hurrying to the porch where Mary's slacks were neatly draped over the railing. "I washed 'em," she said when she returned. She held the slacks up for Mary's inspection.

"Dry-clean only," Mary blurted. "But, uh, I'm glad you washed them. They were filthy," she quickly added, defusing the storm brewing on Girl's face. "Can you untie me so I can dress?"

Girl shook her head. "I'll do it for you." Falling to one knee, she dressed Mary with all the earnestness and care of someone on a mighty quest. Another sickly sweet cloud arose and Mary aimed her nose away. Girl slid the pants past Mary's knees, then paused, leaning into Mary's crotch.

"I beg your pardon," Mary snapped, slamming her thighs closed.

"Careful!" Girl gently forced Mary's legs apart.

"Stop it!" The woman was a brute. Girl leaned closer, peering at a small oblong blister on Mary's inner right thigh. The surrounding skin was a constellation of tiny red dots.

Mary frowned. She was exquisitely familiar with her lifelong skin condition, but this didn't resemble any prior flare-up. Had her psoriasis morphed into a different type? She had no idea if that was even possible.

"You need to call 911! I'm probably having an allergic reaction from that bug attack," Mary said. "People have been known to die from such things."

"You ain't gonna die." Girl bowed her head. When she looked up again, a beatific smile wreathed her face. "This ain't no allergy. You don't feel sick. Do you?"

Mary mentally scanned her body. She felt alarmed, yes. But beneath that, a sense of well-being and comfort in her own skin remained. She'd been asleep for days. Hadn't worked out or stretched since she'd left New York. Hadn't maintained her Paleo diet. Yet her joints felt lubricated and light, her muscles supple and energized.

And her skin. Aside from the rash on her thigh, she felt none of the burning irritation of a psoriasis flare-up. In fact, she would swear her skin was clear, even the spots that had been popping up at the funeral. She spun her wrists against the restraints to study her palms. The cuts from the washtub dunking were almost healed.

"You are not a doctor. Nor am I," Mary said. "Allergies are somewhat mysterious. You can spend your whole life allergy-free. And then be triggered for the first time late in life."

"Oh, they triggered something," Girl said. "And what you felt. It wasn't bites." Her eyelashes dropped to half mast, and she giggled, a fluttery bray.

"Excuse me?" Mary flashed to the interior of the Mercedes, the vibrations stirring her body. She felt herself blushing, an ability she didn't know she possessed.

"The Brood," Girl said.

"Brood? What do chickens have to do with this?"

"Chickens!" Girl dipped into the little pouch dangling from her belt loop and gingerly withdrew a delicate amber shell. She set the cicada casing on Mary's thigh and regained her knightly genuflection. "They put their babies in you. You felt it. Them poking you. Laying their eggs." A giggle-bray and a flash of horsey teeth. "I used to tell you one day it would happen!"

Mary's thigh shot up, sending the cicada shell flying. "Redneck folklore. You would know that if you'd made it past fifth grade." She snapped her mouth shut. She had to calm down, keep the peace with this box of rocks until she gained her trust.

Yet Girl seemed unfazed by Mary's outburst. She completed her valet duties, all the while clucking like a giant featherless hen, then left to putter in the kitchen. She soon returned with two thick slices of bread slathered with butter and jam.

Mary's stomach grumbled. "I don't suppose that's gluten-free?" she asked. Girl gave her a quizzical look.

"Never mind," Mary said, devouring half the slice from Girl's hand. She swallowed, then asked, "Can I feed myself like a grown woman?"

Girl gave a sheepish smile, then tapped the reddened skin surrounding her eyes. "You hurt me bad. Not as bad as that time you caught me in the cave. Remember? That was before I knew. Still thought they was regular bugs."

Mary reflexively drew back.

"But it wasn't really fair. What you did." A shadow waxed across Girl's face. "She called me. Her In The Cave. The Brood was up from the earth. Powerful. The ground was moving. There was so many. I must have been—" She hovered the slab of her hand to indicate the height of a small child. "I didn't know about none of it. How the miners broke open the earth way back when. Shook free Her In The Cave. How some of the cicadas nearby came to be special. To be her eyes and ears. And sing her song."

Girl strummed the lined fabric of her corduroys, then fixed Mary with a thoughtful stare. "Sure didn't know 'bout the Gift. What Her In The Cave gave to our women. To carry the babies. Same as if we were trees. And you and me, the only ones left."

Mary pressed her lips together, containing her objections and her scorn. It seemed unwise to aggravate the woman with matters of science and rationality while she ripped the scab off a decades-old resentment.

"But maybe you weren't ready for me to know?" Girl continued. "Is that why you beat me so bad?" Her eyes widened. "Tore me open! Would have died but for the Brood."

Mary could feel the woman's struggle to tamp down her rage and maintain her cheery demeanor. Her dark eyes had gone cold. The idea that Girl had no intention of murdering Mary suddenly seemed questionable. "Her In The Cave," Mary interjected, in part to distract Girl from her rage, but also for her own understanding. Who was this new character in Girl's elaborate backwoods fantasy? A grandmother? An aunt? Could someone actually be living in the cave who was less of a maniac than Girl? "Is she still there?"

"Couldn't always find her when you were gone. She came and went. But she is here now. We're all here. With the biggest Brood ever was."

Again, Mary glanced through the window nearest the pallet. A full-blown cicada onslaught was underway. The earth disgorged the creatures in relentless waves. Their heavy bodies dipped between trees. They crawled across an outcropping of rock, graceless and gleaming. On all sides, larger creatures—moles, blue jays, raccoons, even squirrels—gorged on an unending banquet of cicadas. Mary remembered the term for what she was witnessing from some long-ago corporate seminar that professed to harness the animal natures of humans for business success: *predator satiation*, an evolutionary strategy of overwhelming enemies through sheer sacrificial numbers. This more-than-you-could-ever-eat buffet of cicadas satisfied the forest critters while leaving plenty of live cicadas for the main event—reproduction.

But why weren't the cicadas exhibiting the swarming behavior they used on her? Her eyes darted toward a corner of the ceiling where a pinhole of sunlight shone through. And what was to keep them from infiltrating Girl's drafty, ill constructed cabin?

"Think I know. Why you didn't say nothing," Girl said. She gestured toward the welt on Mary's thigh. "'Cause of me, ain't it?" The rosy bloom returned to her face. "You know, don't you? Wanted me to say first." She rotated, offering Mary the rolling hillocks of her left side. Slowly, she lifted her shirt. Three pus-filled wounds rose from Girl's flesh.

"Jesus." Mary leaned forward, both repulsed and fascinated. Embedded within each of the watery gashes were dozens of pale growths, each the size and shape of a grain of rice and tipped with a tiny bloodred dot. Mary squinted at the largest of the wounds. A ripple passed through the tiny growths—they were moving.

"I got a clutch, too, Mama. Almost two thousand babies in all."

"A clutch?" Mary repeated, her extremities draining of blood. "What are you saying?"

"Soon, mine'll be hatched. 'Fore too long, yours will look like this." Moisture rimmed Girl's dark eyes as she lovingly gazed at her flesh. When she looked up, sunlight from a nearby window grazed her forehead, illuminating the faint remains of three ocher dots, the points of an inverted triangle.

"Our Brood is growing, Mama."

Mary's body pitched forward, and she vomited all over Girl's leg.

Chapter 5

Mary slumped against the pallet, mind reeling.

"You got a sour stomach," Girl clucked, dabbing bile from Mary's face with an old bandanna. "From the babies. It'll pass." As Girl spoke, she tugged her flannel higher, further showcasing her ruptured skin.

Mary recoiled, tucking her head into her chest and clenching her eyes shut. She felt another retch building and took rapid breaths through her nose.

"Hold on, Mama! I'll get a bucket. Catch your sick."

While Girl searched the cabin, Mary struggled to rein in her panicked thoughts, twisting her wrists in the leather restraints. Her mind zeroed in on the watery gashes in Girl's side. The inner tissue had seemed to move. With what? Eggs? Embryos? Maggots? Could Girl be telling the truth? And now there was a similar rash on her own thigh—a rash that had only appeared after her strange encounter with the cicadas in the woods. Her stomach seized again, on the verge of capitulation.

Enough! she ordered herself, forcing the nausea back. Girl was a lonely fringe dweller, abused and abandoned by her mother. Unable to overcome her trauma, she'd fabricated some bizarre tale to create a sense of belonging or purpose in her empty life. Tragic, pitiable, and completely delusional. Whatever the welts were—boils or an infection—they had only *seemed* to move, jiggling atop Girl's excess of flesh.

As for the rash on her own thigh, she dredged up the maxim she hammered into every intern's head: *correlation does not imply causation.*

Her broken skin was totally unrelated to Girl's. Girl had simply latched on to the idea to bolster her own delusion. In Mary's case, the likely culprit was poison ivy or oak, or some other nasty foliage, picked up while she plowed through the woods in her underwear, trying to escape a madwoman.

Mary opened her eyes to find Girl dutifully presenting the bucket. "You can chuck now, Mama. I'm ready."

"No need. I'm feeling better."

"Let's get your pants on all the way, then," Girl said. She reached for Mary's belt loop.

Mary flinched. "Wait. Wash your hands first. Please." The last thing she needed was for Girl to pass on whatever viral funk she was carrying.

Girl bobbed her head in agreement as she climbed to her feet. "Can't be too careful when they're this little." She strode across the cabin to the hand pump, where she spun a block of soap in her palms.

Mary's inner thigh erupted with itching, as if a legion of angry fire ants was fighting its way through bone, muscles, and ligament. She fought against the wrist restraints, trying to claw the sizzling skin. If this was poison ivy, it was far more intense than she remembered from her few bouts as a child. She clapped her thighs together, hoping the friction would offer relief.

Girl flew back to Mary's side. "You'll hurt 'em!" she yelled. She wedged her fist between Mary's knees, forming a buffer, then fixed Mary with a terrified stare. "They are itty bitty babies!"

Mary opened her mouth to object. But something in Girl's face stopped her. The splotchy skin. The overly bright eyes, pupils pinpricked in alarm. Mary had learned to mask her fear by the time she was five. Yet Girl was wholly without that capacity. Her fear for the imaginary creatures was Vegas-bright.

Mary drew her knees apart, ignoring the riotous itching. "I promise to be more careful. But it could happen again." She furrowed her brow with faux concern.

"No!" Girl squeaked.

"I know what will help. I need to stretch my legs," Mary said. "Walk around outside. That will relax my thigh muscles and calm the itching."

Girl's eyes darted back and forth. Her thumbs wrestled each other, warring walruses on the floes of her large hands. "You gonna run. I can smell it."

"I understand your concern." Mary glanced at her thighs. "But I can tell the . . ." She forced her tongue to uncurl and speak the absurd word. "*Babies*"—she swallowed her distaste—"want to move around."

Girl's face softened. Her eyes grew wide. "They're talking to you. This soon?"

"Yep," Mary replied. "Precocious batch, apparently."

Girl scrambled to her feet. "We gonna walk." She stepped back to scrutinize the binding on Mary's wrists and ankles. "I'll carry you. Like before."

"That defeats the whole purpose. I have to move my body, stretch my muscles. They've made that very clear."

Still, Girl hemmed and hawed, studying Mary and the pallet. She rummaged through a wooden crate, softly grunting as she searched. Dread gathered in Mary's chest. What hellish trial was in store for her now? She leaned forward, but her view was obstructed by her captor's girth.

Finally, Girl returned with a bundle of rope. "Hands are clean," she promised. She looped the rope around Mary's torso, then began adjusting. Sweat darkened the flannel beneath Girl's arms, and a sugary miasma leaked from her pores.

"Excuse me," Mary protested as one of Girl's breasts crowded into her face. She tried not to think of the exotic skin infection colonizing the woman's flesh. When Girl straightened up, Mary found her torso secured in a rope harness with arms and legs free, not unlike the leash attachments parents sometimes used for unruly children. Girl looped the other end of the rope around herself, knotting and tightening until she, too, wore a harness. She unfastened Mary's feet and wrists and gestured for Mary to stand.

"How 'bout it?" Girl asked. The starved look returned as she awaited Mary's praise for her handiwork. Mary's cursory nod triggered a megawatt grin. They shuffled toward the front door with Mary scanning the cabin for knives, a hunting rifle, anything with which to bludgeon, stab, or shoot the hairless mammoth. The single shelf of chipped crockery held the dented porridge pot, no match for what Mary assumed was an exceedingly thick skull. The small pile of wood next to the cast-iron stove looked equally benign. Once Girl corralled Mary onto the front porch, cicada song blasted them. Mary shrank back, searching the yard and surrounding forest for the dark, undulating swarm.

"What's wrong, Mama?"

"What makes them attack?" Mary asked. "Why did they come for me?"

"The babies—" Girl began.

"What about them?" Mary interrupted, gesturing toward a cluster of four cicadas, creeping along the porch railing.

"Sweet things," Girl cooed. "She'll call 'em if she needs 'em."

Mary softly punched her own forehead. How was she to decipher the woman's lunatic answers? When Girl looked away to adjust her end of the rope, Mary flicked one of the bugs from the railings. She jerked back, ready to take refuge in the cabin. The three remaining cicadas continued their waddling progress, paying her no mind. Nor did any of the activity in the yard seem to shift. Cicadas flew in lazy circles, clung to tree trunks, and flicked their wings. They looked on, complacent and still, while their brethren were devoured by woodland creatures. Perhaps the swarming cicadas had been driven to madness by some odor from the car engine? Or maybe she'd interrupted a mating ritual. She decided it didn't matter. If another chance for escape presented itself, she'd take it. She'd rather brave the insects than remain Girl's prisoner.

She scanned the gathering dusk, the quarry with its still waters, the cave bathed in lavender from the setting sun. She ticked through the time since she'd first awoken in the cabin. Four days? She'd been unconscious for long stretches, so five. Maybe even seven. Surely by now someone had found her abandoned car. A hunter, a hiker, a forest ranger. They'd have seen the scratches and dents. Noted the disarray inside. Police would have been alerted and her license plates identified. A helicopter search would ensue. She glanced at the sky, a quiet, empty expanse. Her heart sank.

Or perhaps, she reassured herself, an investigation of all the residences in the area would come first. Girl and the cabin had obviously been here for generations. Local authorities had to know of this place. But whatever the case, she couldn't rely on outside help. As she well knew, there were no guarantees when it came to other people. She glanced back. Girl was feeding the rope through thick-fingered hands that might easily snap one of Mary's arms.

And there was another reason, one she was reluctant to admit even to herself—if she could resolve the situation on her own, she'd avoid broadcasting to the world that she, one of the legal profession's finest minds, had been kidnapped by an ignorant bumpkin.

Mary stepped from the porch. Pain shot through her bare heel as Girl stumbled into her. "Watch it! Please," Mary yelped, cupping her foot. "I could really use shoes suitable for this terrain. For the safety of the babies."

A mysterious smile spread across Girl's face. She tugged the rope, pulling Mary to the side of the doorway. "Stay." She rummaged just inside the door, the rope knotted tightly in one fist. When she straightened, she held a pair of work boots, identical to her own but half the size. She placed them on the porch step. "Kept 'em oiled for you so they wouldn't get stiff."

Mary examined the boots. Assuming these had actually belonged to Girl's mother, they were extraordinarily well maintained after so many years. More evidence of Girl's slavish devotion to her abuser. She loosened the laces and slipped one boot on. A perfect fit.

Girl's face lit up. "Like that fairy story. With the glass shoe."

"Hardly. But these will do." Mary jammed her foot into the other boot. She gave the laces an angry tug, rose from the porch, and set off at a brisk pace. The strange vitality was still with her. Girl fell in behind her, the rope looped over one arm.

"The bugs want to run," Mary called over her shoulder. Without waiting for a response, she broke into a full sprint, hoping Girl had failed to secure some part of the harness. Her experiment ended with the rope jerking her backward and onto her butt. Girl hadn't even grabbed the rope. Her weight alone had been sufficient to counter Mary's momentum.

"Mama! You got to lemme know 'fore you run like that," Girl said. "Somebody's gonna get hurt."

After climbing to her feet, Mary headed toward the dirt road that ran from the cabin down the mountain. At least she could conduct reconnaissance and gain a better understanding of the surroundings. "Step up the pace, okay? These babies are raring to go," she yelled over her shoulder, wondering how far Girl would let her venture.

On each side of the road, the earth rose steeply, studded by small rocks and scarred by erosion from the spring rains. The soft dirt was a crosshatch of tire tracks. She knelt for a closer look, but the rope tightened and her chest twisted backward. Girl had halted, arms spread wide. "Didn't you miss it, Mama? You used to say it was a slice of heaven. Did some work while you was gone. Added screens to the windows. Smoothed the path up to the quarry. Fixed the old springhouse so it keeps milk and such cool as can be."

"Very nice," Mary replied. "I'd love to see the improvements. Especially the quarry path." Perhaps the vantage would reveal an actual, modern paved road or even a distant town. "Can we head up now?" She cringed as a cicada whirred past her. But like the cluster on the porch, the beast seemed oblivious to her.

Girl gnawed her lip, then shook her head. "Mosquitoes gonna be biting soon. Let's head back."

When they neared the cabin, the lichen-covered outhouse came into view. Girl tugged her toward the porch, but Mary resisted. "I need the restroom." Indeed, her bladder ached. But she also wanted to continue her survey of the property.

Girl gave her a baffled look.

"Toilet," Mary clarified, pointing to the small, weathered structure. Girl nodded, then loosened her grip, allowing Mary to proceed. It was Mary's first visit to the outhouse. The times before, when she'd been under the influence of whatever toxin the cicadas had injected into her, Girl had balanced her over a bucket. There may have also been a rudimentary bedpan. Repulsed, Mary pushed the thought away.

They drew closer to the outhouse, Girl at the lead. She pried open the warped door, then stepped back, the rope clasped in her hands, with all the formality of a priest clutching an incense burner.

"Untie me, please." Mary whip-snapped the rope so it cracked at Girl's chest. Girl reddened, then shifted her weight from side to side. Mary could almost smell the consternation churning within the woman's skull. "Girl, I need privacy. I'm going to shut the door. I can't do that unless you untie me."

"Okay. But I'll stomp you if you run. Don't make me, Mama. Please," Girl said, lower lip quivering.

"There will be no need to stomp me. I promise."

Girl leaned her weight into Mary, pinning her against the outhouse wall while she untied the harness. After a final tug, she gripped Mary's arm and steered her inside. She lingered in the doorway, a solid wall of flesh.

"Back. Please," Mary said.

Girl hesitated for a moment, then obeyed. Mary slammed the door, wedging it firmly into the doorframe. "Naturally," she grumbled as her search for a latch ended in failure. The creature likely enjoyed her sit with the door flung open to the great outdoors.

Any urge to urinate fled once Mary was sealed inside. The stench of excrement filled the small space. Flies ricocheted against the worn walls. The toilet consisted of a hole cut into a rectangular wooden riser, the edges worn smooth, presumably by generations of Girl's progenitors. The ancient structure seemed ready to collapse.

Likely there were missing nails or rotten boards. Perhaps she could create an opening and slip away. She drew in a long breath of fetid air, hoping to slow her galloping heart. With shaking fingers, she explored the walls, warped horizontal planks of varying lengths, but uniformly a foot wide.

"You making a big one or what?" Girl called.

"My insides are a mess after the last few days," Mary yelled, hoping her volume would steady her voice and mask the creak of wood as she climbed atop the riser. "You may as well relax. I'll be a while."

The shaking in Mary's fingers had spread to her whole body. She released a long exhale, then positioned herself astride the hole. Plank by plank, she tested the integrity of the back wall. Moisture slid from her underarms. She locked her knees to still her trembling legs. Halfway up the wall, her fingers probed a soft, rotten spot in the wood.

Girl's shuffling and sighs sounded just outside the outhouse door. Mary froze, muscles aching and knotted. When the door remained closed, she carefully, quietly, wiggled a nail from the disintegrating wood. Then another. She'd need at least five minutes to remove the entire plank and slip through the narrow opening. "Is there toilet paper?" she yelled, her eyes on the roll spiked on a nub at the base of the riser.

The grass swished under Girl's heavy tread. A soft thud followed, and Mary imagined the woman's palms on the door. "You don't see none?"

"Privacy!" Mary snatched the inside handle, just as Girl tugged from the outside. Every ounce of her body weight was needed to keep the door from flying open. Her heart slammed her ribs. "I see it now. Thank you."

She slipped her fingers around the plank's edge and began a delicate maneuvering. As each nail came free, she pocketed it, coughing or sighing to camouflage the procedure. Before the final tug, she mimicked a bowel-stricken groan and wrenched the board away.

She tumbled backward, pinwheeled one arm, then caught herself, her fingertips tented on the doorframe. The plank dangled from the fingers of the other hand. Trickles of sweat became a flood, flowing down her sides. She fought to silence her ragged breath.

The door shuddered with Girl's weight. "You okay, Mama?" she asked. "Got some chamomile. That'll fix you."

"For God's sake, leave me in peace. Your interruptions are not helping."

She tensed her abdomen, curling herself forward and regaining her position on the riser. Carefully, she leaned the plank against the wall. Cool evening air drifted through the gap, a rectangular slit measuring a foot wide and four feet long. The cicadas had fallen silent. For once, Mary wished for the cover of their earsplitting din. But perhaps their silence signaled a retreat to their rotten little burrows, or hives, or wherever the hell they spent their downtime. She shivered, remembering yesterday's attack. Then it occurred to her that she could probably outrun them. After all, they hadn't fallen upon her until she'd slowed to a walk, and then again when she was trapped inside the car.

Gripping the opening, she slid one leg through the gap. She planted her boot on the grass, then shimmied her slender frame sideways, until most of her body was outside. Quietly, with excruciating slowness, she withdrew her remaining leg. She poked her head back into the outhouse. "Almost done. Thank you for your patience."

"Welcome, Mama." Girl's voice tinkled with delight.

Mary squinted into the evening gloom. The backyard was a tangle of low undergrowth, canted along the mountainside and descending into the forest.

"Need more paper?" Girl called.

Mary bolted toward the trees, uncertain of her route. The shadows of the backyard seemed to merge into a central pool of darkness. A hulking figure rose up, blocking her path. For a moment, Mary thought Girl had caught her, that the light of the setting sun had distorted Girl's shape and draped her in shadow, stretching her to seven feet tall with shoulders the width of a car. But she quickly realized her mistake. This was no person. The figure's inhumanly thick arms rested against a broad midsection, which widened into mountainous breasts. Great hips flowed into continental thighs. But there were no feet. Instead, the figure hovered inches above the ground, emitting a low hum.

Shock flooded Mary, paralyzing her mind and body. Behind the hovering form, the forest loomed, a dark expanse writhing with shadows. Mary goaded her limbs into motion, sprinting left. The figure mirrored her, swift and silent, blocking her path. Mary faked right, then juked left. The figure glided with ghostly ease, anticipating Mary's every move. It passed through a ray of setting sun, flickering with iridescence, then fractured into a thousand smaller forms.

Cicadas.

Mary screamed, backing toward the outhouse, one hand stretched behind her, eyes locked on the swarming monolith. When her fingers touched the wood, she whirled around. Girl's dark eyes shone through the gap Mary had created to escape. Her thick fingers waved Mary inside. She spoke in a low, quavering whisper. "I'll protect you."

Mary torpedoed her body through the opening, her face and breasts scraping against the raw wood. Girl clumsily gripped Mary's waist and jerked the rest of her body through. Mary's head rammed into Girl's torso, unleashing a burst of flatulence. The gas mingled with the odors of the outhouse, forming an overpowering stench. Coughing and gagging, Mary struggled to free herself from the folds of Girl's body, but the confines were too tight. She dug her elbows into Girl. Her feet kicked wildly.

"Be still," Girl hissed. She rattled Mary into an upright position and held her tight, powerful thumbs digging into Mary's arms.

Outside, the horde of hovering cicadas kept an eerily quiet vigil, circling the outhouse, disappearing then reappearing every few seconds. Every other revolution, the blob would pause in front of the opening in the wall, stretch to eight feet, then ten, before shrinking to its original size. Mary trembled, fighting the urge to draw closer to Girl. The seething mass of cicadas appeared menacing. And intelligent. This wasn't the natural swarming behavior of insects.

Wedged next to Mary, Girl's panicked mouth-breathing intensified. Her sweat soaked into Mary's clothes. Mary tried not to gag, terrified that the motion and noise would draw unwanted attention. "What—" Mary began, her voice barely audible. But Girl clamped her thick fingers across Mary's mouth. Her great heart thundered in Mary's ear.

Suddenly, the swarm collapsed into a seething basketball-size sphere of eyes, legs, and wings. For a moment, the iridescent orb hung in midair. Then it detonated, flinging yellowish ooze against the outhouse and through the gap.

"Jesus!" Mary spat, sloughing discharge from her face.

Girl threw open the door, locked her arms around Mary, then hustled across the weed-choked yard. At the same time, Mary's itching kicked into overdrive. She shrieked, her cries echoing through the valleys of Girl's enormous ear. But the woman barreled on. When the root cellar came into view, Mary's shrieks grew louder. She hammered her fists into Girl's thighs. Girl's embrace tightened, constricting Mary's rib cage.

"Got to show her I got you in hand. That the babies are safe," Girl huffed, her sugary breath perfuming Mary's screams of pain. She pinned Mary's arms, flung the cellar door open, and thrust her inside. Mary stumbled, then twirled around to face Girl. Lunging forward, she sank $20,000 of cosmetic dentistry into Girl's earlobe, praying her veneers held. Girl howled and fell backward, leaving a chunk of flesh in Mary's teeth.

Mary shot forward, but the door slammed, sealing her in darkness.

Chapter 6

The blood of Girl's earlobe coated Mary's chin, salty and warm. She spat and gagged, rubbed her forearm across her mouth, then pounded the root cellar door. "Girl!" she yelled. "You will rot in jail for the rest of your insignificant life! My colleagues will have tracked my vehicle by now. Do you understand how meaningless a person like you is to society? A jury will relish locking you in a cage!"

With each word, she beat the rough wood, splinters lodging in her palms. The dam of her self-possession had been breached. She had not clawed her way to the top only to perish in the hovel of a lonely lunatic with mommy issues.

The waning daylight leached through the filthy sliver of window. In the cellar's dark recesses, she could sense critters stirring. And what of the thing she'd seen out there? True, it had been dark, with the setting sun casting shifting shadows. But it had moved, blocking her path, like a willful, intelligent entity. Maybe she was losing her mind, or hallucinating. But Girl had seen it too. And the disgusting yellow ooze, still drying on her skin, was all too real.

She probed the darkness until her fingertips grazed the door, then slid to the ground, resting her back against the rough wood. She raked fingers through her hair, her meticulous curls now tangled and streaked with slime. There had to be a rational explanation for all of it: the hovering silhouette, the cicada attack in the Mercedes, the itching rash, and the strange and steady vitality of her fifty-seven-year-old body despite the laundry list of injuries she'd suffered.

And Girl. The image of her roughened face arose in Mary's mind. The scalding from the porridge was still evident. But in less than two days it had shifted from a vicious third-degree wound to something more akin to sunburn.

Science would provide a reason. Or psychology. Once all this was behind her and she had research and investigative resources at her disposal. For now, the priority was escaping this backwoods nightmare.

She swabbed her bloody chin with the sleeve of her blazer and considered the likelihood of Girl transmitting a blood-borne disease. The woman was a fringe dweller, but assuming her stories of childhood were true, her depraved mother had pimped her out. The first order of business after Mary returned to the land of the living would be a megadose of antibiotics.

All around her, the cellar's permanent residents were waking up, skittering along the dirt floor, clicking and chirruping, with the addition of a new noise, a distinctive squeak that suggested the presence of a rodent. She jumped to her feet, resolving to prod every inch of the cellar in search of a weapon or a tool. She'd either free herself from this homespun jail cell or clobber Girl senseless when she next showed her bovine face.

She shuffled forward until she felt the narrow edge of one of the shelves of mason jars she'd spied during her first internment. Patting the length of the surface, she encountered a grime-encrusted object, but it disintegrated in her hands. She continued walking her fingers forward, cobwebs lacing her hands, until she felt cool glass beneath a layer of dust, capped with a metal top. She palmed the dense, heavy jar. No doubt chock full of pickled animal parts or some other Depression-era delicacy.

The shelf contained seven more jars, each of which she placed on the ground. She then attempted to wrest the shelf from the wall, imagining a battering ram for Girl's midsection. But the wood was bolted into place. She searched the entire cellar, gritting her teeth through dangling filth of unknown origin and numerous insectile caresses. But she found nothing more substantial than the jars. Shelves and shelves of them.

She weighed a jar in her hand, then grabbed another. The shards of broken glass would do the most damage. But how to safely and accurately smash two jars together in total darkness? She would need light, which meant waiting until morning. And Girl might pop by for a visit before then. Perhaps a blow to the head with one of the jars? She'd need to bring the jar down with sufficient force, as Girl had already displayed a remarkable tolerance for pain.

As she indulged the vision of crushing Girl's head, intense itching erupted on her inner thigh. She cried out in agony and fell to the dirt floor. Tearing open the zipper of her slacks, she plunged one hand down her pant leg and dragged her nails along the skin. She sprawled in the dirt, arm propped behind her, skirting the edges of pleasure and pain. Finally, the itching subsided, and she withdrew her hand. A sticky film coated her fingertips. She felt queasy, remembering the pus-swollen slashes in Girl's skin and the unmistakable movement within.

Restlessly, she dried her palms on her slacks, rubbing harder and longer than was necessary. She was still certain her rash was some virulent strain of poison ivy or a similar toxic plant. Yet Girl's outlandish tale preyed upon her thoughts. Could any aspect of the superstitious drivel be true? Once again, she forced herself to confront the idea. Broods and clutches and caves, and a mysterious female figure who ruled over it all. An impressive level of description for someone who clearly had very little education, if any. But bugs mistaking her thigh for a tree, or whatever the hell they normally used to incubate their eggs, was beyond the pale. She'd spent a lifetime assiduously avoiding pregnancy and motherhood. There was no way in hell she'd been knocked up by a swarm of bugs.

Her first and only brush with pregnancy had been as a sophomore in college. After a late night at the campus pub, a philosophy professor she'd worshipped had fallen from his pedestal into her shocked, and unwilling, embrace. She'd immediately dropped his class and later, when she found out she was pregnant, scheduled an abortion. Nineteen years old and the recipient of a full scholarship to a respectable private college, she would not allow herself to call what had happened in the pub's dumpster-choked alley a rape. That would have implied powerlessness and lack of agency, in her mind dangerous admissions that might send her backsliding to the victimhood she'd only recently shed.

She'd briefly considered having the child, another human in the world with whom she'd share blood ties. But she was terrified that her past lay dormant in her, a ticking time bomb, waiting for the right conditions to awaken her own capacity to abuse. She left the abortion clinic the same way she'd arrived, alone. And with a firm intention to remain childless.

Birth control pills had been her initial solution, but by the time she was in her early thirties, she'd switched to an IUD, a choice that had the unexpected benefit of eliminating her periods. She'd never grown accustomed to menstruation, the strangeness of arguing in court or bullying the opposing counsel at the negotiating table while warmth gushed from her body and pelvic muscles garroted her abdomen. Her male colleagues, especially Teddy, would have been reduced to quivering blobs if they'd been similarly afflicted.

Like clockwork, she'd replaced the device every eight years. Until one day her gynecologist had hinted at menopause, suggesting the IUD was no longer serving a function. And just like that, an aspect of her biology she'd relegated to the shadows as an afterthought, or a symptom to be suppressed, came to an end.

She cast aside these musings and closed her fingers around one of the mason jars. After testing her grip on the dusty glass, she took up her post near the door. Her thoughts returned to the hovering apparition. In those terrifying moments behind the outhouse, the thing had seemed an inflated silhouette of Girl. But a different image now came to mind. The prehistoric Venus of Willendorf figurine, a grotesque exaggeration of the feminine form she'd first seen when it was emailed by one of her male colleagues to the rest of the partners. A lout and a cornball, he'd captioned the image *cave man porn*.

She drew in a sharp breath. The hovering form also resembled an object encountered more recently. The carved wooden doodad nestled next to Mary on the pallet on the first day she'd awoken in the cabin. She reflected on Girl, her religion of one, and the look in her eyes, an admix of adoration and fear, when she spoke of "Her In The Cave." And the three faded red dots on Girl's forehead in the shape of an inverted triangle, which matched what Mary had seen on her own forehead in the car.

Why would Girl have anointed them both with the upside-down triangle? Maybe a childish impulse to create similarities between them. Or did the paste contain poison, a sedative, or some kind of hallucinogenic? She wiped her palm across her forehead, feeling as if her mind were pushing up against some hidden truth.

Slivers of moving light broke the dark outline of the root cellar door. She gripped the mason jar and quietly got to her feet. The padlock bumped against the weathered wood. She slid to one side of the door, arms above her head, mason jar locked and loaded. The door creaked open.

"Mama?" Girl filled the doorway. Her flashlight illuminated the back wall. A pair of bright rodent eyes fled. Girl poked her head inside. "You awake?"

Mary brought the jar down with all her might. There was a dull *clunk*, followed by shattering glass. The flashlight hit the ground, then rolled upright, spotlighting Girl's stunned expression. Peaches slid over a gash on her cheek, then plopped to the ground. Fruit syrup, threaded with blood, dripped from her hair, down the fading raccoon-mask burn, onto her shoulders.

Stunned, Girl swayed in the doorway, cow eyed and mute. Mary broke from the shadows and shot through the door, slipping past Girl. She sprinted along the side of the cabin, where a kerosene lamp cast a forlorn glow through the window. When she reached the front porch, she sped on, past the pickup truck and toward the road. As she descended the rock-strewn driveway, her inner thigh exploded with itching. The sensation was ferocious and unbearable, as if a horde of tiny disembodied mouths were chewing through her flesh, bones, and viscera. Her limbs contorted and her feet twisted upon themselves. Her body launched several feet down the sloping driveway. She slammed into the hard-packed earth, immobilized by the inferno of itching. She writhed on the ground, shrieking, too crazed to even scratch, her unseeing gaze fixed upon a sky ablaze with stars. A sheet of frigid water rained down. She was vaguely aware of Girl at her side, clutching an empty washtub like a hollow shield. The pallet waited nearby.

Girl scooped Mary from the road and slammed her into the wooden frame. The icy water had quelled the torturous itching, and Mary fought, punching Girl while she was being strapped in.

"Be still!" Girl's voice was shrill, birdlike. Her closed fist slammed against Mary's head. Mary slumped, ears ringing as Girl hauled the pallet back to the cabin. Dragging the wooden frame up the porch steps, Girl cursed her mother with the same ancient rage she'd unleashed on the first day of Mary's captivity. She thundered into the cabin. In one fierce motion, she flung the pallet into a corner, knocking the rustic furniture aside. She stomped across the floor, then loomed above Mary, fists clenched.

Mary was seized with terror, even awe, at the magnitude of Girl's fury. The woman seemed ready to demolish Mary, the cabin, the entire world. Yet Girl's eyes betrayed an inner conflict, as if they'd been stitched into the wrong face, twin islands of sorrow adrift on an ocean of rage.

The fury won. The ocean rose up, engulfing the islands. Girl's hot breath blasted Mary's face. Her thick fingers tightened around Mary's neck.

"Wait." Mary's airless plea was barely audible. Her wrists bucked against the restraints.

Girl's grip tightened.

Dark blots congealed at the edges of Mary's vision. A puff of air escaped her collapsing throat.

Girl squeezed harder. A sob broke from her, a howl from a desolate plain.

Mary's lids fluttered. As her heart beat out its final rhythm, the words she needed to survive rose to her lips. "I'm sorry," she wheezed.

Girl's face went slack. Tears traced a bright rim along her eyelids, then doused her near-strangled victim. She peeled her fingers from Mary's bruised neck.

Air rushed into Mary's lungs, then blasted forth in a fit of coughing. Her body convulsed as oxygen returned to her blood and brain. Her heart raced to catch up. She slumped forward, head hanging, until her breathing quieted and her vision cleared. The room was a chaos of overturned furniture, tracked with dirt and brambles. The blue-black night filled the windows and poured through the open front door.

Mary could make out Girl on the porch steps, a softly sobbing figure draped in shadows. Abruptly, Girl turned toward Mary and rose from the steps. Darkness seemed to melt the features from her face. Her silhouette ballooned, then fragmented into a multitude of winged creatures. A towering form—a larger-than-life Venus of Willendorf—hovered for the length of Mary's held breath. Then it disappeared.

Without saying a word, Girl put the restraints back on Mary and left the cabin.

Throughout the night, Mary awoke from fitful dreams of the Venus silhouette. She would rub her wrists and ankles raw against the restraints, then listen for Girl's blubbering or her heavy tread. But the woman was gone.

During one of these awakenings, Mary peered bleary-eyed through the window in the direction of the cave. The cave mouth seemed to flash with deep green, then orange, before returning to black. She tried to brush off the strange sight, reasoning that her eyes must be fatigued, the oxygen levels in her blood still deficient. It was hard to know what any of this craziness meant, but she had to remain disciplined in her thinking and correct for her own misperceptions. She had to continue to study her captor, her weaknesses and wants, so she could engineer her escape.

When she was thirteen, Mary was ordered inside the small, dark closet beneath the basement stairs of Saint Agnes's for the last time. It was Good Friday. Sister Francis, a shuffling arthritic who the children had secretly dubbed "Quasimodo," meted out the punishment. Mary had long ago stopped fearing the closet. In fact, she'd come to enjoy the brief refuge from the chaos of the orphanage, a place to devour the sweets she'd begun swiping from the larder. Her expanding body now necessitated the removal of the cleaning supplies before she could be properly sealed in.

But on this day, the prospect of the closet filled Mary with despair. Sister Francis had interrupted an important mission that had begun many weeks ago. Mary had chanced upon a homemaking magazine tossed in a waste bin near the front entrance by a young couple hoping to adopt. The couple left after discovering the orphanage had no infants.

Mary had first been elated with the treasure of new reading material. She'd already consumed the contents of Saint Agnes's meager library several times over. But then, while reading the magazine front to back, she happened upon Dr. Calloway's Medicated Balm, guaranteed to clear the worst skin ailments, including psoriasis. The dragon-lady taunt still resurfaced occasionally. And great effort was required to secure her often too-tight clothing over the encrusted patches of skin. But the pain was the worst, a deep, throbbing burn that could keep her up at night. To raise the five dollars needed to purchase the ointment, she'd tapped into the informal economy that flourished between the orphans, trading her labor to complete another child's chores and selling a pair of new socks pilfered from the donations room. For the final dollar, she'd resorted to bullying a younger bully into loaning her the funds.

After weeks of waiting, Mary was en route to the bathroom for the first application of Dr. Calloway's when Sister Francis intercepted her. Toilet usage was only permitted during certain periods of the day, and Mary was out of bounds. While the nun dragged her toward the stairs, Mary considered overpowering her, something she could have easily done. But there were punishments far more sinister than the closet for such behavior. She'd have to wait until she was freed to apply the ointment, usually after two or three hours. Or maybe she'd try in the closet. She had grown skilled at maneuvering in the darkness. Halfway down the stairs, Sister Francis froze. Though her body was compromised, her eyesight was eagle sharp. Her fingernails clawed Mary's closed fist, and the Dr. Calloway's fell to the floor. The nun peered at the label, pretending to read, though all the orphanage knew of her illiteracy. She then stuffed the tube in the folds of her habit.

Mary stumbled alongside Sister Francis down the remaining stairs. Tears burned her cheeks as she removed the cleaning solutions from the closet, followed by mops and buckets.

"In you go," Sister Francis said when the work was done. The nun pulled the door closed, but Mary jammed her scuffed loafer into the opening. Sister Francis's face trembled. The grayish skin folded into rageful crags. She jerked Mary out of the closet and slapped her hard across the face.

Her cheek stinging, Mary held the nun's gaze. Her desperation for a cure, her long-nursed desire for normal, pain-free skin, the anguished waiting for the ointment to arrive—blasted her mind clear. A strategy arose, inspired by a snippet of conversation overheard two weeks ago while she emptied wastebaskets in the administrative offices on the ground floor.

"I know you can't read," Mary said.

Another powerful tremor shot through the enraged face. Another ringing slap met Mary's cheek.

"That paper they want you to sign," Mary plowed on, ignoring her fresh tears. "It's so they don't have to pay for your doctors and medicine if your cancer gets bad."

Sister Francis's open palm, poised to strike, froze midair. Fury drained from her complexion, revealing an aged, ravaged countenance, the eyes hollow and terrified.

"Before you sign the paper," Mary said, her voice strengthening, "bring it to me. I'll read it to you."

The nun nodded. A humbled, compliant child.

"But you have to give that back," Mary commanded, holding out her open hand. Sister Francis pulled the ointment from the folds of her habit and dropped it into Mary's palm.

That night, Dr. Calloway's Medicated Balm induced a torturous inflammation that sent Mary racing through the shadowy corridors for another off-limits activity, a shower. In the darkness, she rinsed the caustic ointment from her skin, muffling her sobs to avoid discovery.

In the morning, Sister Francis found Mary beneath a maple tree at the edge of the orphanage grounds, huddled against the trunk, feverish with pain. Mary read the letter aloud, her hands shaking but her voice steady. She directed the sister to secure a dictionary, and together they looked up words like *liability*, *breach*, and *indemnify* until they both understood the full meaning and consequences of the letter. When Sister Francis died three years later, it was after receiving reasonable health care, every penny fully covered by the diocese. Psoriasis continued to plague Mary. But from then on, she understood the power of trading against another person's weaknesses, and the keen force of her own mind.

When Mary next opened her eyes, the cabin was flooded with morning light. Girl had returned and was puttering around the room in a sleeveless undershirt. Her earlobe bore faint teeth marks, the only trace of Mary's vicious bite the night before, though she was sure she'd taken a chunk out. But Mary barely registered the fact of Girl's rapid healing. Her attention was drawn to Girl's breasts, which had undergone another drastic transformation, as if a plug had been pulled, draining their plumpness.

Girl stretched one arm toward the shelf above the water pump. Her right breast flashed in the wide armhole of her shirt. The flesh hung like a sail on a windless day. Yet she seemed oblivious, or inured, to the loss of her great bosom overnight. If anything, she was energetic, even sprightly. Her cheeks were rosy, and she hummed a nonsense tune while scooping a whitish goo, resembling lard, from a rusty can into a wooden mixing bowl. Every few moments, Girl glanced through the open cabin door to the cave. A secretive smile would steal across her face and one arm would encircle her waist, like a woman beset with images of last night's lover.

Mary knew it was possible to lose tremendous amounts of weight in a short period of time. In her forties, she'd trained with a former Olympic wrestler. But surely Girl hadn't been up all night, her chest encased in cling wrap, pounding sit-ups and jumping rope. And this was the second time it had happened. But truly—who gave a fuck? Hillbilly enemas, redneck herbal douches, spa day at the crick. "Just get me the hell out of here," Mary muttered.

Girl started at the sound of Mary's voice. She quickly donned a flannel shirt, but not before Mary caught sight of two wet circles on the front of her undershirt. Girl poured the contents of the mixing bowl into a plastic cup. "Breakfast," she chirped, carrying the cup to Mary. All traces of last night's trauma were gone. Had the lunatic already moved past how she'd almost strangled Mary to death?

Mary peered inside the cup, disturbed to feel her stomach rumbling at the sight of the disgusting sludge. "You didn't put that lard in this, did you?"

"Course there's lard." Girl snorted. "You forget how to make Mother's Milk? Yours was better than mine."

"White sugar?"

"Tree sugar." Girl flashed her blunt teeth.

"Like sap?"

Girl nodded. "Got to fatten you. For the babies. Else you'll lose 'em."

Mary grimaced. No wonder the woman emitted a constant stream of flatus.

Girl shook the cup, sliding it gently into Mary's hand. "For the babies," she said.

A plan for escape flashed clear and bright in Mary's mind. Simple, even obvious, as a good plan should be. She almost wept with relief.

"I won't be consuming this. Or anything else," Mary said.

Girl's smile faltered. She clutched the cup like a chalice. "You hungry, ain't you? Heard your belly. Ain't fed you since yesterday."

"I need you to focus, Girl. To hear me loud and clear. Unless you release me—and by this, I mean either call an ambulance or bring me to the nearest hospital—I will starve myself and by extension . . ." She swallowed her distaste. "The babies."

Girl shook her head. Her fingers slid up and down her corduroys. "Hospital don't know about this," she breathed. The loose skin of her chest quivered. "Ain't no doctor ever seen Her In The Cave. Or the miracle of the cicada babies born of our women. You know that."

"I'm sure the doctors will do their best." Mary sealed her lips as Girl again brought the cup, with its noxious, fatty contents, closer.

Girl pulled the cup away, dancing from foot to foot, her face a swamp of confusion.

"These are my terms." Mary fixed Girl with a long stare. "I will starve myself. And them. Unless you agree."

Chapter 7

Ignore the ignoramus, Mary counseled herself. Girl had been pacing nonstop since Mary announced her hunger strike earlier in the morning. Mary had long ago mastered the art of tuning out distractions, and humans, great and small. Her line of work rewarded it. She figured Girl would cave by tomorrow morning, latest. Especially as Mary cranked up the drama on her starvation of the "babies."

In the meantime, she mentally ticked off her list of action items for her return to the land of flushing toilets and electricity. Her unwashed skin was coated with a week's worth of grime. Her clothes were stiff with dirt, yellow ooze, and splotches of Girl's blood. Her pants were ripped along the inseam, the tear inching down her thigh. After initiating Girl's arrest, she would seek medical attention and then continue on to Cape Cod. During the drive, she'd phone her personal masseuse so he could meet her at her island estate shortly after she arrived. Two or three hours of Swedish and she'd be feeling like herself again. The following morning, rested and back in the saddle, she would set up an emergency conference call and fire everyone on her staff. Yes, she'd ordered them not to contact her. But goddammit. *Not one of them* secretly kept tabs on her? Tracked her phone or car by GPS? Pointed a sniffer at her IP address? Her firm regularly employed these very techniques to dig up dirt and bolster their cases.

Her staff's failure to surveil her struck Mary as blatant incompetence. Or worse, complacency. She was the firm's most valuable attorney. The rainmaker who enabled their privileged lifestyles. A staff worthy of her would have found a way to override her wishes for seclusion without her knowledge. They had not. For that, they would be jettisoned.

Mary glanced at Girl, whose face was a thicket of worry. When the woman's despairing eyes met her own, Mary fluttered her lashes and lolled her neck, as if on the verge of fainting. Girl halted her pacing and rushed over with a cup of Mother's Milk. Mary sealed her lips and shook her head emphatically. Girl fretted for a moment, then brought the cup to her own lips, gulping down the pale sludge. Her breasts were already regaining their plumpness. The gruel must contain a massive amount of calories. Within seconds, the room filled with Girl's sweet stench. She slumped away to stare through the screen door, as if some neon-flashing solution would flare forth from the great outdoors.

While Girl polished off the revolting Mother's Milk, Mary reconsidered the sequence of her release. Should she stick with her demand of a hospital first? It might make more sense for Girl to pull over at the first gas station. There, Mary could enlist the clerk's help to call the police. Then again, she had to remember she was in cornpone central, where ignorance was king. There was a risk that the high school dropout of a clerk would fail to register the gravity of the situation. Girl might then renege on the bargain and permanently imprison Mary in the root cellar. Or worse. For all her pigeon-toed docility, the woman could turn violent on a dime.

A buttery aroma pulled Mary from her thoughts. Girl was hunched over a row of pancakes on the woodburning stove. Girl cast a furtive glance at Mary. "Mm-mmm," she grunted. "Buckwheat johnnycakes. You like that." Oil popped and sizzled, triggering another grunt.

Mary drew in a long breath, silently reminding her digestive system of a decade of abstinence from blood-sugar-spiking carbs and her hard-won sculpted legs, narrow waist, and firm glutes. Still, her stomach issued a noisy plea. Mary was unperturbed. In the contest of mind over body, her mind always triumphed. And how different was this from the many rigorous cleanses and fasts she'd endured even while attending decadent business banquets and unending client dinners?

She steered her thoughts back to reentering her life. After the conference call, she'd turn her attention to the MaxFauna trial. Weirdly, her current impasse with Girl had inspired a new line of thought. Girl's attachment to the "babies" bore parallels to Mary's star witness. The woman checked all the boxes for a credible witness: an engineer who managed a high-performing, all-female team; a single mom with a benign social media life centered mostly around her daughter's cancer diagnosis and treatment; a churchgoer. The woman's testimony would cast doubt on the accuser's character, undermining her claim that workplace misogyny, embedded in the company's culture, had led to her alleged rape. The witness was also extremely loyal to MaxFauna.

But had Mary fully exhausted the potential benefits of this witness? The current approach was sufficient if everything proceeded as planned. But what if the opposing council introduced a surprise witness or piece of evidence? She had to be prepared to mount an emergency defense, in which case less savory tactics might be required—such as influencing her star witness to emphasize, or de-emphasize, certain aspects of the testimony. No outright lies, of course. More like a well-crafted suggestion or insinuation. As it stood, the witness's sole contribution was to contradict a key piece of the accuser's timeline. What if she introduced new information? Or recontextualized a damning fact?

The witness's greatest preoccupation was her daughter's health care and the associated costs. During their initial meeting, Mary had gently teased out this information until she determined the true source of the woman's loyalty to MaxFauna—she'd just survived a round of layoffs that would have imperiled her daughter's health insurance. For now, MaxFauna's excellent plan fully covered the complex treatment needed for the daughter's rare childhood cancer.

Like Girl's undying devotion to the "babies," the woman's concern for her daughter's well-being left her vulnerable to manipulation. Mary could tap into this, incentivizing the witness to shape her testimony as needed. During the next prep meeting, Mary would hint at the possibility of facilitating an arrangement for the daughter to gain access to experimental treatments or some hotshot doctor. The hospital administrator she'd represented last year came to mind. He'd pledged eternal indebtedness after she'd steered him through a settlement with an on-the-job paramour.

Girl stomped toward Mary, sending tremors through the rustic furniture and homespun tchotchkes. Even in her reduced state, the woman's girth was impressive. One hand held a spatula, the other a tin plate with a steaming stack of pancakes slathered in butter and syrup. She placed the food on a stool near the pallet. Saliva flooded Mary's mouth.

"Syrup's right from the tree," Girl said, her voice bright with forced cheer.

"I have no doubt of that," Mary replied, a fleck of spit escaping her mouth.

"See. Your mouth is juicing. You want it."

Mary's nostrils flared. She lengthened her neck. Her thick curls, tangled with dirt and twigs, spilled over her shoulders. "Girl. I've told you what I want."

Girl waved the pancakes beneath Mary's nose. The hunger pangs surged. Had Mary's hands been free, they would have flown unbidden to the plate. Suddenly the plastic cup with gray gruel was at Mary's lips.

"Mother's Milk is the same as these pancakes," Girl cooed. "Sweet. I even warmed it."

Mary clenched her jaw and jerked her face away. When Girl pressed the drink closer, Mary slammed her forehead against the cup, knocking it from Girl's grip. Girl recoiled, her hand cupping the earlobe Mary had sunk her teeth into.

Mary steadied her voice. "I'm deadly serious, Girl. I'll eat nothing. Unless you bring my purse with my phone. Or drive me to a hospital. Otherwise, the babies will starve."

Girl remained silent. She removed the pancakes, swiping the top two and nibbling as she shuffled back to the washtub.

"You can, however, bring me water," Mary said.

Girl scurried to fulfill Mary's wish, returning with a chipped coffee cup, still chewing the pancakes. Mary shook her head. "You should never keep a chipped cup. Bacteria collects in the crack." Girl returned with a mason jar of water, which Mary quickly polished off. Mary pointed to her face, straining against the leather wrist restraints. "Would you please wipe my face? With a clean cloth and fresh water?"

After Girl wiped away the grime, Mary considered asking for a hairbrush. Or something that might function as a hairbrush. But the risk of Girl presenting her with an object meant for an animal, or some hairy part of Girl's own body, was too great. She'd have to return to civilization with a rat's nest.

She studied Girl putting away the pancake ingredients. In her dejection, she was clumsy and slow moving. Mary decided to turn the screws a bit more, not enough to trigger Girl's rage but enough to let her know this wasn't some idle threat.

"I once lived on nothing but water for a week," Mary called across the cabin. "It's a treatment out in California. A water fast. They claim it resets your system. Reduces inflammation. On average, more than half of participants fail to complete the program. But honestly, I could have gone another week." After a long sigh, she continued, "Unlike these precious babies. They're weak with hunger. On the verge of expiring." Girl twisted toward Mary, her eyes glinting in the shadow of her brow. Mary pushed on. "I haven't heard from them in at least an hour. They were already distressed after what happened last night." She flashed her neck, where Girl's hands had nearly crushed her windpipe. Girl staggered backward, uttered a cry, then fled the cabin.

"Might be a good time to get ready for our trip to town!" Mary yelled through the screen door. Her eyes followed Girl's plodding figure until she disappeared behind the back of the house. A vague unease crept over her. What was the creature up to now?

Mary tested the wrist and ankle restraints. The straps barely budged. She was weak with hunger. She needed to accelerate this whole process somehow, before her brain and body turned to mush. A buzzing sound overrode the panic building in her chest. She peered through the screen door. Girl was visible beyond the grassless patch where the truck was parked, at the top of the rocky driveway.

At first, Mary attributed the buzzing to a few dozen cicadas amassed on the tree overlooking the Ford pickup. Freed of their amber shells, the insects busily traversed the trunk and fluttered between branches. Their translucent wings sparkled with orange iridescence against dark, segmented bodies. Mary homed in on a pair of cicadas, strangely still, seemingly bonded at the base of their abdomens. Suddenly, one of the pair took flight, leaving half of her squirming mate on the tree trunk and half still attached to her backside. Mary flinched as the horrid spectacle flew toward the screen door, then veered away.

The buzzing grew louder, and she caught sight of the true source of the noise—a chainsaw wielded by Girl, who was trimming back a low-hanging tree branch from the driveway. As the saw gnawed at the branch, a small cloud of cicadas appeared, swirling above Girl, then landing on her rough cap of hair, her arms, and, surprisingly, on the chainsaw itself. Girl powered down the saw and began speaking. Mary strained to make out the words, but the distance was too great. After a few minutes, the swarm took flight, billowing gently above Girl's head. Smiling, Girl reached upward, seeming to tickle the swirling cloud before it congealed and drifted away.

Charming, Mary thought. The chainsaw buzzed back to life. She turned her attention to working her wrists out of the leather restraints. But the chainsaw fell silent once again. Mary's gaze returned to Girl. Even from a distance, it was clear the woman's entire body had stiffened. Mary traced Girl's wide-eyed stare to a descent in the driveway where a figure had appeared—a tall, thin man whose knobby knees protruded from baggy hiking shorts. A wide-brimmed hat cast his face in shadow. He raised his hand in greeting. Mary summoned all the force of her hunger-racked body and screamed "Help me!"

As the words left her mouth, the throbbing cicada chorus swelled, perfectly matching the pitch of her voice, swallowing her scream. The man paused and cocked his head. He gestured toward the surrounding trees, then addressed Girl, mouthing a greeting Mary couldn't hear.

"Here!" Mary screamed, her throat burning with her raw cries. "I'm in here! Kidnapped!" Again, her sound was instantaneously overwhelmed by a sequence of earsplitting bursts from the cicadas. The man grinned broadly and covered his ears.

Mary gathered her strength, this time emitting a long, wordless howl. The cicadas responded with a tidal wave of song that so tickled the man that he performed a jig. As Girl watched him dance, her stiff, predatory posture suddenly relaxed, an arrow released from its bow. The heavy burls of her shoulders dropped. Mary's raw screams continued, seeming to orchestrate a cicada symphony. Girl sidled closer to the man, sharing his pleasure. He remained intensely focused on Girl while she pointed to the ground and the trees. Finally, he shook her hand and strode back the way he'd come. Mary slumped against the rough wood, hoarse and exhausted.

Girl stared in the direction of the man's retreat long after, Mary surmised, he would have disappeared down the steep road. At last, her reverie broke, and the chainsaw roared to life. Impatiently, Mary followed Girl's progress until the branch had been removed, lopped into smaller pieces, and stacked neatly aside the porch.

"Well?" Mary rasped when Girl had plodded up porch steps. "Who was that?"

"You okay, Mama? Sounds like you swallowed rocks."

"Most likely a symptom of the starvation you're forcing the babies to endure. Who was the man out there?"

"Nobody. Just a hiker."

Mary narrowed her gaze. Was the goose actually blushing? "But you chatted for a while. Was he some kind of . . . companion? A boyfriend, perhaps?"

"No!" Girl shrieked. In two thunderous strides, she was at Mary's side. "He's not like those men you brought." Her fist hammered the pallet, barely missing Mary's face.

"Of course not!" Mary gasped. "I just meant, I'm happy to see you've made a friend."

Girl's gaze met Mary's, dark and uncertain. "He came because of the Brood. He loves them. Like we do."

Mary forced a smile, deciding to leave the topic unbroached. For now.

Dusk darkened the cabin and the world outside. All afternoon, Mary had nodded in and out of sleep, powerless against the somnolent haze that overtook her. The boredom. Her weakness from hunger. The toll of hours and hours of hypervigilance. Not even her obsession with the arrival of the stranger earlier in the day could keep her awake. Who was he? Some kind of nerdy cicada enthusiast? Her pulse raced with the thought that he might be an undercover cop, posing as a hiker. She curtailed the most disturbing inquiry—whether the cicadas had displayed an intelligent sonic defense to prevent her rescue—deciding that in her hunger and duress, it must have only seemed so.

The scent of grilled meat drifted from the woodburning stove, where Girl maneuvered above a hot skillet, sweat occasionally dripping into a pan with burger patties. A quiet groan of hunger escaped Mary. Had Girl snuck away to buy ground beef while she slept? Or was this some fresh-killed creature from the woods? She craned her neck and stared through the screen door. A few cicadas crept along the dented hood of the truck. Could Girl have started that junkyard specimen without awakening her? She swallowed, draining her watering mouth. "Girl, if you take me to a diner, I'll eat two of those and wash it down with a Mother's Milkshake. Otherwise, you can eat those burgers yourself."

Girl again enacted her foolish bait-and-switch, waving the burger under Mary's nose and then thrusting the Mother's Milk at her. Mary was grateful the hamburger wasn't the goal. At this point, she didn't think she could resist. Even the gray lard smoothie was starting to look good.

"Just a itty bitty sip," Girl wheedled. "Please."

Mary jerked her head from side to side, clenching her teeth. Girl danced around, struggling to bring the cup to Mary's lips while staying out of biting range. Mother's Milk sloshed onto the floor. Girl mopped up the spill on hands and knees while Mary assailed her with the suffering of the fictitious babies.

"Oh no!" Mary tilted her head toward her thigh.

"What?" Girl froze. She gripped the rag, soaked with Mother's Milk.

Mary's brows rose. She shook her head. "It pains me to say, another one has passed."

Girl jumped to her feet, round face flushed, eyes unblinking.

"Dead. Forever."

"No!" Girl sobbed.

"Yes," Mary said, softening her voice. "And you could have prevented it. Heartbreaking. But it's still within your power to put a stop to this."

Girl lunged for Mary's waistband, tugging at the button and zipper.

"Back the fuck up!" Mary's snapping teeth snagged a tuft of coarse hair. She yanked with all her might. Strands wedged between her teeth. Girl snatched away her hand, snagging the tear in Mary's inseam and ripping it farther. "This is wrong! As you are fully aware! Let me go!" Mary screamed.

"I can't!" Girl wailed, drawing closer to Mary. "You know it! I would. Even though it would hurt me bad. Or I'd come with you. But She ain't gonna let you go. You saw with your own eyes."

"Figure it out, Girl. Buy a dozen cans of Raid. Wrap me in flypaper and smuggle me out in your truck. I don't need to know the details. Just do it."

Girl wrung her hands and let out an anguished cry. Her eyes darted to the screen door. "The Brood is coming on. Hard. Biggest ever." She froze midsentence, then dropped to her knees.

Mary tensed. Now what was happening? Was the lunatic preparing to pray?

"You're growing, Mama. And changing." Still kneeling, Girl crept forward until she was inches from the pallet, her eyes riveted on Mary's inner thigh. "Faster than I ever seen."

A chill shot through Mary. She forced herself to follow Girl's awestruck gaze. Visible through the newly widened gap of the ripped inseam was a strip of Mary's inner thigh, the same spot where Girl had discovered the small blister two days before. The lesion had tripled in size and was now a raised, six-inch oblong. She hunched closer, eyes probing the ruptured skin.

"Hold up!" Girl scrambled to her feet, rustled around the kitchen, then returned with a kerosene lamp. She adjusted the flame, spotlighting Mary's lap, then produced an old magnifying glass with a missing handle. Mary curled forward even more. The blister zoomed in and out, at the mercy of Girl's wobbly grip. But at one point the lamplight and the lens aligned perfectly. Mary's body gripped and shuddered. The light pierced the blister's fluid-filled membrane, revealing rows and rows of tiny, slender ovoids sprouting from a cleft in the underlying tissue. The creatures nestled side by side, a gleaming, tumorous white. Rice-like, as Girl's had been, only now seeded in Mary's flesh. Mute with horror, Mary could only gawk while Girl adjusted the glass, revealing two faint dots at the uppermost tip of each living grain. Girl cooed, "Eyes are coming in already. Soon, li'l baby legs. Mouthparts. Head feelers. Once they hatch, we call 'em nymphs . . ."

A howl burst from Mary's throat. Girl fell back. The magnifying glass thumped to the ground and rolled off. The lamp tumbled, spilling kerosene on the graying floorboards. A small flame sprang up. Girl pounded the fire with her boot while keeping her frightened gaze on Mary.

"You saw 'em, didn't you, Mama?"

"Go! Out of my sight!" Mary yelled. Girl stumbled out of the cabin.

Arching against the pallet, Mary slammed her legs together, hoping to burst the hideous swelling. But she was weak with hunger and restrained at the ankles and managed only a feeble clap. Her bound hands curled into claws, aching to dig the flesh from her thigh. She retched and sobbed, no longer able to deny the unthinkable—insects were nesting within her, colonizing her thigh with their parasitic presence. She trembled, desperate to escape her own contaminated body, powerless to halt the metamorphosis unfolding within.

Girl's earlier words rang through her mind: *"You're growing, Mama. And changing."*

By the time Mary reached adolescence, she was escaping to the orphanage's basement closet almost daily. In the secret darkness, she binged sweets, especially syrup, feeding with a wild, suckling hunger. As the sweet thickness of the syrup broke across her tongue, her spirit calmed. She untethered from the rules and capricious discipline that permeated every second of her life. For a moment, she felt sated. She knew comfort.

Her thirst for sweets on top of Saint Agnes's starch-heavy menu amplified the growth and changes of her body. Moving through the institution's dim hallways, she felt like a huge, rounded balloon with hands and feet glommed on, inflated with syrup instead of air. This sensation filled her with shame, but also an odd sense of safety. She'd witnessed the bodies of older girls with slender physiques loudly broadcasting the onset of womanhood, regardless of how the girl might feel about that change. It didn't matter if she was ready for it or wished to hold off a bit longer until she could be sure of what it all meant beyond the walls of the orphanage. She'd also observed the reactions these changes triggered in the boys, and sometimes the male staff, of Saint Agnes: gibbering idiocy, leering glances, or overt hostility. But for Mary, the budding breasts, strange tufts of hair, and mysterious blood flow were all blended and obscured by her wide, rolling contours and angry swaths of psoriasis. She moved about her small world armored within her own flesh. In exchange, she suffered the sting of nasty taunts and hours of kneeling on rice for her gluttony. But those consequences felt like they were on her terms and her time, the closest she could get to control of her body and her destiny.

In college, her body evolved, along with her understanding of its capabilities. Her enrollment had been a miraculous occurrence initiated by an eager young social worker who'd talked her way into Saint Agnes to present college and financial aid options to a small group of kids aging out of the system. Mary took a required fitness class and learned to run, flushing her body with a new kind of intoxicant: endorphins. She experimented with weight training, the only woman in the university's workout room, and learned that she was naturally strong. The most thrilling discovery was the ability to sculpt her body into a new form. In between her studies, she tinkered with various regimens, calibrating nutrition and exercise until she'd fashioned a body that signaled strength, perfection, and self-discipline. When the urge arose to nurse the difficulties of the day on sweets or she was beset by the nagging feeling that she was a scruffy, unwanted castaway among privileged youth, she would subject herself to a grueling weight session, then run late into the night until she fell exhausted to the track. But the greatest suppressant was the feeling that her desolate past was never far behind. Her balloon-self lurked in the shadows, ready to reembrace Mary if she were to fall.

Later, when her success was established and finances allowed, she'd turned to cosmetic reinforcements: breast augmentation in the late eighties, Botox and rhinoplasty in the early 2000s, ongoing lifts and touch-ups to eradicate flaws and slow the march of time. The purest low-fat food, fistfuls of supplements, personal trainers who charged hundreds an hour, unrelenting self-discipline—this was her formula for mastery of her physical self, her defense against the vagaries of people and the world. She took in only that which strengthened her and walled out anything that did not.

At some point during her exhausted stupor, Mary's head had rolled forward, and she dozed. Her eyes cracked open to the sight of her torn inseam and the sluglike swelling on her thigh. She inhaled sharply and averted her gaze. Shadows stretched across the cabin. A looming figure darkened the doorway.

"You," Mary said, tongue thick in her dry mouth.

Girl stepped forward, fingers gripping the handle of a battered pail. "Brought this. Case you gotta make water."

Mary forced her gaze to her lap and regarded the swelling. The *clutch*, as Girl had called it. "The babies are real," she muttered, almost to herself.

"Course they're real. You think I was lying? That why you was so mad before?"

"They are inside me. Growing."

"Sure are." A half smile wormed across Girl's face. "You ready, then? For Mother's Milk?"

"I am desperately thirsty. The babies even more so."

"I'll get you water first then," Girl said, turning.

"Wait. Do you know how long a human being can survive without water?"

Girl clutched the pail to her bosom and shook her head.

"Three days. Something as fragile as these babies, maybe two. Maybe less."

Girl fled to the kitchen. The creak of the water pump soon followed.

Mary called out, "I have a new offer for you to consider." The creaking stopped. Girl shuffled from the kitchen, a water-filled jar in hand. Shoving down her desperate thirst, Mary continued, "No

Mother's Milk. And now, no water. Until you take me from this place. To a health clinic. To a phone. To a motel. Any or all of the above."

Mary tensed, waiting for Girl to wail and plead. But her captor only cocked her head toward the screen door, where the hoarse trill of cicada song wafted in on the evening breeze.

"The babies. Her In The Cave," Girl said, breaking her silence. "Only goodness I ever been a part of. Far as anybody else, I'm dirt. Lower than dirt." She let her gaze linger on Mary. "I will protect Her. And what's Hers. With my life."

Staring into the dark loam of the woman's eyes, Mary replied, "Then you better think long and hard about how you want to resolve this situation. Because you are on the verge of breaking your vow. And hear this." Her voice hardened. "My body belongs to me. Not to her. Not to you." She fanned open her thigh. "Not to these."

Girl retracted the pallet, lowering Mary into a horizontal position for the night. She stepped away, murmuring, "You was always like iron."

Mary studied the woman's face, relieved by the deep resignation she saw there. "I'm glad we're starting to understand one another."

Girl left the cabin for another of her nocturnal rambles. Mary's attention flew to her thigh, the tiny tumescent creatures, the promise of other body parts to come. Gritting her teeth, she repeated Girl's words, *like iron, like iron*, again and again, beating back the panic. She was like iron, forged from a thousand moments of hurt and abuse, recast through her unyielding willpower. This was just another horror to be survived. And conquered. Her breathing steadied. Until then, she would focus on the narrow set of facts pertinent to her survival: The lesion and the bugs were confined to a small part of her body, less than 0.01 percent of her mass. Aside from her hunger and thirst, the rest of her seemed healthy. Eventually, her doctor would nuke the creatures to kingdom come with powerful antibiotics, probably the kind used to treat exotic parasites picked up on cruises or from raw meat.

And she had Girl's infestation to look to as a test case. Presumably, Mary's condition would follow a similar course. Girl still seemed her powerful, behemoth self despite the presence of her *babies*. She winced. To what depth of loneliness did one have to sink to refer to an insect infestation of the flesh as "babies"? As she drifted into fitful sleep, the running track of her college years flickered in her mind, empty except for her, pushing herself through laps late into the night.

When she awoke, dawn had gilded the earth in shimmering rose. The sheen invaded the cabin, illuminating the water pump, the battered old trunk, and Girl, who quietly approached Mary to lever the pallet into the upright position. After that, Girl was in and out, slinking between the cabin and the truck.

"You're doing the right thing," Mary said, when Girl returned from the truck. "The cave witch will understand."

"Witch?"

"She'll probably reward you for exemplary service. Going above and beyond for the babies." Mary's voice was hollow with hunger. Her thirst blazed like desert sand. She struggled to organize her thoughts. "A promotion, perhaps. Now kindly untie me and help me to the truck."

The first ray of full sunlight shone forth, illuminating Girl's hangdog countenance. A thin plastic hose dangled from one hand. A metal funnel occupied the other.

"I'm sorry, Mama. This is gonna hurt."

Chapter 8

At the start of Mary's affair with Teddy, after their first afternoon of torrid sex in his pied-à-terre, he brought her to his favorite five-star French restaurant. The sparkling crystal and silverware intimidated her, as did the hovering, diffident waiters. She also felt alarmed by the *gras*, fat of all varieties lurking in the mysterious dishes. At that point, she'd only been thin for six years. The hard-won victory over her body's impulses seemed fragile. The specter of weight gain haunted every meal, each bite a dangerous necessity that could send her careening back to chaos. Through trial and error, she'd arrived at her perfect regimen: breakfast, consisting of dry toast, an apple, and black coffee; lunch, skipped because she was "too busy"; and dinner, an enormous salad topped with tuna, a near orgiastic experience after the day's deprivation.

That first meal with Teddy, she'd donned a perma-smile to hide her distress as course after course arrived at the table. How he'd enjoyed pressing butter-drenched escargot against her lips, or greens wilted with bacon fat, or his favorite, pâté de foie gras. She'd adapted, developing a strategy of extended chewing and long, flattering monologues that fed Teddy's ego while he fed himself. The result was that Teddy, always a glutton, polished off most of the meal. Her strategy also included excusing herself to quietly purge the few bites she'd ingested while Teddy attended to the check. She'd emerged stronger, having seeded the beginnings of a food protocol for social and business interactions that would serve her for the rest of her life. It was one of the many ways that she never entered a situation unprepared.

For years after the affair ended, Teddy continued to gift her with Christmas tins of foie gras, a reminder, she supposed, of what he saw as his role in her success. Each time, she'd take a whiff, reaffirm her disgust, then toss it in the trash. One year, a new intern caught sight of the gift on her desk, opened but not yet trashed, and launched into a polemic on how the unholy stuff was made; specifically the gavage or force-feeding regimes the ducks and geese had to endure. He described in graphic detail the process of artificially fattening the livers to create the mush that Teddy relished. While Mary agreed with the intern that the practice was barbaric, she immediately terminated him. Her firm was ill suited for activist types.

It was the intern's horrific description that wheeled through Mary's mind as she took in Girl, the metal funnel, and the plastic hose that escaped the woman's fumbling fingers and flapped across the muddy floor. Mary's emaciated body stiffened. Her belly, a dry, shallow concave, pumped wildly with panicked breath. Girl drew closer. Mary managed a hoarse scream, then snapped her jaws, angling to bite. But Girl edged behind the pallet, out of reach.

Mary jerked her head to and fro in a futile attempt to catch sight of Girl. She struggled to interpret the swishes and creaks that accompanied Girl's heavy tread. Rough fabric brushed her forehead and darkness fell. "Stop! What are you doing?" she cried, straining to see through the blindfold. The cloth tightened until her skull was flush with the pallet. Another strip of fabric was layered on top of the first, Girl's thick fingers maintaining a constant grip on the crown of Mary's head.

Mary stiffened her neck, straining against the cloth. A hard surface slid into place on one side of her face, and then the other. Her head and neck were now slotted to face forward, totally immobilized. "Girl! Slow down. Let's talk this through." Mary failed to keep her voice from trembling.

Shadows flickered through the fabric covering her eyes. She thought of the hose escaping Girl's clumsy hands, bouncing along the filthy cabin floor. "Wait! I'll eat. Bring on the Mother's Milk. And water! Please." But there was only a long piteous sigh. The floorboards groaned, first at Mary's side and then behind her. "Girl! Listen to me! You do not want to do this. You could harm me, tear my esophageal lining or damage my stomach." The wood floor creaked. Liquid gurgled nearby. "I said I would eat! Do you hear me!" The ring of metal on metal. "You'll give me an infection. Kill me and every one of those babies. Is that what you want?"

A sob broke through Mary's words. As her panic mounted, she found herself cursing Teddy, the long-ago affair, even her choice to continue with his firm. Why had she attended his funeral rather than heading straight for Cape Cod? She'd rescued the lech from his predatory behavior time and time again. Now her connection to him had spawned this nightmare, at a time when she'd considered her life nightmare-proof.

Oweee-oooo. Oweee-oooo.

The beastly chorus spilled in through the open window. Her cheeks and neck tingled, as if tiny wings fluttered past. When fingers gripped her chin, she snapped her teeth, her only defense, on empty air. She arched her back and bucked her hips until she felt Girl's bulk pin her midriff. Breathless from the pressure, she wheezed for oxygen, praying that the rickety pallet would collapse and free her. But the old wood miraculously held. One by one, three new restraints tightened around her torso.

"I'm sorry, Mama," Girl grunted, tugging the slack from the final restraint. "You say you gonna eat. And drink. But I don't believe you. You skinny as a hound. Not good for you. Not good for the babies."

Again, the ring of metal. Thick fingers dug into Mary's cheeks, prying her mouth open. Unable to move her head or neck, Mary locked her jaw, snorting and gasping. The flesh of her inner thigh warmed, pulsing with a suckling rhythm. Her teeth ached with the force of her clenched jaw.

Girl pinched Mary's nostrils, trapping her breath. Still, Mary fought to keep her mouth sealed. One minute passed. Her heart hammered against her ribs. Another minute. Two more. Until her skull seemed on the verge of detonation.

Her consciousness wavered. The room dimmed. Her mouth fell open.

Oxygen poured into Mary's lungs. The plastic hose breached her lips, gashing her tongue and grinding the back of her throat. Bile doused the torn tissue, burning and acidic, and flooded her airway. She sputtered and choked, on the brink of drowning in her own fluids. Writhing and convulsing, she fought for air. The plastic tube advanced, drilling into her soft insides. She felt as if she were being split in two, as if muscles and flesh were peeling away, recoiling from this unnatural intrusion.

Lard and syrup invaded her body, the vessel she'd controlled for decades with rigor and devotion. Her face was awash in tears, mucus, and blood. With each sob, the hose raked her insides. But Girl held the plastic tube steady as the sludge dumped into Mary. Soon Mary's stomach felt like it was filled with stones. When the mixture ran down her chin and neck, Girl withdrew the hose. Mary heaved, her throat brimming with Mother's Milk, but she stopped herself. If she reversed Girl's horrible handiwork, the woman would only repeat the process.

"It's over," Girl sniffled. Gingerly, she removed Mary's blindfold.

For a moment, they locked anguished gazes, hazel with earth.

"You fucking animal," Mary wheezed, then hocked a mouthful of blood-flecked saliva in Girl's face.

Wordlessly, Girl swabbed Mary clean, leaving her restraints in place, then disappeared into the night. The darkness reverberated with what seemed like all the world's creatures, humble and horrid, come to serenade Mary's humiliation.

Mary was awakened by her throbbing and scraped mouth, her scorched throat, her aching body. She scanned the room, finding the now-familiar menstrual tapestry, the raw-wood floor, the screen door hammered and patched in a million places.

She slammed her skull against the pallet. The engine of her rage sputtered to life. She did not belong here. Hers was a world of glass and steel, elevators rocketing through the clouds, obsequious maître d's, cowed attorneys, and eager underlings. A world she manipulated with ease. A world she would return to.

Who was this bowlegged dirt-eater to torture her with force-feeding—polluting and injuring her body? She pressed her nails into the heels of her hands and screamed with all her might. In reality, she emitted a barely audible croak. But in her mind, her sound was bloodcurdling and fierce.

When Girl reappeared, her prodigious breasts restored to fullness, her skin glinting with an amber sheen, Mary's heart detonated. She would have torn Girl's head from her body and gleefully lapped the blood, had she been able.

Girl's knees locked. Her eyes dulled with animal dread as she clutched the thin hose to her chest. "Just a couple more times, Mama. That's all."

"I. Am. Not. Your. Mother," Mary hissed. Her own hot breath burned the raw insides of her mouth.

Girl shuffled past, head bowed, shoulders slumped. With each step, her hulking form seemed to collapse further into itself.

The blindfold slid over Mary's eyes. Darkness swallowed the world.

"Who would want to be your mother?" Mary cackled, the words traveling from another time, another place, another mouth. "You are a piece of shit. I hate you."

The hose again plunged down Mary's throat. Pain razored through her and Mother's Milk swelled her stomach, but she was gone, inside a memory. She could only see her own small hands reaching for a face she'd long ago forgotten. Lopsided with drunkenness, the face spat out the exact words Mary had just spoken to Girl. *Who would want to be your mother?* The face contorted with derision, then lit up with the pleasure of cruelty.

When Girl returned in the afternoon, hose in hand, Mary was again possessed by a potent, all-consuming hatred. The blindfold descended and the hose drilled down. The pain summoned Sister Jillian, a nun renowned for her devastating insults and deft use of shame, especially when it came to young Mary. Sister Jillian's towering figure arose in the darkness behind Mary's blindfold. She was engaged in the ritual berating of Mary's seven-year-old self, when fear turned the letters and phrases of Mary's primer into hieroglyphics. "Your brain is defective. You will never amount to anything." Mary redirected the hateful torrent from her past onto Girl, even as the plastic hose ground the words into wet, indecipherable pulp.

With each feeding, Girl fumbled through the horrible chore, moaning and weeping, muttering a thousand apologies, and carefully cleaning Mary's face and neck afterward. Mary struggled to track the passage of time, by number of feedings, angle of sunlight, onset of darkness, Girl's appearances with the horrid convex of wood she'd fashioned into a primitive bedpan. But the effort was beyond her strained mind. At some point, morning or evening, Girl bowed and scraped before the pallet, belly overtopping her corduroys, hair dark with sweat, a timid smile cracking her lips. "Last one, Mama. You did it. I hurt you. I know. But I had to. Her In The Cave . . ."

Mary said nothing. The blindfold brought the darkness. The hose made its final descent.

This time Mary was visited by her foster father, hurling hateful words at her when she was a four-year-old. She saw herself squatting in the barren expanse of dirt that served as a backyard, her eyes wide with terror. *You worthless, spineless nothing.* She tried to fling the words at Girl, reaching through time with small hands. But the words were too heavy. They clung to her, as if they belonged, as if they were embedded in her skin.

◆ ◆ ◆

Mary trudged behind Girl, navigating the porch steps on shaky legs while shielding her eyes from the bright summer day. The rope hung between them, heavy and slack, as if waiting for a schoolgirl to awaken it with chants of *Cinderella, dressed in yellow*. Still tethered, Mary trailed after Girl to a frigid creek, where she washed filth from her hair and body. Beyond caring about her nudity, she shed her suit and underwear, managing to maneuver them from beneath the harness, so that Girl could wash them in the gurgling water.

When Mary rose from the creek to dry on a sunny rock, Girl broke out in ecstatic cooing. There was no need for Mary to investigate the source of Girl's delight. She was well aware of the growing bulge on her inner thigh. There were other bulges on Mary's body as well. Her belly was now distended to a degree she hadn't experienced since childhood. She felt an alien heaviness to her step, as if the earth's gravitational field had changed. Small rips had appeared in the shoulder seams of her blazer.

After washing, Mary settled on the steps of the front porch, wrapped in a worn quilt, the damp rope harness chilly against her skin. Her wet toes imprinted the dusty steps. The nail polish was chipped and peeling, except for her right pinky toe. At some point during her ordeal, the nail had been ripped away and now only the raw nail bed remained. Girl draped Mary's wet blazer, slacks, and underwear on the porch railing, then withdrew a whittling knife and a half-finished wooden figurine. One rounded breast had been completed, along with the sloping belly and full hips that tapered into a sharp point.

Mary could sense her tattered will trying to repair itself, each shred attempting to bind to the others, to galvanize a plan, a strategy, an escape. But her iron will seemed unavailable to her. Even the all-consuming rage she'd experienced during the force-feeding had gone cold. She stared dully at Girl, her mind dissolving into the motion of the knife carving the wood, calling forth the shape Mary had sighted behind the outhouse and then on the porch steps.

"Mama."

Mary blinked, forcing herself to focus on the shimmering terrain of Girl's broad face. The aching need for mother's love still lurked in the woman's gaze. But the sight no longer disgusted Mary.

"A little present. For you. And the babies," Girl said, holding out the figurine.

Mary stared at the figurine, then accepted it. "Thank you, my dear. This gift is fitting for what I'm about to say." The words arose with no forethought, like dry leaves drifting up from the emptiness within her.

At the endearment, Girl's rough complexion flooded pink. Her dung-colored eyes darted, birdlike, from Mary to the ground and back again. Mary ran her fingers along the figurine's rounded surfaces, focusing calmly, inexorably, on the one path that was left to her.

"I confess," she said, holding Girl's gaze. A breeze stirred the dense forest. Leaves whispered among the agitated branches. "I'm your mother. I've come back with the Brood."

Girl's forehead knotted. She searched Mary's eyes, stifling the joy that threatened to overtake her. Waiting, Mary sensed, to be the butt of the joke.

"You were right," Mary continued. "When you said I was denying the truth of who I am. You were always better than me. More loyal. A better helper to Her In The Cave." No mockery tainted her words. The mythology arose spontaneously, as if she had truly lived it. "I can't say for sure, but I think Her In The Cave sent me away on purpose. I think she knew I was rebelling. On the inside."

On the porch step below Mary, Girl had been reduced to jelly. Her tears pockmarked the weathered wood. Her thick fingers shook. Though she'd never voiced any doubt that Mary was her mother, she seemed overwhelmed, even flummoxed. She raised her tear-slicked face to Mary.

"Why didn't you just say? Why'd you make me hurt you?" Girl's bottom lip crept forward, timid and pink, a creature venturing outside its shell.

"Because I'm weak, Girl. I never wanted to be a mother." The quilt slid from Mary's leg, exposing her sharp kneecap. "I rejected that honor. That is my sin. I hope you can forgive me. I hope Her In The Cave can forgive me." She repositioned the quilt, then entwined her slender fingers. The emerald-cut diamond twinkled in its platinum setting.

Girl rolled her eyes skyward. Tears washed her rounded cheeks. "I'm a sinner too. I hated you when you left. Hated you since you been back. Cursed you behind your back." Her closed fist thumped her chest.

"That's all behind us now." Mary's gaze strayed to the harness. Now was not the time to ask to be untied. It was important for Girl to come to the decision on her own. And there was no real urgency at this point. What was there to defend against now that she'd accepted the role of mother? And strangely, for the past hour, she'd hardly felt the harness on her body or been aware of the restraint.

Her tongue hollowed and thrust forward in a suckling motion. "Any Mother's Milk left, daughter dear?"

Chapter 9

The now-familiar sickly sweet odor engulfed Mary. She turned, expecting to find Girl nearby. But the woman was on the far end of the porch, shoring up a sagging handrail, the rope between them vibrating with the rhythm of her repair work. Mary snuggled deeper into the musty quilt, then glanced at the empty mason jar on the porch step at her feet. The rim was crusted with dried Mother's Milk.

Of course, Mary reflected. *Eat like Girl. Stink like Girl.*

Even still, a mere glance at the chalky remains caused a flutter within her thigh and a yearning for more of the concoction. What was happening to her that she craved the loathsome, lard-laden Mother's Milk? Worse, why did she no longer feel the urge to retch when she thought of the pale, red-eyed embryos gestating within her thigh? Instead, she somehow felt insulated from her own disgust, swaddled in cottony apathy. Something akin, she imagined, to the dope fiend who, cocooned in a fresh hit of heroin, stares curiously at a cluster of festering track marks.

Surrendering to her cravings for Mother's Milk triggered shame, as did the possibility that the horrid pupae might be somehow calming her, blunting her emotions by leaching neurotoxins into her system. But her mind was still intact, despite this bizarre and gruesome ordeal. The suppression of her outrage and disgust was surely part of the reason. She drew in a deep breath. And underlying this protective calm was the slow and steady reemergence of her iron will and her determination to save herself.

The yearning broke over her again, with greater intensity. Mary yanked the tether and Girl looked up from her repair work. Wordlessly, Mary held up the empty mason jar. When Girl beamed with satisfaction, Mary swallowed the insults that instinctively rushed to her mouth. Today was about being a mother to Girl and cementing the trust that would lead to her untethering. If that trust grew strong enough, Girl might even lend her dear old mom the keys to the truck.

"Ask you something?" Girl said when she returned with the refilled mason jar.

Mary glugged half the viscous liquid, then wiped her lips with the back of her hand. "By all means."

"The way you talk. It's different from before you left. You sound . . ." Girl studied the scuffed toes of her work boots, frowning as she searched for words.

Mary sipped her slimy cocktail until the woman's face twitched to life.

"You talk," Girl continued, dangling the hammer between her great thighs, "like the news people on the TV." Mary refrained from reminding Girl that she'd raised this very point early on as proof that she was not Girl's mother.

Instead, she flashed to the old busted TV inside. At some point, the cabin must have had electricity, providing Girl with her only exposure to the world at large. She pictured preadolescent Girl, gnawing on cast-off chicken bones while her maniac mother cursed the talking heads on the screen. Girl's last broadcasts probably occurred when Americans still received news from the same sources, regardless of political leanings. Then, as now, a homogeneity in TV accents prevailed, against which regional dialects were judged to be ignorant or blue collar, a form of stereotyping with which Mary was all too familiar.

Mary had entered college with an accent almost as hideous as Girl's. During her years at Saint Agnes, her enduring act of defiance was to resist the attempts of the nuns to quash what, as an adult, she'd identified as an Appalachian dialect, probably West Virginian. Clinging to the aggressive twang and vowel swapping gave her a sense of agency, small and desperate though it was.

On the first day of her freshman year, the Intro to Philosophy professor asked each student to share their career aspirations. She'd mumbled that she hoped to attend law school and be hired—which she pronounced "hard"—by a New York firm. Thereafter, her presence at social or school gatherings elicited snickers from the middle-class students and outright scorn from the blue bloods. It didn't help that her voice was reedy and she finished most phrases with an obsequious upward lilt.

Second semester, after witnessing a club of exchange students performing a recitation of Shakespeare's sonnets, she'd enrolled in a voice-and-articulation workshop. The only native English speaker in the group, she struggled alongside ESL students from around the world. Afterward, she'd taken Oral Presentation in Literature and Poetry, then repeated both courses.

Purging her accent and modulating her voice to a lower register had been the second major victory in Mary's battle to recast her fate. The first had been losing her childhood blubber. She pinched the new layer of skin brimming over her waistband, unsettling an old despair—that her body was beyond her control, that it would drag her down to the chilly depths of her past, that she would never be free.

She drew in a sharp breath and forced the maudlin thoughts from her mind. She'd dropped the weight once; she would do it again. And for the moment, she had no choice. She shivered, remembering the horrid tube plunging down her throat.

"You're right. My accent has changed." Mary smoothed her hair, attempting to tame its coarse wildness. "I like to keep a low profile.

My accent—our accent—called too much attention to me. If you ever decide to venture out, I advise you to do the same."

"Venture out?" Girl snorted. "Ain't gonna. Never." A note of derision rang through her words. Her eyes darkened, storm-churned rivers, reminding Mary of the unknown risks that came with taking on the role of Girl's mother.

"And why would you?" Mary threw her arms wide. "When you've got this?"

The twinkle reentered Girl's eyes. "Twenty-seven years. What did you do out there?"

"Learned about the law to understand how the world works." Mary paused, striving to connect her world of power, luxury, and ambition to the survivalist existence of Girl and her mother. Her eyes dropped to the wooden figurine nestled in the valley of her quilt-covered thighs. "To better equip myself to keep this place safe."

Girl's eyes widened. She pawed her knees. "Her In The Cave is stronger than the law."

"I'm not suggesting she isn't strong. But I felt it was my duty to learn everything I could, in service of Her." Mary quaffed the last dregs of Mother's Milk. "Besides, there are things you don't know about. Between Her and me."

Girl's dark eyes filled. Her bottom lip rolled forward. Mary found herself patting Girl's knee, a small boulder encased in corduroy.

"Never thought about you and Her In The Cave having secrets. Without me." Girl dropped her eyes and picked at the rough skin crowning her knuckles. "Guess there's important stuff I'm too dumb to know." After a few more sniffles, a shy smile appeared. "I got a secret too." She raised her eyes to Mary. "He came again." Rosey splotches blossomed across Girl's face.

"Who?" Mary straightened. "Your boy—" She paused, remembering Girl's violent reaction when she'd referred to the gangly hiker as *boyfriend*. "Your new friend? The one who loves the Brood?"

"Dale." Girl nodded, improbably radiating a petaled, girlish freshness. "While you was sleeping. This time we talked an hour."

Mary's nostrils flared. Sleeping? More like unconscious from exhaustion after a force-feeding session. Again, she wondered if the man might be undercover, searching for her. If so, his investigative skills were sorely lacking.

"Oh, Mama!" Girl leaped to her feet, taking no notice when her broad boot tipped the mason jar off the porch step. "He knows so much about the cicadas. A different kind of knowing than ours. He calls them *Magicicada.*" She cradled one fist inside the other. "Magic! Ain't that wonderful? And he gets just as mad as we do when somebody calls them *locusts.*"

"Highly offensive," Mary said.

"He was so excited! He called ours a *shadow brood.* Says there's lots of other broods that come out at different times in different places. Everybody knows about those ones. But nobody knows about ours. Neither him. He found it on accident. Followed the song. Isn't that sweet?" She paused, tucking her chin into her chest, like a hen preparing to roost.

"He succumbed to the siren song."

"Sirens?" Girl cocked her head. "Guess the cicadas sound like that sometimes. Afternoons. When it's hot."

"Think he'll come again?" Mary asked. Dale was sounding more and more like a bona fide bug hobbyist rather than an undercover cop. And an odd bird, judging from his ability to hover at the same conversational altitude as Girl. But he still represented the outside world, a possibility for escape.

"Don't know." Girl's face fell. "My mouth got moving too fast. I accidentally told him the most magical cicadas were up in the cave. He said no. Cicadas wouldn't spend time in a cave. That made me mad. So I shut my mouth until he left. Did I mess up?"

"Far from it. He probably thinks you're playing hard to get. I'm sure he'll be back. Did you notice a vehicle?"

"He hiked up the road," Girl said, then giggled. "Says he likes to be inside nature. Not inside a car."

"Charming. And Her In The Cave. She didn't try to stop him?"

"Why would she do that, Mama? He ain't out to hurt us. Or mess with the miracle of the Brood."

A single cicada landed on Girl's forearm, its six jointed legs perched on her dust-streaked skin. She drew it close, staring tenderly into the globular red eyes. "Hello, sister," Girl cooed. The creature flicked its wings, delicate panes of orange iridescence, hinged to the green-black thorax.

"They're almost done," Girl said, shifting her gaze to Mary. "Seventeen years underground. Each one all alone in her own little cave. Nobody to talk to. No one to love." Her eyes glistened. "Breaks my heart. Ours'll leave too," Girl said, lifting her shirt. The three fluid-filled membranes were only slightly larger than at the last viewing. But the stirring within the watery cocoons was much more pronounced. "You got to be ready. For that sadness."

Mary tried not to flinch. Apparently, the suppression of her disgust for her own infestation did not extend to Girl's. "Precious," Mary said, forcing her puckered mouth to form the words while focusing on a patch of skin just above the eruptions.

Girl lovingly stroked each swelling in turn, the cicada still perched on her moving hand, then lowered her shirt. "We are blessed, Mama. You and me."

Mary jumped to her feet, detaching from the woman's love-soaked gaze. "I'd like to stretch my legs," she said. Her eyes cut to the quarry and the cave above. It was late in the day. Already twilight was creeping into the golden afternoon, staining the leaves of the hoary oak above the cave.

Mary slapped the figurine against her palm and eyed Girl. "The cave. Has it changed much since I went away?"

Girl's rumpled forehead smoothed. Her eyes grew dreamy. "It's more . . . clear. More alive. We used to have to do so much guessin'. Remember?"

"Sure," Mary said.

"What to do. When to do it. Like when we had to figure out the sacred marking. All on our own." She gestured to her forehead. The three ocher dots forming an upside-down triangle had long since faded. Mary reflexively brushed her own forehead though she assumed the symbol had disappeared from her skin as well.

"Dale." Girl blushed as she said the name. "He calls them *ocelli.* Three simple eyes between the regular ones." The cicada crept along her wrist. Gently, she pointed at the flat space between the two red eyes where three shiny points, barely larger than pinpricks, formed an inverted triangle. "He says their only job is to see light and darkness. I didn't tell him he was wrong about that one. No way he could know it's really a sign between us and the Brood. That we mark ourselves with their crushed-up shells and the blood-sap of the trees." She eyed Mary's inner thigh. "How else would they know we're ready to hold the babies?"

The cicada took flight. Mary scooped the mason jar from the ground and replanted it on the steps. A chill swept through her. Girl must have anointed her forehead with the three dots before the attack in the Mercedes. Had that really summoned the bugs, like some bizarre fertility ritual? Again, she considered the unsettling notion of a collective intelligence shared between the cicadas. Again, she sought a more rational possibility. Perhaps the paste used for the markings contained a pheromone that drove the bugs to deposit their eggs in humans. Old Dale would have a field day with that one.

Mary steered herself back to her mothering role. "Maybe it's not the cave that's clearer now, Girl. Maybe it's you."

Girl's hands tumbled from her hips and sought refuge behind her back. Her shy smile widened. "Never thought about it like that. But maybe. Like now. I know what she wants."

Mary's spine tingled. "She wants to see me," she guessed. Or was it a guess? Did she, at this moment, feel something? Not a physical sensation, like her craving for the Mother's Milk. Something mental. Emotional.

Maybe. But it was only intense curiosity. Not some paranormal voodoo hoodoo. There was a mystery within that cave to be revealed or debunked, be it the discovery of a lonely madwoman's imaginary friend, a geologic phenomenon, or something yet to be explained. Plus, she was sick of the cabin, sick of the porch, sick of Girl's face. The interior of a dark cave would be a welcome change.

Girl unfastened the rope harness so Mary could exchange the quilt for her mostly dry clothes. Somewhere between the creek bath and whittling, Girl had sewn the tear in Mary's inseam. When Mary thanked her, she blushed and rammed her fists deep in the pockets of her corduroys. Mary dressed, noting Girl's averted gaze. Perhaps it signaled a growing trust.

They stepped from the front porch onto the hard-packed dirt that served as Girl's driveway. Passing the pickup truck, they veered right onto a footpath. Mary studied the trail, following its meandering course through a short expanse of prairie grass, around one end of the quarry, and up the steep mountainside. She estimated fifteen minutes to reach the quarry pit and round the lower quarter, and another ten to navigate the three switchbacks that would bring them to the cave mouth. Above the cave, the ancient tree rippled against the sky. The leafy crown seemed overly verdant, more suited to jungle than mountainside.

Mary took the lead, remaining several paces ahead of Girl as she trudged through the knee-high grass to the edge of the quarry pit. Deep within the blasted bowl, the water was cloudy and still. A piercing cry echoed against the gutted rock walls as a bird of prey swooped past. The footpath soon broke away from the pit to traverse a small plateau before the main ascent. Warm evening air churned with the buzz and flicker of swarming cicadas. Nymphs marched en masse across the ground in search of a molting place. The plateau's few small trees bowed beneath throngs of winged bodies fused in the mating act. It seemed all stages of the insect's life cycle were on display.

Mary swatted wildly, a wayward cicada caught in her curls. She glanced back at Girl, who seemed unfazed by the five or so hitchhiking atop her broad skull.

The grating vibrato of cicada song cut through the collective din.

Oweee-oooo. Oweee-oooo.

Mary's hand flew to her forehead, rubbing aggressively in case any of the red ocher paste remained. She halted on the trail, waiting for Girl to catch up. The woman's outsize physique suddenly seemed a safe harbor in this landscape roiling with cicadas.

"You know the law good?" Girl asked, raising her voice above the pulsing hum.

"I do," Mary replied, feeling more confident as Girl drew closer.

"There's a man comes by," Girl said, absently tugging the rope at her chest.

Mary stopped short, then quickly resumed walking, trying not to seem overly interested. She rounded the first of the switchbacks. The trail grew steeper. Large chunks of reddish-brown and ash-colored rock appeared, freestanding or partially embedded in the mountainside. Many of the rocks bore a red mineral rash that sparkled from one angle and appeared dull and ulcerous from another. When nothing more was forthcoming from Girl, Mary gently probed. "You mean, your new friend?"

Girl snorted with disdain. "No! This man is a no-good. Comes couple times a year. First time, snuck in on foot. But I caught him. Heading up to the cave. I pounded him, but he came again. In his truck."

Girl hesitated. Mary fought the urge to turn heel and shake the words from her. So the man had come more than once. Perhaps he was with the county or state? But even Girl wasn't so stupid as to assault a government employee.

"Sounds unpleasant," Mary said. "Sorry you had to go through that. But well done on the pounding. What did he want?"

"Asking about buying the land. Last time was fifteen days ago. I smashed his windshield."

"Brava." Mary turned and pumped her fist in the air. "That's my girl."

Girl's face lit up, a full moon flashing in the darkness. "He was with two others. All of 'em oily and smiley. Wondering about the paper for this land."

"You mean the deed?" Mary asked. With each step, the rope slapped against her leg. Glassy crimson gravel danced along the trail, dislodged by her hiking boots. She powered over a cluster of large rocks, then waited for Girl to clamber through.

"Said it'd be easy to kick a trash woman like me off the land." Girl tottered as she crested the final rock. Mary jerked the rope, shifting Girl's center of gravity forward. "Thank you, Mama," Girl said, her boots landing firmly on the path. "Said I got no kin. And no paper. Said he'd do it. Or some big company."

"Did he say what he was after? What made the land so valuable?"

Girl shook her head. "Iron ore is long gone. Garnet ain't worth nothing."

Mary glanced at the rust-colored ulcerations in the rock and the glassy crimson fragments. "Okay, not iron. Not garnet. Could be fracking. It's effectively illegal in the state of New York, but powerful interests are lobbying to change that. Could also be real estate development. We need to find out what his angle is, who he's representing," Mary said, rounding another switchback. She was enjoying the steady uphill exertion and the unexpected treat of a legal conundrum. "Secondly," she sang out to the gathering twilight, her mind sliding into a familiar groove. "You said you've—" She halted. "*We've* been here for generations. The women of our family. Caring for the Brood. For Her In The Cave."

Girl grunted her assent.

"Even if there's no official deed to the land, squatter's rights were established decades ago."

"Who's a squatter? Not me." Girl stomped the dirt, raising a cloud of dust. Tiny garnets bounced along the trail.

"I don't mean you're a squatter. It's an informal legal term. Shorthand for 'adverse possession.' Have you kept up with the property taxes?"

Girl's face reddened. "Yes. I don't like it. But I pay. Takes almost all the money I make helping farmers with their apple harvest."

"And you've resided on the property continuously, correct? Never shared it with anyone else while I was away?"

"Just Her In The Cave."

"I'd have to look into it a bit more, but I believe you have an unimpeachable claim to adverse possession. I'd recommend beginning the process immediately. It will protect you from bottom-feeders like that man. I'd be happy to initiate the claim," Mary said.

"Oh, Mama! Thank you!" Girl panted, her midsection bellowing like the throat sac of a toad. She lurched toward Mary for a hug but became tangled in the rope, pulling them both to the ground. Mary narrowly missed cracking her skull on a stone.

"Enough!" Mary said, fighting off Girl's bumbling attempts to help. When they were both on their feet, Mary offered Girl a reassuring smile. "No thanks are necessary. This is my home too. I'll just need to drive to town and file the papers."

Girl's brows drew together. Her fleshy lips disappeared into her mouth. "I have to see," she mumbled. "Tomorrow's busy. Lots to do." She turned and kept walking.

"Up to you," Mary said, softening her tone. "But advice from your mother? We shouldn't let this drag on. We need to protect ourselves."

They covered the last few yards in silence, Mary shoving down her frustration at Girl's lingering distrust. She would continue to work this angle. After all, Girl had raised the issue. Plus, the slimy speculators were sure to return. When they did, Mary would raise holy hell and sound the alarm. Assuming she was still alive—the thought of keeping up the mother ruse for much longer was exhausting. A sigh escaped her.

Girl whipped around. "I know what you are feeling, Mama." Directly behind her, the cave sank into the mountainside, the opening a rough, dark aura to Girl's thickset shoulders and legs.

Mary threw back her head and gazed at the tree above the cave mouth. It was a strange confluence of overground and under, the tangle of roots flung wide to expose an earthen womb. Despite lustrous leaves, the tree had an imposing, haunted quality. Knobby outgrowths and deep hollows suggested misshapen mouths and leering eyes.

The cave mouth was wide enough for three people to enter, shoulder to shoulder. Chill air rushed from within, filling Mary's nostrils with a dank, fungal odor. She shivered, imagining some sinister place, legions below, where the strange smells and icy drafts arose. The rays of the late afternoon sun pierced the cave's dark interior. "Jesus!" Mary flinched and fell back. A throng of albino snakes dangled from the cave ceiling.

"Come on, Mama!" Girl laughed, then clutched one of the snakes. Dirt sifted down, dusting her shoulders. "That's roots. From the Guardian Tree. Up top. You forget?"

"I suppose I did." Mary frowned, eyeing the pale tree roots. Feeling foolish, she dropped her gaze to the muddy floor and immediately regretted it. A tide of cicada nymphs swarmed past, marching from underground, out of the cave, and into the remains of the day.

Ignoring Girl's ogling, Mary slipped the wood figurine into her pocket and dropped to one knee, pretending to tie her shoestring. Her head throbbed. Her pulse was wiry and insistent. Was she really going in there? What did she plan on doing? Playing patty-cake in the muck with Girl while awaiting a visitation? She shivered, imagining another encounter with the creepy hovering silhouette. She should be focused on the land deed, stoking Girl's fears so she'd relent and loan Mary the truck. Then escape—back to her well-ordered, well-heeled life.

"Stay left. On the wall, there," Girl said, pulling a flashlight from her corduroys.

After a brief hesitation, Mary rose and moved deeper into the cave. She had to. This place was critical to understanding the mysterious terrain of Girl's psyche.

"Not there, Mama!"

Suddenly Mary was sliding across the downward-sloping cave floor. The walls narrowed, and she picked up speed, her body a mud-slicked torpedo speeding down a chute. Her boots plowed the space in front of her, leaving a spray of disintegrated cicadas in her wake. Throwing her arms wide, she clawed the cave walls, shrieking as a fingernail split in two.

All at once, the floor seemed to fall away. She plummeted several feet, then jerked violently to a stop, hanging midair, like a fly dangling from a spider's thread. Twisting and twirling from the rope harness, she struggled to get her bearings. Forty feet below, an underground pond was visible, illuminated by light from an unknown source. Stalagmites protruded from the slimy water, eager to impale her if Girl's homespun harness broke.

The wooden figurine slipped from Mary's waistband, tumbled end over end, and splashed into the shallow waters. She could hear Girl grunting above and prayed that she had a firm toehold.

"Don't worry, Mama," Girl huffed, her voice echoing from the chute in the ceiling from which Mary had catapulted.

"You drop me, I will break my back!"

"I know. The Pure Pond washes our sins, but it's rocky."

"No shit!" Mary screamed. Twirling above the jagged stones, she caught sight of a narrow fissure in one of the cavern walls. Through it, a smaller, adjacent cavern was visible, illuminated by what was unmistakably daylight, suggesting a second entrance to the cave, or at least a crack in the rock face that led outside.

As Girl muttered and fretted above, the sunlight wavered, as if dampened by a passing cloud. When full sunlight returned, a flash of metal caught Mary's eye. "Motherfucker," she exclaimed.

"Don't be afraid, Mama!" Girl grunted.

Mary remained silent, her eyes locked on the opening to the adjacent cavern. Through the crack she could just make out a damaged bumper and part of a hood. She'd found her Mercedes.

Chapter 10

Mary gripped the rope knot at her chest, spinning in quickening circles. She craned her neck at crazy angles. Far below, the opening to the adjacent cavern flashed past, again and again. With each rotation, a tantalizing flicker of her car's hood flared forth. Dizziness overtook her, and she squeezed her eyes shut. No wonder the car hadn't attracted a search party. Mary remembered the wet thunk when she'd tried the ignition, as hordes of cicadas swarmed the vehicle. Whatever damage they'd caused must have been temporary; however strong she was, Girl couldn't have dragged the car up the mountain. And Mary didn't remember seeing a winch or other device on Girl's truck. So the Mercedes still worked. It could still help her escape. When had Girl found time to hide it? Obviously the bumpkin was more capable of subterfuge than Mary had given her credit for.

Grunts echoed from above. A small avalanche of pebbles spilled onto Mary's forehead from the chute in the cavern ceiling. Her eyes jerked downward. Her guts roiled. Forty feet below, the stalagmites formed a toothy cluster, rising from the center of an oily body of water, the stagnant surface broken by trickles of condensation from the fractured cavern ceiling. Girl had called the pool of water the "Pure Pond." More likely toxic runoff from an old mining operation.

She studied the taut, creaking rope extending from her chest to the jagged chute from which she'd fallen. She prayed Girl hadn't used a legacy rope, proudly handed down through generations of kinfolk. One rotten or frayed portion would send her dropping like a stone. If the stalagmites didn't kill her, then the toxic sludge surely would.

"Any day now," she shouted. Girl grunted, a straining beast of burden. Another drizzle of rocks broke free.

The cavern formed a dome about thirty feet across. The walls consisted of flowing, striated rock interspersed with ruptured indentations and recesses that had been dynamited or chipped away. Ghostly remnants of a railroad track were visible near the fissure leading to her car. The opening could have been part of the track system that carted out the extractions.

The cavern ceiling flowed into a broad natural chimney from which drafts of fresh air and flickers of sunlight emanated. She stared up into the chimney. The glowing aperture in the dark rock momentarily blinded her before her eyes adjusted. Where on the mountain did the chimney emerge? Perhaps a high ledge overlooking Girl's property, or even the peak itself.

"What the hell is going on up there?" Mary shouted, unnerved by the Girl's silence and the stillness of the rope.

Girl raised a bestial cry. The rope tightened and drew closer to the chute. Mary could now make out Girl's shining face and huge knotted forearms.

"Another two feet!" Mary cried. She glanced down at the opening to the adjacent cavern. Only a small portion of the hood was visible from this higher vantage. She scanned the wall above the opening, desperate for some defining feature in the rock that she might later use to make her way to the car.

A gasp sounded above. The rope slackened. Mary plummeted several inches.

"It's stuck," Girl howled.

"Well, free it!" Mary shrieked. "Before I get skewered."

"I'm trying," Girl huffed.

A fist-size rock clunked against Mary's forehead. Blood flowed into her eyes. Her body yo-yoed on the trembling rope. The chute was farther away than when she'd first fallen through.

In desperation, she tucked her thighs into her chest, angling to flip her legs up and around the rope. If Girl was not up to the task, Mary had to somehow scale the line on her own. She tried repeatedly to whip her legs upward. All the while, a whispery drone swelled around her, filling the wide void of the cavern. The sound spiked into a grating metallic whine, pulsing and pulsing.

With horror, Mary identified the familiar sound—the sonic heartbeat of the Brood. The oppressive pulse had surrounded her on the road in the woods, just before she became a live human host.

She redoubled her efforts, clutching at the rope, gasping and grunting. Her muscles quivered. A sob broke from her as her limbs surrendered to exhaustion.

Abruptly, the rope vibrated, as if plucked by the hand of an unseen giant. She was thrown into a rapid spin. The cavern's ocher walls whirled past. She craned her neck upward, fixing her gaze on the chute in the ceiling. She yelled out to Girl until nausea overtook her.

Then she was falling, the severed rope clutched in her hands. Her insides rushed up.

Her screams blasted the domed chamber, overwhelming even the screeching cicadas.

"Mama!" Girl's anguished bellow seemed to fill all the world.

Mary's eyes fell to her body, waiting for the stalagmites to break her in two.

But instead, she floated, carried on a shifting, jittering magic carpet. Thousands of tiny movements rustled beneath her body. The abrasive din of the cicadas mellowed to a gentle hum.

A wail split the air, followed by the sound of Girl's clomping descent into the cavern.

Spread-eagled on the teeming, amorphous mass, Mary felt her mind stutter, then grind to a complete halt. A great shadow moved along the cave wall, mirroring her flight.

Soon she was poised above a small plateau of rock beneath the chimney, illuminated in a pool of sunlight, her body tilting upright. Her boots touched rock. The gusts of a thousand tiny wings rushed across her skin. A dark hovering shape arose before her, assembling itself into the towering silhouette she'd first encountered behind the outhouse.

"Mama!" Girl's holler blasted from behind. She came pounding across the cave floor.

Mary remained mute, unable to tear her gaze from the flickering, gyrating form, composed of insects. Insects! By all appearances, the swarm of bugs had collaborated on her rescue, lifted her mass over a distance, exercised will, saved her rather than harmed her.

Saved the babies, she corrected herself.

Girl whimpered and fell to her knees before the hovering silhouette. Her great, bewildered eyes sought Mary's, imploring Mary to do the same.

The dark mass swirled and glinted like a woman-shaped portal to another world. Mary's fear turned to giddiness, fueled by the impossibility of what she was seeing, of what had just happened. But kneel alongside Girl? It seemed a bit much.

The silhouette dissolved into thousands of winged cicadas, blowing past Mary and Girl and leaving behind a sweet, moldering odor, like honey-drenched rot. The swarm flowed up the chimney and out into the orange-gold sky.

"A miracle," Girl breathed. But moments later, her face drooped. Her dark eyes filled. "I almost killed you. And the babies," she wailed. Her fingers spidered toward Mary's thigh.

"Correct," Mary said, swatting Girl's hand away.

Mary's eyes roved the chimney walls. A stupor threatened to override her reasoning mind. She had no rational explanation for what she had just experienced. No set of data points to refer to. Or precedent she could cite. Perhaps one day she'd find one. But right now, explanations were not a priority. She had to stay focused, to keep her eye on the prize—surviving this nightmare.

She steadied her breathing and turned to Girl. "Flashlight?" When Girl proved too distraught to comply, Mary plucked the light from Girl's trouser pocket. She aimed light upward, illuminating the naturally occurring minerals embedded in the ceiling of the cave—garnet and quartz, judging from the flashes of crimson and brilliant sparkles. Her eyes wandered directly overhead, to the chimney. Traces of gemstones were apparent here as well, glinting in shafts of sunlight. Small clusters of cicadas crawled along the chimney walls. Had these bugs been part of the hovering silhouette? Progenitors of the special class currently gestating in her thigh and Girl's torso?

She shifted her gaze to Girl, who was still kneeling, head bowed. The woman was enormous, but surely even she wasn't capable of hosting enough of the creatures to make up the swarm they'd just encountered.

Though the hovering shape was gone, a strange resonance lingered in the cavern, heightened by the ongoing hypnotic pulse of cicada song.

Mary's breath caught. She was suddenly overcome by an acute nostalgia, of sunlight and woods, welcoming arms, bare feet in grass. A longing broke open in her, so powerful that her legs buckled. She fell to her knees, stone against skin and bone.

Yet no such home, wooded and welcoming, had ever existed. Not for her. It had only been a childish fantasy.

There had been one brush with adoption, when Mary was fourteen, ancient in orphan years.

An elderly woman, thin boned and quiet save the ever-present click of rosary beads, once took her away. Mary later learned the priest of the church affiliated with Saint Agnes had encouraged the old woman to foster an older female orphan as a companion and helper. If the arrangement went well, the woman would consider adoption.

For the first time, Mary had her own room, an attic bedroom that once belonged to the woman's oldest boy. In his small collection of books, she encountered and relished *Adventures of Huckleberry Finn.* At night, the sloped ceilings glowed with glued-on constellations.

The chores were light. And the woman, if not warm, was appreciative, even devoting a rosary to healing Mary's psoriasis.

But she died in her sleep three months later. Mary returned to the orphanage.

When Mary came out of the memory, Girl was offering her the molted shell of a cicada that perhaps even now was ascending into the bright oval at the top of the chimney. Mary surprised herself, accepting the amber capsule and examining its horrid perfection in the flashlight's beam. The tiny antennae; the minute, clawlike forelegs; the thick scalloped abdomen. A fragile memorial to a life cast off, morphed into something new.

But a memorial to what, really? She frowned. A meaningless speck in a multitude of others identical to itself. A brief, doomed life teeming with chaos, driven only by the need to reproduce.

The longing for home intensified, though this time it was her penthouse on Central Park South that beckoned, with its skylight in the master bedroom, where she could see only the heartiest stars, the brightest few that survived the glow of Manhattan.

Her life was hard edged, dog eat dog, competitive. She'd built her fortress and was its sole occupant. But it was hers. Not the golden, green-grassed kind of home. She'd discarded that childhood wish long ago. What she had created, though, that was hers. And she would scorch the earth to return to it.

The cicada chorus penetrated her thoughts, swelling to a crescendo, then piercing her with raw intensity. She jerked her gaze to the chimney and around the cave walls. Why were the little beasts revving up again?

The sound boomed forth, then narrowed into a compressed vibration that plunged into the center of her being, warming her heart, belly, and genitals. Her breasts tingled; her nipples ached. She gasped. Wetness was spreading across her silk blouse.

"What the hell?" She shot Girl an accusatory glance. "Make them stop! Jesus!" She stretched her damp shirt taut as her nipples continued to leak.

Girl raised her dark eyes. Fresh tears pooled and spilled down her pillowy cheeks. A pair of cicadas circled above her rumpled hair. Another perched on her flannel shirt where two wet circles had appeared. Three more cicadas landed. Soon dozens were creeping across Girl's shoulders and chest. She fumbled with the buttons of her shirt. Insects fluttered toward her, swarming farther into her chest as each button came undone.

Mary stumbled backward, dropping the cicada shell and crushing it underfoot. The flashlight fell from her fingers, slamming against the rock floor and landing at Girl's feet.

Girl's eyes rolled to gleaming white. Her lids lowered. She moaned, withdrawing one heavy breast. Cicadas rushed across the white flesh, converging on the nipple. Others joined, scrabbling across the creatures already feeding until Girl's bare chest was a shuddering plane of wings, jointed legs, and dark heads. Briefly, her eyes flickered open. "Sit, Mama. The Brood is thirsty."

Mary recoiled. Her teeth chattered. A cicada landed on her shirt front and crept toward her breasts. Frantically, she flung it off. "No fucking way!"

Girl's eyes cracked open. She fixed Mary with a drugged-out gaze before again succumbing to the feeding, rocking back and forth in a rhythmic pulse.

Slowly, Mary backed away from Girl, shuffling across the stone plateau until she reached the stagnant pool. One edge of the black, glassy pond was aflame with light from the dying sun, pouring through the chimney.

She had to get to her car. Her legs felt rubbery and unreliable as she began to pick her way around the noxious pool. Her heart slammed against her ribs.

Another moan escaped Girl. Mary looked back, unable to resist.

Girl hadn't moved from her strange genuflection. The winged beasts swarmed across her body, droning peacefully even as they writhed and twisted, angling for greater access to Girl's breasts. Girl's face was the only area unclaimed by the beasts. A waxing, beatific moon. Radiant. Devout. The reason for the dramatic swings in Girl's bust size was now appallingly clear.

Mary hurried on, pausing frequently to search for the crevice through which she'd seen the Mercedes. But the topography she'd memorized dangling from the ceiling was unrecognizable from the ground. Rocks of various sizes were scattered along the pond's circumference, many bearing the same rust-colored blemishes she'd seen outside. Others were coated in a treacherous layer of slippery green moss.

Beyond the reach of the sunlight, the rocks became a jumbled, shadowy maze. She scrambled over a boulder, lost her balance, and splashed into the pond. She froze, listening. A groan of ecstasy echoed through the cavern. Mary grimaced, then gingerly plodded through the shallow water back to the rock-strewn edge.

She slowed as a boulder-size protrusion came into view, six or seven feet up the cavern wall. Its translucent quality contrasted with the surrounding rock. A dark form seemed suspended within, like a creature trapped in amber. Was this a fossil? Some prehistoric bear or mountain lion frozen for all eternity?

A warm flutter caressed her cheek. Then another. Soon a small cloud of cicadas swirled around her, homing in on her breasts. Cursing, she dropped to her knees at the edge of the Pure Pond and began dousing her shirt pockets, the fetid water streaming through her shaking fingers and rinsing away whatever unnatural substance her breasts were excreting.

Her body seemed alien to her, no longer her own. A strangled sob rose to her throat and a powerful yearning rose in her: for release, to let the creatures feed, to experience the pleasure so evident in Girl's radiant expression and soft moans.

Decades of militant discipline came to Mary's aid. She dug her fingernails into her thighs. Chomped down on her own tongue. The pain blew aside the longing to nurse. She shoveled another handful of water onto her chest, then regained her feet.

Moving through swaths of shadow and light, she traced the edge of the pond. Metal tracks appeared. She increased her pace. Perhaps the railway was part of the same rudimentary system she'd spied from above, curving toward the opening and her car. But the discovery led only to a rough-hewn stairway ascending through the ceiling, presumably the one Girl had stumbled down earlier, after Mary had nearly fallen to her death.

"Mama . . ." Girl's low, guttural cry drifted across the Pure Pond.

Mary halted at the foot of the stairs, listening intently, until Girl's voice dissolved into intoxicated murmurs. She raced headlong up the stairs, deciding to continue her search for the adjacent cavern above ground. An eastern-facing entry point must exist, she reasoned. One that connected to some godforsaken dirt road. How else would Girl have stashed the car?

It was imperative she find the Mercedes before Girl woke from her bug orgy or Her In The Cave dropped by for another visit.

The stairway was little more than a pitch-black tunnel curving upward through the rock. Her battered forehead erupted in fresh pain as she rammed into the low ceiling. She hunched in the claustrophobic space, shoulders brushing against narrow walls. How on earth had Girl forced herself through?

Finally, she emerged in the cave's anteroom, brushing aside dozens of twisted, pale tree roots to stumble into the mild summer evening. Regaining the trail, she jogged in the opposite direction of their arrival, hoping the path continued around the mountain to the cavern sheltering her car. But the trail quickly dead-ended and the mountainside became impassably steep.

She dashed back to the cave, where she recalled a series of exposed roots laddering up one side of the cave's exterior to the ancient oak. Grabbing hold of the lowest root, she heaved herself up and climbed, fingers gripping the rough bark, the work boots holding her steady. As she scrambled upward, her scalp prickled. Her skin erupted in gooseflesh. She jerked her head, glancing over each shoulder. Every boulder-cast shadow became the hovering silhouette. Every flutter of leaves an attack intended to suffocate her or rip the incubating creatures from her thigh. She prayed that Girl's disgusting ritual was somehow occupying its attention.

With a final heave, she scrabbled atop an outcropping of rock and earth that had melded to the oak's lichenous trunk. A turret-shaped mound hunkered just behind the tree, the top of the cavern's chimney, she guessed. She spun around, surveying where the mountainside tapered to lower altitudes. Three hundred feet below, Girl's cabin glimmered, a blue-tinted doll's house, its rustic imperfections obscured by distance. The charcoal scribble of road descended into the valley. Miles away, headlights winked to life, then died just as suddenly.

To her left, the mountain flattened to a ledge that quickly curved out of sight. If her mental calculations were accurate, the ledge should eventually lead her to the car's hiding place. She leaped from the outcropping, ignoring a branch that scraped her cheek. After plunging through a patch of thorny undergrowth, she found herself a foot or so from the ledge's steep edge.

She rounded the mountain and a small stand of trees appeared. Beyond the scraggly trunks, the rock-strewn earth sloped to an old carriage road. "Fuck yes," she whispered, trembling, excitement and fear waging a tug of war.

She broke through the trees and began a steep headlong descent. With each step, she grew less cautious, fear and adrenaline flooding her body. She tripped over a tree root, narrowly avoiding a face-plant. Hands on knees, she halted beneath a low-hanging branch, commanding her breathing to slow, her mind to stay vigilant. She could not afford to be sloppy. Not when escape was so near.

She straightened up, bumping her forehead on a soft papery object hanging from the branch. Immediately a wild buzzing awoke. She whipped around to discover a football-size hornet's nest, the angry inhabitants emerging at an alarming rate. A huge stinger sank into her neck.

Her shriek shattered the evening air.

"Mama!" Girl's roar seemed to rise from the bowels of the earth.

Mary powered down the ledge, tripping over rocks and tree roots, tumbling and regaining her feet until she reached the carriage road. She ran, pumping arms and legs into a full sprint. With every ragged breath, a single thought pounded through her mind, spurring her on.

Get to the car.

Evening shadows shrouded the carriage road and surrounding forest. A rock face swam into view. A six-foot-by-six-foot archway had been dynamited into the base. *This has to be it,* Mary told herself.

"Mama! I'm coming!" Girl roared, seemingly from beneath Mary's feet, much louder than before.

Mary charged toward the shadowy archway.

Girl's anguished yelling continued. Mary halted, disoriented. The woman's voice was drawing closer with each passing moment. And it seemed now to be coming from within the cave. She peered into the darkness. Her eyes adjusted, and an insane, gleeful laugh flew from her mouth. The silhouette of the car floated before her.

She bulleted through the cave entrance. A flashlight speared the darkness, then retreated. Girl's huffing echoed through the space.

Mary reached the Mercedes and placed her palms on the cool metal. A jolt of triumph shot through her. She jerked open the car door, nearly weeping to find it unlocked, and threw herself inside. Her purse was on the passenger seat where she'd left it, just before the cicadas had invaded the car.

She slammed and locked the door, then punched the ignition button. The motor roared to life. Girl had neglected to remove the key fob from the car, once again. "Yes!" she gasped, trying to steady her trembling hands on the wheel.

The headlights flared on the back of the cave. Girl's pale face and deep, unblinking eyes stared into the high beams. She emerged from a crevice in the rock wall, her broad body as formidable as the boulders around her. In the blaze of the lights, she froze, making no effort to block the car. Her face was a wound reopened. Despite Mary's desperation to escape, she was gripped with pity for this forlorn being, twisted and broken by her depraved mother before she ever had a chance at life. Shunted to the fringes. Used for some disgusting ritual. Abandoned.

But Mary had to get the hell out of here. Now.

She threw the car into reverse. Girl sprang to life, rushing forward to pound the hood. "Wait!"

Mary's breath came in rapid gusts. Her hands felt clumsy on the wheel, as if the car belonged to someone else. The tires spun uselessly, impeded by oversize scree.

A loud thump sounded. Mary screamed at the sight of two massive hands suctioned to the driver's side window, framing Girl's stricken face. "I'm sorry! I love you!" she howled.

Mary punched the accelerator, released, then punched again. The engine revved. Pebbles bulleted the undercarriage. The car rocked in place.

The window rattled beneath Girl's pounding fists. Mary jerked away, expecting shards of glass to explode into the car. But it was Girl's face that seemed to fracture, morphing from disbelief, to anger, to hurt, and back again.

Mary revved the accelerator, backed off, then floored it. The tires sprang loose. The front end of the car slammed against the edge of the dynamited archway, nearly pinning Girl to the rock. Mary cut the wheel hard, reversing onto the carriage road, then sped off.

A wall of mountain slid past on one side, a blur of trees on the other. Through the darkness, her real life beckoned, the crowded sidewalks of Manhattan, the spired skyline, the majestic green of Central Park visible from her terrace. A garbled cry left her mouth, half sob, half victory howl. As she picked up speed, a flash of light exploded. Followed by another. The car slumped and careened. She slammed the brakes. Another explosion and the front end of the car bottomed out, slamming Mary's face into the steering wheel. The Mercedes skimmed the mountainside, then slid to a stop.

Mary lifted her face, her forehead gushing blood. A figure emerged from the dusky shadows, lanky and fluid, striding toward the car. Mary fumbled to open the door. The night breeze rushed in, laced with Girl's faraway howls.

"Please. Help me. I was kidnapped by that crazy woman back there."

The figure paused, straightening broad, angular shoulders. A silhouetted rifle hovered nearby. "Bitch. You call my daughter crazy again, I'll blow your head off."

Chapter 11

The night sky sparkled above Mary, flaunting its cold, distant beauty. She was on her back, her dew-soaked body spread-eagled across the hood of the Mercedes. Her wrists and ankles were bound by ropes threaded beneath the car's undercarriage. The hood's wrecked front section canted her body at an odd angle, forcing her to squirm periodically so her leg wouldn't go numb. Her neck throbbed, still hot with venom from the hornet's sting. Her forehead ached from slamming against the steering wheel. The car was in front of the cabin, partially shaded by the elm tree overhanging the patch of dirt that served as Girl's parking area.

Mary clenched her fists. An hour ago, she'd been in the back seat of the Mercedes with a semiautomatic rifle pressed against her gut, wielded by Girl's mother, her *Real* Mother, as the car thumped the half mile down the mountain on flattened tires. This was followed by the ordeal of Real Mother instructing her daughter in the art of securing a human being to a car hood, "just like deer-kill."

Initially Girl suggested they imprison Mary in the root cellar. But when Real Mother learned of Mary's false claim of motherhood, she'd ordered the lashing to the car. At one point, Mary had pivoted toward the woods, sensing an opportunity to run. But Real Mother had fired a round from her weapon, cutting a shallow moat into the earth at Mary's feet. She'd promised the next round would sever Mary's head from her neck.

Mary's impression of Real Mother's physical appearance was hazy: a shadowy figure on the carriage road; wide, cunning eyes glimpsed beneath the car's dome light, with irises of twisted hazel undergrowth; lean, muscular forearms flashing as Mary was bound to the car hood. And Real Mother's voice—mocking and relentless as a finger jab to the forehead.

Now, bathed in the light of the cabin's porch windows, Mary had a front-row seat to the mother-daughter reunion. At least audibly. The cabin's interior was above Mary's line of sight, but she could hear the women's voices with near-perfect clarity.

At this moment, Girl was presenting the menstrual tapestry to her mother, a verbatim recitation of that first horrible day of Mary's captivity. Girl must have practiced this speech thousands of times while fantasizing about her mother's homecoming.

Mary was treated once again to all the lurid details: Real Mother's vow to thirteen-year-old Girl that when her "first blood" came she'd no longer be pimped out to strange men, Girl's grief that her mother was long gone when it happened, and her determination to preserve the proof until her mother's promised return with the seventeen-year cycle of the Brood.

"When the cicadas crawled up seventeen years ago. And you didn't come. I almost gave up. But I didn't. I put my mind on this year. And here you are."

"Come here, sweet thing. You did good." Real Mother's voice drifted through the windows. "That's right. Next to Mama. Put your big old head on my lap." Girl's sobbing soon followed. "It breaks my heart that I missed your first blood," the woman continued. "But I had no choice. I was called. And I always knew Her In The Cave would set you right. And now look at you. Full grown. And then some."

"Thank you, Mama," Girl blew her nose vigorously.

"And don't you worry about *that* piece of trash out there," Real Mother said, her soothing tone falling away. Mary's skin prickled.

Through the cabin wall she felt Real Mother's attention turning toward her.

"I'm dumb for thinking she was you." Girl sniffled. "But she showed up right when you was supposed to. I was missing you so bad. Guess my head fooled me." Another gush of tears. "Where you been all this time?"

"I'll tell you all that when I'm good and ready. Important thing is I'm here now, and we can welcome the Brood. Together."

"Cleanse in the Pure Pond. Speak our blessings in the cave. Bow before Her. Like we used to," Girl said.

"Like we used to," Real Mother repeated, followed by an eerily recognizable call. "Oweee-oooo. Oweee-oooo."

"Oweee-oooo. Oweee-oooo." Girl's full-throated response pierced the cabin walls, her mimicry more precise than Real Mother's.

"Your sound truly honors Her In The Cave. Makes me want to get up there. Maybe even this afternoon. But first, Mama's gonna handle that fucked-up situation out there."

Mary's blood turned to ice water. She raised her head, straining to catch the rest of Real Mother's words. But the voice had quieted to a low whisper, punctuated by Girl's sniffling apologies or professions of love.

She inhaled deeply to slow her racing heart. She reminded herself that she was reunited with her car, half-wrecked though it was. Her laptop and mobile hot spot were probably still in the trunk. Even though immobilized, she was within inches of contact with the outside world. The thought gave her some small comfort.

She strained against the ropes. Her hands budged an inch or two, her feet not at all. Judging from the expert knotwork, she suspected this was an oft-used method of restraint for Real Mother. God only knows what sort of life she'd been leading. But Mary wagered it involved criminal activity, possibly even prison time.

She let her head fall back on the hood. Might Girl let her go now that she knew Mary wasn't her mother? Or would she fear Mary going to the police once released? Perhaps Mary should revisit the idea of the NDA with Girl. Promise discretion. And money.

And then go to the police.

But Girl was so far removed from the legally binding world in which Mary lived, a world of agreements and trade-offs, intricately structured deals designed to inflict both pain and benefit, to protect careers, power, and in this case, her own life.

But not Real Mother. She'd been out in the world. Or at least the underworld. Perhaps Mary could strike a deal with her, which of course Girl would acquiesce to. The NDA, cash, plus legal action against whomever was trying to push them off the property.

And what of the infestation now bulging against the inseam of her slacks? The thing had grown rock-hard. Would Girl still care about the creatures metamorphosing there, now that she knew Mary wasn't her mother? If so, would she force Mary to stay? Until what? The things hatched from her thigh? Or slithered? Or exploded into a case of gangrene?

She pressed her back into the hard metal hood, again and again, fighting the urge to shriek into the night.

The early morning sun gilded the wild grasses surrounding the cabin in green gold. A breeze awoke the elm tree above the Mercedes, gently stirring the leaves. Mary squinted up into the branches where a newly molted cicada twirled helplessly in midair, its moist wing trapped within the empty amber shell.

For the millionth time, she wrenched her wrists against the rope binding. Tears stained her cheeks from the agony of skin rubbed raw. The night had been endless. She'd trembled violently, hour after hour, racked with cold and fear. Her back ached from the torturous curve of the hood. Her leg was numb from the dented metal. She was soaked with dew and urine, her bladder having finally overpowered her will.

Slowly, she turned her stiffened neck to study the vehicle now parked next to her car, a diminutive version of a monster truck. The orange-gold Ford, probably from the eighties, was in mint condition.

The outsize tires were caked with mud. Girl's truck had been relegated to a weedy patch of ground near the outhouse. The Ford was here when Real Mother, Girl, and Mary had arrived last night. Most likely, Mary thought, Real Mother had cased the cabin before making her surprise appearance on the forest carriage road.

A creak sounded from the porch. Mary raised her head to find Girl emerging from the cabin, a mason jar of milky liquid in one hand. Saliva flooded Mary's mouth, escaping her lips. She tucked her chin into her shirt, hoping to absorb the upwelling of drool. Girl's bulbous eyes remained glued to the ground until she was at Mary's side. When she met Mary's gaze, her shoulders slumped. Her broad palm slipped beneath Mary's skull with the formality of a health-care worker.

Ignoring her craving and the stirrings within her thigh, Mary stared past the jar, searching Girl's face. "I tried to tell you the truth. Numerous times. But you wouldn't listen."

Girl's lips blanched as she pressed them together.

"What was I supposed to do?" Mary asked. "You gave me no choice but to lie."

Again, Girl held the cup to Mary's lips.

So the babies still matter, Mary thought. "I promise I'll drink," she said. "Just please hear me out."

Girl's eyes darted to the jar, insistent.

"Fine," Mary said. She glugged down the liquid, almost choking in her rush to drain the jar and plead her case while she was alone with Girl.

The screen door flew open. Real Mother strode onto the porch and into the bright morning sunlight. Mary guessed the woman was in her mid- to late fifties. Her storm-gray hair was pulled into a braid, a thick whip that fell below her waist. Wide, sharp cheekbones shaped the rugged, handsome face. Hazel eyes flickered with vulpine wariness. Weathered jeans clung to long, agile legs. Her upper arms were taut and sun weathered, her forearms a pastiche of tattoos. A chunky, oversize bracelet dangled from one wrist. A black sleeveless Metallica T-shirt accentuated her sinewy neck and shoulders. The rifle was casually cradled beneath one arm. Another large tattoo stamped her chest, a design that in the past would have been meaningless to Mary. Now she immediately discerned the green-black head of a cicada, its bulging red eyes peeking over the low neckline of the T-shirt.

Mary was loath to admit it, but she could understand why Girl, twenty-seven years after the abandonment, had mistaken her for this woman. In another life, they could have been relatives, even sisters. They both stood at approximately five foot eleven and, before Mary's recent weight gain, shared the same narrow waist and broad shoulders. Mary had seen enough court drawings of herself to recognize her own bullish confidence in the woman's stance. The vicious sensuality of the lips and trace of a cleft chin were also unnervingly similar. The resemblance was less pronounced in the woman's complexion, which told a story of decades fully exposed to the sun and a life lived without the benefit of the Botox needle.

Girl's tales of abuse circled through Mary's mind, being pimped out as a girl to strange men, the vicious beatings, the neglect, the indoctrination into a bizarre cult of cicada worship. Recalling Real Mother's sadistic gusto when she coached Girl through binding a human body to a car hood, Mary now fully believed it was true. Girl was psychologically twisted, but considering the deviant now clomping around the cabin's sagging front porch, it was a wonder she wasn't more so. Girl's swings between rage and servile "love," her determination to regain her mother at all costs, a chance perhaps to redo her unthinkable childhood and quiet the voices in her head—it made more sense to Mary than she cared to admit.

Emitting a low whistle, Real Mother regarded the red-eyed cicadas dipping through the air and swarming the surrounding trees. "Just look at 'em all," she breathed. "Hello, beauties! Bet you're happy as hell to see me!"

Girl let out an excited giggle and hurried to Real Mother's side. Breathlessly, she watched as Real Mother approached a lone cicada scaling one of the porch's lumber posts. She extended her hand toward the insect and snapped her fingers. When the bug continued to creep along the wood, she snapped again. "Come on now."

"Watch, Mama," Girl said, snapping three times. The cicada buzzed onto her open palm. "See?" She returned it to the post.

Real Mother tried once more, snapping three times. But the cicada only flicked its wings.

"A shy one," Girl cooed. She seemed ready to demonstrate again. But Real Mother was already ambling down the steps, her eyes veiled in something almost resembling hurt.

Mary raised her head, doing her best to adopt the unblinking gaze she reserved for negotiations. "I have a proposition that could benefit you greatly. Then we go our separate ways in peace. No harm. No foul," Mary said.

Real Mother drew next to the Mercedes, Girl at her heels. Her hazel eyes glittered, roving over Mary's splayed figure. Her thick eyebrows arched with pleasure, curiosity, or both.

"Your daughter showed me hospitality," Mary continued. "It's only right that I compensate you both for that."

Quick as a viper, Real Mother's fist struck Mary's jaw. "Girl told me all about that silver tongue of yours." She removed the chunky bracelet, which Mary now realized was a roll of duct tape. She ripped off a strip and sealed Mary's blood-filled mouth.

"You thought this one was me, Girl?" Real Mother returned the duct tape to her wrist. "We ain't nothing alike. Maybe *you* and her. Specially round the midsection." She grabbed a handful of Girl's belly fat and twisted. Girl flinched, then giggled nervously. Real Mother reached for Mary's stomach. Mary's rope-bound wrists bucked forward as the woman's nails sank deep into the newly fattened flesh.

"Tubby. Both of you," Real Mother said. "Not my style." She gestured to the mason jar. Dried Mother's Milk coated the glass. "Never touch shit like that. Lard. Sugar. Nasty in. Nasty out." She blew out her cheeks and curved her arms around an imaginary belly.

Real Mother turned and strutted a few feet from the car, her braid a swinging rope. She paused, widening her stance before curling one arm into a biceps flex. She lovingly stroked the muscle, her eyes fixed on Mary and Girl. "I eat meat and water. Nothing else." She spun around, this time flexing both arms. Her back flared into a solid plane of muscle and bone. "No booze. That's the real secret. None of that opioid shit neither. Just meth." She swaggered back to the car, clearly enjoying her own lanky physique.

"You were always strong, Mama," Girl murmured, her voice adoring and shy.

"Lean and mean!" Real Mother whooped. She paused to listen to her words echoing across the valley, her face rent by a lazy grin. "God, it's good to be home." She wrapped Girl in a rough hug.

"I love you, Mama," Girl whispered, somehow seeming small within her mother's arms.

"Lean and mean," Real Mother repeated, releasing Girl. Her voice was now quiet, almost reflective. "That's what confuses me." She cocked her head. "How my only kin thought I was this here dough girl. How'd that happen? Huh?" She pump-faked slapping Girl's skull. "Huh?"

Girl flinched, then stumbled backward. She laughed, an obsequious bray, but her eyes were clouded and uncertain.

"You always were a sweet little dummy, Girl," Real Mother said. "But still." She scowled at Mary. "And she smells like piss."

Mary's mouth and chin were stiff with dried Mother's Milk. Her body, heavier than it had been in decades, suctioned to the hood of the car. The rope burned her wrists. Blood dripped down her throat.

A wave of shame tore through her. She felt the urge to justify herself to this maniac, to explain that normally she was slender and fit. Kept a strict Paleo diet. Paid thousands each year to a personal trainer. Was not a slob. Was not a fat piece of shit. Had not lost control of her own body.

In this moment, Mary felt grateful for the duct tape. The confessional urge terrified her more than the rope restraints, more than the rifle. She slammed her head against the car hood repeatedly and dug her heels into the metal, to feel her muscles, to remind herself of her own strength, to defy the impulse to give a fuck about what this cretin thought of her.

"Throw all the temper tantrums you like, Silver Tongue," Real Mother said. Then she paused, catching sight of the newly molted cicada on the branch above, its wing still trapped in the shell it had just shed. Girl followed her mother's gaze, then hurried to her side.

"Best put her out of her misery," Real Mother said. She reached up on tiptoes to swat the cicada. But Girl's hand shot out and caught her mother's wrist.

"No!" Girl roared. Her eyes glinted. Her heavy jaw was set.

The cocksureness drained from Real Mother's face. Mary tensed, awaiting one of Girl's bursts of violence. Girl plucked the cicada from the branch, then released Real Mother's wrist. Gently, she teased the wing from the shell before returning the cicada to the tree.

"You put your hand on me, daughter."

"I'm sorry, Mama. But she wants to live. Even though she can't fly."

Real Mother glared at Girl, chest rising and falling. Her gaze drifted past the tree, in the direction of the cave. "Your heart is in the right place. But you ever grab me like that again . . ." Her face hardened like scorched earth. "I will split you like kindling for the fire. Now get the meat out of the cooler in my truck and make me some sausage." After throwing a dark glance at Mary, Real Mother returned to the cabin.

Softly, Girl patted Mary's impregnated leg, whispering, "Don't forget about *them*, Mama. I mean, Mary," she quickly corrected, glancing fearfully toward Real Mother.

But Real Mother was clomping across the porch. She paused to pull a flip phone from her pocket and disappeared inside the cabin.

"The babies," Girl continued in a low voice. "Got to protect them. Don't go thrashing around like you did before. Please." Her eyes again darted to the cabin.

Mary stared into Girl's churning brown eyes. A certainty sprang to her mind. *Real Mother doesn't know about the babies.* Girl had kept it from her.

Before Mary could contemplate the meaning of the omission, Real Mother reappeared. She began a slow lap around the car. "Just talked to my fence. Even though Silver Tongue fucked up this fancy rig, we can still get something for it. As is. Or maybe we'll chop it." She grinned at Girl, then continued her circling.

As she rounded the hood, she froze, eyes nailed to Mary's feet. "I'll be goddamned. You even got this bitch wearing my boots." She grabbed the boot on Mary's impregnated leg and began wrenching it off, not bothering with the laces. Mary screamed through the duct tape while Real Mother roughly torqued her leg. Girl rushed to her mother's side.

"Let me get it, Mama," Girl said, maneuvering her bulk between her mother and Mary's foot. She hastily unlaced the right boot and Real Mother turned her attention to the left. When the boots were off, Real Mother grabbed them and began yelling while buffeting Girl's head with the hard soles, each word accompanied by a clap to Girl's skull. "I. Hurt. People. Who. Steal. My. Shit."

Girl whimpered and fell to one knee. Blood flowed from one ear. Real Mother pushed past her toward Mary. She ripped the duct tape from Mary's mouth. "Did she steal my boots and give 'em to you? Or you stole 'em on your own?"

Beyond Real Mother, Mary caught sight of Girl. She was motionless as a stuffed bear. The understanding telegraphed between them that Mary's response would dictate which of the two of them got the shit beat out of her.

Some enraged, vengeful part of her wanted to rat out Girl. She certainly deserved it. Force-feeding, kidnapping, imprisonment. Not to mention designating Mary as a human petri dish without her consent.

Real Mother nosed the muzzle of the rifle into Mary's cheek.

"She gave them to me," Mary started.

Real Mother charged Girl, the rifle butt aimed at her face. Girl dropped to the ground, curling into herself, broad hands shielding her skull.

"To help Her In The Cave!" Mary screamed.

Real Mother halted in midstride. She spun around to face Mary, the gun butt still poised to strike Girl.

"The only shoes I have are pumps," Mary raced on. "There was a problem in the cave." She racked her brain for details from Girl and Real

Mother's earlier conversation about their microcult. "A small cave-in by the Pure Pond. Where you speak the blessings." Real Mother lowered the gun. Mary continued, "Girl is strong. Normally she could handle it. But she'd just fed the cicadas." She steeled her face to hide her distaste. "Her energy was flagging. So she loaned me the boots to help her clear the passage. That's why we were up there."

"You mean before you tried to run away." Real Mother parked a hand on one hip.

"Well," Mary replied, unable to help herself. "I think we're all in agreement that I never should have been kept here in the first place."

Real Mother rushed forward. Her fist rammed Mary's chest, knocking the breath from her body. "That's the thanks you give my daughter for saving your life? And loaning you my boots? Feeding your fat face out of her own pocket? How 'bout I borrow some of your stuff? Like this ring, for starters." She jerked the emerald-cut diamond ring from Mary's finger. "Think I saw a fancy purse in there too." She whipped open the car door and withdrew the Fendi handbag. After digging through the contents, she found the wallet. Silently, she thumbed through ten crisp hundred-dollar bills, Mary's withdrawal from the ATM in the lobby of her firm's building the day before Teddy's funeral. It felt so long ago now.

"That ought to do it. For starters," Real Mother said. She eyed Mary's driver's license, pocketed it, then tossed the empty wallet back in the bag. "For you, pudding pie." She extended the Fendi to Girl, the gold buckle glinting in the sunlight.

Girl glanced at Mary uncertainly. Her hands remained at her sides.

"The fuck you looking at her? This purse is mine to give," Real Mother said. "Fair compensation for this bloodsucker. You got enough with the nymphs milking you dry. Don't need this one too."

Once again, Real Mother's words improbably stung Mary.

And Real Mother, that sneering bitch, somehow knew it.

"Take it, sugar. You earned it. Fair and square." Real Mother dangled the purse. Obediently, Girl slid her arm through the handles.

Chapter 12

Blood filled Mary's mouth. She turned her head to spit and winced as her cheek was scalded by the sunbaked metal of the car hood. She imagined UV waves blasting through the nuclei of her skin cells, disordering the DNA, grinding unnatural textures into her face and hands, like the dynamite used to eat away at the mountain now overshadowing her.

An unhinged chuckle welled up as she contemplated her decades spent battling the sun's rays. She felt a strange release at the futility of preserving her complexion, followed by the certainty that sun, exhaustion, and the absence of real food were slowly eroding her sanity.

Girl and her mother had disappeared into the cabin over an hour ago. She caught snippets of their chatter as Girl prepared Real Mother's sausages.

"The key fob's in the purse," Real Mother said. "You mean to tell me you left that hag's car unlocked and ready to start?"

Apparently, the vittles had been consumed, and they'd moved on to rummaging through the Fendi bag.

"Didn't know what that doohickey did, Mama. Looked all over for a key till I figured out about the button. Don't look nothing like my pickup," Girl replied. "It's like a spaceship in there."

"They been doing it like that for years, you knucklehead. With the button. And it shows the picture of the lock right there on the key fob. Even you could figure that out."

"Saw that. But I was scared to try without knowing for sure how it worked." Girl's voice softened to a whine. "'Cause of what happened before."

"Hell are you talking about?"

"When I was little. Playing in your truck. Locked the keys inside. You was mad, mad. Remember?"

Real Mother remained quiet. Mary detected the faint jingle of the handbag.

Girl continued, "That time with my arm. When you—"

"I remember!" Real Mother blurted. "Don't need you to tell me what's already in my own head."

Another silence dragged on. Mary shuddered, trying not to imagine what punishment Real Mother had meted out to young Girl for the innocent mistake.

The closing of a snap sounded, and a zipper in motion. Real Mother cleared her throat. "What the fuck are all these little bottles and jars?"

"Smells like honeysuckle," Girl said.

Mary pictured the backwoods duo puzzling over her prescription-grade facial products even as her skin sizzled on the car hood.

"This red jar," Girl murmured, "smells so good I could eat it."

"What a surprise." Real Mother chuckled. "My Girl eats anything that doesn't eat her first."

"Ru—Reh . . . Tie . . . Nal," Girl intoned.

"Gimme that," Real Mother said. "Retinol cream."

"You read quick as can be."

"No. I read normal. You are just slow. Always have been. Not your fault." Real Mother paused. "Retinol cream. Women like that, all they care about is keeping the men interested. With their looks, their creams and perfumes, their shiny underwear. It's women like that old slut out there that give men the upper hand. Keep the rest of us from getting anywhere."

"How dare you! You depraved hayseed!" The words erupted from Mary's mouth.

The cabin fell silent. Footfalls pounded across the wooden floor. The screen door flew open and Real Mother burst forth, eyes blazing from the roughened bark of her face. “Nobody talks down to me, you talcum-powdered hag. You’re still alive at my pleasure. And it’s only ’cause I ain’t decided whether to gut you and feed you to the wild hogs or string your parts round the cave as an offering to Her.”

She stormed down the steps and came to rest at Mary’s side. “Hogs. Or cave. Pick your poison, bitch,” she hissed, the odor of sausage wafting across Mary’s face.

“There’s a stick with bristles at the end of it in my purse. Called a toothbrush. I recommend using it.”

Real Mother’s fist slammed into Mary’s face repeatedly. Old wounds reopened. New ones formed. The pulsing thrum of cicadas spiked to a high-pitched keening, though Mary still clearly discerned the quiet pop of her nose breaking. From deep within her well of pain, she wondered why she was provoking this woman, inviting this pummeling, endangering her life. As Girl wedged herself into the fray, shielding Mary from the rain of fists, Mary read the answer, clear and bright, in the inferno of Real Mother’s eyes.

In Mary, Real Mother saw everything she hated: the wealthy and effete, the polished professional, the removed one-percenter who manipulated a world greased with their capital. Because Mary and the people like her saw Real Mother and Girl as caricatures, ignorant rednecks, clueless about the ways of the world, incapable of bettering themselves even if they had the inclination.

A lesser class of human.

Had there been a time when Real Mother tried to climb out of the hole into which she’d been born, before she became an abusive parent and a pimp to her own daughter? Had she, like Mary, seen beyond the life of failure and mediocrity others presumed for her?

Maybe. But Real Mother hadn’t succeeded in reshaping her destiny. Mary had. That fact drove Mary to meet Real Mother’s violence with her own righteous rage, to explode whatever ideas the lunatic had about who Mary was and the contours of her character.

"Don't waste your energy, Mama," Girl huffed. "She ain't worth it."

Cursing, Real Mother dropped her tattooed forearms to her sides. She wiped her blood-flecked knuckles on her jeans. "Your stupid ass put us in this situation!" She headbutted Girl, then marched toward the monster truck.

Girl scurried after her, rubbing her forehead. "Where you going?"

"I got business to take care of."

"What about Her In The Cave?" Girl asked. "We were gonna visit this afternoon. You said."

"I just got here, dammit. I need to settle in."

"She's waiting."

"Let her wait!" Real Mother's scream exploded across the mountainside. She gestured toward the elm tree with its cicada-encrusted branches, then to the porch where the dark, winged bodies studded the posts. "You ever seen a Brood this big?"

"No. But—"

"I brought 'em! Me!" Real Mother bulldozed Girl's words. "They felt me coming! Unlike you. Turd for brains."

Visibly trembling, Girl again glanced toward the cave and the ancient tree above the dark, gaping mouth. The leaf-choked branches stirred, though the air was stifling and still.

Real Mother aimed the heel of her steel-toed boot at Girl's rump. "You've been setting on your fat ass while I've been chasing broods all over the country. Montana, North Carolina, Michigan. Even chased the thirteen-year broods to Louisiana and Mississippi. There are broods like ours, Girl. Not many. But a few. I was out there. Loving them, calling to them, marking myself." She lifted her Metallica shirt to reveal her bare chest.

The cicada tattoo ascended between bell-shaped breasts tipped with dark-rose areolas. Gossamer wings spanned the muscular lattice of her upper chest. Her abdomen had been stained green black with the insect's thick thorax, which terminated at a soft swell of belly, her only reserve of fat. "Meanwhile, the rest of the world is trying to kill 'em off. Cutting down the mother trees, pouring shit into the ground." She dropped her shirt. "So quit riding my ass. I'll go to Her when I'm good and ready."

She threw open the door of the orange-gold Ford, swung into the driver's seat, and slammed herself in. The engine roared to life, and she tore out of the driveway, shrouding Mary and Girl in dust.

"Why haven't you told her?" Mary's wounded mouth sprayed blood as she spoke. Her broken nose throbbed with each word.

"Time for your Mother's Milk," Girl said, with forced brightness. Her broad back hunched as she slunk toward the porch.

"Forget the Mother's Milk!" Mary sputtered as Girl disappeared into the cabin. Though, disgustingly, she longed for the sweet grog.

The sun had shifted slightly, draping Mary's face in shadow. The pain of her broken nose and bruised jaw drenched her in a hallucinatory fog. She stared into the tree, where thousands of cicadas writhed along the branches. Her gaze softened, and tree and cicadas merged into a kaleidoscopic pattern, surging in one area, dispersing in another, surrounded by the call and response of their chorus. Were they plotting Mary's death? Maybe they were singing lullabies to the creatures in her leg or tattling to Her In The Cave about Real Mother's refusal to pay homage. Then again, maybe they were just being dumb bugs.

Girl's pale countenance swam into view. Her eyes had transformed, the flat brown color now richer, with more depth. But then Mary realized it was her full lips that had darkened, shifting her eyes into relief. "Etienne," she said, recognizing the shade of her Chanel lipstick. "Very nice." Girl covered her mouth, as if she'd forgotten about the lipstick. But joy flickered in her eyes while she fed Mary the Mother's Milk.

The solution slid down Mary's throat, followed by the familiar warm stirrings in her thigh. A thrumming energy radiated from her leg to her hips and belly. When it reached her chest, the bruising from Real Mother's punch cooled. Her breathing became less constricted.

The energy moved to her pulverized face, soothing the volcanic pain to an everyday headache. She sighed. Her lids grew heavy.

"That's right," Girl cooed. "Heal up. Sleep. Put you inside when Mama gets back. Got to get her permission."

Mary forced her eyes open. "Why haven't you told her?"

Girl averted her gaze and shuffled toward the cabin.

"You don't trust her," Mary called. "It's okay. I understand. It'll be our secret."

Girl spun on her heels, sputtering in her rush to speak. "Course I trust her! She's my mama!"

"Then why not tell her? She's a part of this whole . . ." Mary paused, searching for an adequate term to describe the surreal nightmare in which she was ensnared. "*Thing* with Her In The Cave. Isn't she?"

"I'm gonna tell her. At the right time."

"What about when she gets back? Maybe it'll make her less hostile toward me. We could do it together. Or maybe just me. It's my body, after all. My *babies*."

"They are never ours!" Girl wailed, her dense skull bowed over restless hands. She made her way down the porch steps and placed the empty mason jar on the hood.

"The babies are always for Her In The Cave," Girl said. "We are like the mother tree. We just carry them while they grow." She cupped the bulging clutches beneath her shirt. "Get used to that now. Before they come."

"Trust me. There will be no fight for custody on my end. Does your mother know about yours?"

"Course." Girl's brows peaked. "She's happy as can be. Specially since she can't. At least not yet."

"You mean your mother has never . . ." Mary glanced down at the bulging inseam of her slacks. "The bugs haven't used her this way?"

Girl shook her head. "But it could still happen. Like with you."

Mary remained silent, considering this surprising detail. Is that why Real Mother ran off years ago? She felt insulted or excluded. Or even inadequate.

"And yet you haven't told her about me. Why not?"

"I don't know why I haven't said." Girl glanced up at the tree. A smile stole over her face as she watched the busy goings-on. The smile faded, and her gaze returned to Mary. Her voice shrank to a whisper. "It's just. She hasn't gone to see Her In The Cave."

"Neither did I. But that didn't stop you from kidnapping me and keeping me here against my will."

Girl's gaze turned inward. Her eyes softened to opaque brown pools.

"What?" Mary asked.

"After that first day." Girl's voice was strained, as if she were speaking against her will. "I think I knew. Deep down. You wasn't her."

"What! Are you kidding me?" Mary screamed, reopening a wound on her lip. "Why didn't you let me go?"

"But then you got blessed! With babies!" She gestured toward Mary's leg. "Then I knew you had to be my mother." Her brow furrowed.

"Only because you smeared that pigment on me. Those three dots. With pollen or whatever the hell attracts them!"

"They wouldn't have paid you any mind if you weren't meant for it. Even with the dots. 'Fore she left, Mama put dots on herself. A bunch of times. Didn't matter. She was never blessed."

"How blessed will I be when your mother kills me?" Mary asked.

Girl's mouth quivered.

"There something you don't trust about her," Mary pressed. "You need to pay attention to that. We need to stick together. Share information. Find out her intention."

Girl's face grew pinched. Gingerly, she returned the cicada to the branch. "I do trust her," she said, her words breaking at an odd pitch. "And I'm gonna tell her."

"She treats you like garbage, Girl. The same way she treated you before she left." Unable to gesture with her bound hands, Mary threw her gaze over the landscape. "Everything you've built here. Leveling off the path up to the quarry, the screens you added to the windows, the work on the springhouse. You did all that to make a home for yourself. Think of how peaceful you've been all these years. Without her."

But Girl had turned away, her broad hands clamped over her ears. The screen door slammed behind her. Mary howled Girl's name, again and again, desperately trying to draw the woman who'd been her captor, still was her captor, into an alliance against her own flesh and blood. Finally, exhaustion overcame her, and she fell silent. When Girl reappeared what seemed like hours later, it was because the roar of an engine announced Real Mother's imminent return. Frantically, Mary again took up her plea while Girl remained planted on the steps.

"She didn't even bother to give you a name. 'Girl' is not a name."

"She ain't got a name neither," Girl muttered.

"How do you know? Maybe she's never told you."

Girl's downturned mouth carved through her soft cheeks. The engine grew louder. Soon the creaks of Real Mother's truck could be heard as she navigated the rocky dirt road.

"She disrespected Her In The Cave," Mary said. "That's not okay."

Tires crunched gravel at the driveway's end. The screech of a heavy metal guitar riff cut through the steaming air.

"Please don't say nothing about the babies. Not yet," Girl said through clenched teeth. She plastered on a smile and waved. The truck skidded to a halt. Real Mother shrieked along with a devastating falsetto climax, then killed the radio.

"Still sitting around on your fat asses?" Real Mother's voice blared through the open window. "I been hard at work," she said, climbing from the truck. "Moving the needle on turning this hunk of junk into cash." She planted herself at the front of the Mercedes, then razed Mary's bound body with a hateful stare. "My fence is sending a tow truck. We need to get this bitch out of sight. Lock her in the root cellar."

She mounted the porch, then froze. Slowly, she spun around, then reached for the mason jar, still resting on the hood of the car, coated with viscous residue.

"That's the second helping of that sugar-lard today," Real Mother said. She held the jar in front of her face, one eye doubling in size through the glass. Her gaze ricocheted from Girl to Mary and back again. "Why you feeding her so much Mother's Milk?" She flipped the jar in her hand, and with lightning speed, whipped it at the front of the cabin. Glass shattered against the wall. Girl let out a strangled shriek.

Real Mother sauntered over to Mary, her heavy braid uncoiling from her shoulder. "And look at that pretty face. Boo-boos almost all better. You'd never know I beat it to a pulp just a couple hours ago." She leaned close, her breath warming Mary's still-swollen lips and the cuts healing on her chin, cheeks, and forehead.

The green-black cicada head reared from Real Mother's T-shirt, scarlet eyes glowering. Coarse hair tufted her underarms. "Congratulations," Real Mother breathed. Abruptly, her mouth was on Mary's, tongue squirming past Mary's lips, filling the cavern of her mouth.

Mary recoiled, horrified. At first because of the leathery creature's assault. But then at the sudden, unbidden desire flooding her body. Had her hands been free, she would have pulled Real Mother's lanky frame down onto her. Was random arousal another bizarre by-product of the incubating creatures? She jerked her head against Real Mother's grip, struggling to quell the yearning that had overtaken her body.

"Well, well," Real Mother murmured when at last she withdrew her tongue. "Who knew a withered old thang like you could get knocked up." She sprang her upper body off the hood in one spry move. "And to think my own sweet daughter didn't tell me a damn thing about it."

Girl blanched. Her massive legs quaked. A wet circle appeared at her crotch and rapidly spread.

"Jesus! Enough with pissin' your pants. You fatties need to learn how to use the shitter!" She jutted her sharp chin at Girl. "Now show me. 'Fore I rip off her clothes and find it myself."

Girl pointed a trembling finger to Mary's right inner thigh. Real Mother snorted, then stormed to her truck. Hoisting herself to the open passenger-side window, she rummaged briefly inside, then returned with a pocketknife.

"Wait! No!" Mary screamed, unsure of where the blade might land.

Real Mother pulled Mary's pant leg taut then sliced the fabric from knee to ankle. Seizing the flayed pieces, she ripped the inseam open to the crotch, exposing Mary's clutch. As she studied the swelling, Real Mother remained expressionless, save a twitching left eye. Mary was keenly aware that however she felt about the clutch in her thigh, in the eyes of Girl and Real Mother, she had succeeded where Real Mother had not.

Real Mother's fist flew out, like a rattlesnake from the shadows, catching Girl square in the face. "You piece of shit," she spat. "You let an outsider corrupt the purity of our Brood. I should have known you would fuck up any- and everything while I was away." She pulled her phone from her pocket and glanced at the screen. "I would take care of this myself, but unfortunately I can't do every goddamn thing." She slid the duct tape from her wrist.

Mary's voice rose as Real Mother approached. "Look! I don't want this thing in my leg any more than you do. I know a very discreet doctor. He'll remove this for me tomorrow. Today!"

Real Mother's face swooped down to Mary's, her eyes narrowed with a savage gleam. "You don't *want*? You don't *deserve*!" She sealed the tape over Mary's lips, then retrieved her rifle from the porch.

"Untie her. Now." She waved the gun at Girl, who'd begun quietly weeping.

Girl fumbled with the knots. Mary tried to catch her eye, but Girl avoided her gaze, loosening the rope until blood rushed painfully back into Mary's wrists and ankles.

Still weeping, Girl marched Mary along the side of the cabin, her thick fingers nearly swallowing Mary's neck, one arm clamped around Mary's waist.

Mary stumbled along, sensing Real Mother's rifle trained on the back of her skull, hearing the swish of the woman's long stride through the unkempt grass.

As the root cellar drew near, Mary's body stiffened. Girl tugged open the rough wooden door, releasing a chill draft from the earthy darkness. Directly behind Mary, Real Mother inhaled sharply.

A sudden blast of gunfire exploded. Girl and Mary both screamed and fell to their knees. Real Mother's rawboned figure appeared before the root cellar door, the rifle pointed to the heavens, her thumb tucked in the pocket of her tight-fitting jeans. "Now," she began, her voice penetrating the gunshot still ringing in Mary's ears. "I'm going to give you a chance to redeem yourself, Girl. For your colossal fuckup. You want that?"

Girl nodded frantically, jiggling the beard of tears and mucus collecting on her chin.

"Good," Real Mother replied. She shoved Mary inside the root cellar with such force that Mary landed belly-down on the dirt floor. "I'll be back in an hour and thirty." She pointed the muzzle at the bulge in Mary's leg. "That better be drained dry." She punched Girl in the chest. "Understand?"

"Yes."

"Tell me, then, Girl," Real Mother said.

Tears broke across Girl's cheeks, but her voice rang clear.

"Kill 'em. Kill the babies."

Chapter 13

Mary lay sprawled on the floor of the root cellar. Real Mother stood just outside the doorway, haloed by afternoon sunlight, the semiautomatic aimed at Mary's heart.

Groaning through the duct tape, Mary pulled the torn fabric of her slacks over her exposed thigh and groin, compelled to at least attempt this small gesture of self-dignity.

"Nuh-uh," Real Mother said. "Take 'em off. Easier for Girl to get betwixt your legs. Probably more action than you've seen in the last twenty years."

Mary shook her head violently in protest, but when Real Mother menaced her with the butt of the rifle, she relented, sliding off the pants and casting them aside.

Behind Real Mother, Girl appeared in the yard, the wooden pallet Mary had been confined to pinned under one brawny arm. Mary winced, noting the small metal pail in Girl's hand, bristling with utensils and a filthy plastic bottle of some solution. Her mind churned with the implications of Real Mother's orders. Some part of her felt relieved. On several occasions, she'd come close to clawing at the pus-filled welt on her own, hoping to excise whatever was incubating there. Then she pictured Girl performing what amounted to minor surgery. The pain. The risk of infection and gangrene. The danger of a botched job that might send the creatures burrowing deeper. Her stomach lurched.

As Girl drew closer, an eerie whimpering leaked from her bloodless lips. She angled the pallet into the root cellar.

"Quit your sniveling," Real Mother said. "You're doing the right thing. This clutch was a mistake. I figure Her In The Cave tuned into your mush for brains and picked up on your stupid idea that this old hag was me. Better to put a stop to the abomination now."

Real Mother waved the gun at Mary. "Get your ass out of the way. And get a move on, Girl."

Girl arranged the pallet, guided by the sunlight streaming through the doorway. When she was finished, the pallet lay open to the full horizontal position. Mary shivered. Had the great galoot designed a strategy for slicing into Mary's leg? Or was she just going to wing it, experimenting with one sharp instrument after another, probing Mary's unanesthetized flesh until she got it right?

Or horribly wrong.

Mary tried to catch Girl's eye, to somehow wordlessly remind her of how she'd called the creatures "miracles" and clucked over them like a maniacal mother hen. But Girl avoided her gaze.

The metal pail released a muted clink as Girl lowered it to the ground. In addition to a thin piece of steel, the pail held a Bic kitchen lighter. And another object, darker and nonmetallic.

Mary's scream melted to spittle behind the tape. The dark object was the carved wooden figurine, its lower end sharpened to a point.

The butt of the gun crashed down on Mary's shoulder. She yelped and fell to one knee. "Shut it!" Real Mother growled. "That silver tongue's gonna be wagging from the grave, ain't it?"

Girl scooped Mary from the ground, forced her on the pallet, and bound her with rope. Mary howled and lashed out, even as Real Mother's gun tracked every movement.

"Those ropes are crap." Real Mother tapped Girl with the toe of her boot. "Use this." She tossed a fresh roll of duct tape at Girl. "Stronger. Once you dig into that leg, pain's gonna crank up her adrenaline."

Girl made her way around the pallet, binding Mary's arms and legs with multiple layers of tape. Real Mother grunted her approval. "Don't forget the head. If you can find one under that rat's nest."

When Mary's arms, legs, and head were restrained, Real Mother shoved Girl aside and tested the bindings. She added another layer to Mary's wrists, already raw from hours spent lashed to the car hood, then torqued Mary's right knee into an odd angle, fully exposing the swelling on her inner thigh.

Mary's eyes strayed to the turgid lump, now the size of a large halved potato. Light slanted from the doorway, illuminating tiny movements within the watery cocoon. She turned her face aside, weeping at the prospect of Girl's work-roughened hands extracting the thing.

"See that, Girl," Real Mother scoffed. "She can't look at them babies. She ain't deserving." She stepped back and lowered the gun. "I'm leaving this up to you, daughter. Prove to me that you aren't a total waste of my womb."

As Girl bobbed her heavy skull, Real Mother paused, eyes scanning Girl's mouth. She flicked a thumb across her own wet tongue, then violently rubbed all traces of lipstick from Girl's face. Girl stumbled backward. "Keep still," Real Mother barked, attacking Girl's chin. "And stay away from that whore's paint."

Before leaving, Real Mother clutched Girl in a one-armed embrace. "Now hop to it," she said. As Girl nuzzled deeper into her mother's chest, a look of distaste flashed across Real Mother's face. "When you're done, we'll celebrate. Shoot something for dinner. You and me. Then get a good night's rest so we can go to Her In The Cave early morning."

"Yes, Mama," Girl whispered.

After Real Mother left, Mary screamed protestations through the tape, hoping that Girl would unseal her mouth. But Girl seemed to have turned inward. Muttering softly to herself, she examined the metal pail. "You got to. Or she'll leave again. For good. You got to."

Mary arched her whole body against her bindings, eyes straining to one side as she tried to discern which instrument Girl was after. When at last Girl rose, her face was slick with tears. The wooden figurine was nested in her plump fingers. A muffled scream filled Mary's throat. Girl ceremoniously presented the object to Mary, hands shaking. "I carved it. It means something," she said.

After testing her thumb on the sharpened tip, Girl reached into the pail once more and withdrew a pocketknife. In a half-dozen strokes, the tip was razor honed. All the while, tears burnished the great bowls of her cheeks.

Using the stove lighter, Girl scorched the figurine's sharpened point. The flame cast trembling shadows on the cellar walls. Mary's heart raced while she observed the DIY procedure. Could wood even be sterilized?

Girl loomed above Mary's thigh, positioning the sharpened point directly over the swelling. Mary squeezed her eyes shut, bracing herself as the familiar warm energy flared beneath her skin. Outside the root cellar, the plaintive cry of cicadas peaked and ebbed in an irregular rhythm, as if their protective impulse was confused by Girl's hand in the damage and her tortured, conflicting emotions. A searing pain pierced Mary's thigh. She roared, ballooning the duct tape and emptying her lungs of air. Her eyes flew open, darting to the incision Girl had made along the inflamed margin of the swelling. Aside from a tiny trail of ooze, the watery cocoon was still intact.

The figurine clattered against the wooden slats of the pallet, coming to rest near the edge. "Can't do it," Girl whispered. She reached for the pail, withdrawing a dishcloth to stanch the trickle of blood flowing across Mary's leg.

"So little," Girl wept. "Never hurt no one. Just wanting to live. To be happy." A huge sob racked her hulking body. "Ain't no fault of theirs."

Girl dragged her forearm beneath her running nose and stared through the open door. For several minutes, she remained motionless. Gradually, her sodden expression cleared. Her drooping mouth shifted upward. She hammered her thigh with her fist. "This is my fault. Shoulda told Mama about the babies. Right away. She don't really want to kill 'em. She would never, ever, ever do that. She's mad, that's all."

Girl clapped Mary's tape-bound hand. Mary yelled out in pain. "Sorry," Girl said. Flecks of hope gathered in her eyes. "Don't worry. We're gonna save 'em. I'm gonna talk to her. Make her understand."

Mary screamed at Girl's retreating figure, gripped by the certainty that if Real Mother returned first, she'd employ a much more expedient method of killing the creatures.

She'd kill the host.

Through the half-open root cellar door, Mary peered at a sliver of yard behind the cabin. In her rush to plead her case to Real Mother, Girl had neglected to shut Mary in. Or maybe she'd done it on purpose, to let light and air into the stagnant space. It wasn't as if Mary was going anywhere. Real Mother's skill with duct tape was formidable. Mary was as helpless as a pinned beetle in a glass case. And the root cellar was far enough behind the cabin that the tow truck driver was unlikely to hear her muffled screams. A chill shot through her at the thought of her car's dismantling. She allowed herself to ponder a question she'd been avoiding.

Why was she still alive? Why hadn't Real Mother turned her flesh to confetti with the semiautomatic even before she knew about the creatures in her leg? It was possible the grizzled maniac had a more ambitious plan. Perhaps she hoped to force Mary to empty her bank accounts *before* killing her. Complicated, requiring multiple interactions with the outside world. But not impossible.

Or perhaps ransom. It was simpler. A one-shot deal. Real Mother had discovered Mary's driver's license. No doubt she'd rifled through her business cards as well. For all Mary knew, Real Mother had already contacted the firm with a price for her life. Theoretically, ransom was a best-case scenario. Assuming Real Mother kept her word. And the firm put up the funds, which wasn't a certainty. At least two of the partners would secretly celebrate her demise.

But then again, the firm would be screwed without her on the MaxFauna case. Millions were at stake. And the firm's reputation. So in all probability, the sharks would deem it in their best interest to save her life.

How it warmed the cockles.

She craned her neck, pushing against the tape encircling her head, angling for a better view through the half-open door. The shadows had lengthened, striating the pale knee-high grasses and tangled undergrowth. She guessed Girl had been gone for over an hour. She had no idea if her Mercedes had been carted off. Or how Real Mother had received Girl's plea for a stay of execution. At least she hadn't heard gunshots. It was possible Girl hadn't even broached the subject yet and was cowering on the sidelines, waiting for the right moment.

Movement stirred the dappled light at the edge of the woods. Flat on her back, Mary strained to see. Eyes aching, she struggled to focus, terrified that someone was skulking toward the root cellar. The movement soon sharpened into a shadowy form flickering between the tree trunks. She shuddered. Perhaps it wasn't a human after all.

But when the shadow finally stepped from the trees, she clearly discerned a man. As he forded the tall grass, knobby knees flashing, his wide-brimmed hat slipped from his head and dangled by the drawstring. He stepped briefly out of Mary's sight, beyond the doorframe. When he came back into view, he was closer to the root cellar, studying a sapling and the cicadas swarming its willowy trunk.

Mary's breath caught. It was Girl's oddball love interest. A powerful scream gathered within her. The duct tape tore at her lips as her mouth swelled with sound.

Just as her cry for help crystallized, an eruption of cicada song blasted from the trees, the mountainside, even from the dirt floor of the root cellar. At the sound, the man swept his gaze across the landscape, his smile widening. He turned in circles, eyes sliding past the cabin, the root cellar, the sky, and the woods, arms flung outward in spastic joy.

The sound died in Mary's throat. Her coiled muscles slackened. She recalled her last exhausting and futile effort to scream for this weirdo's attention. The bugs, Her In The Cave, would not allow it. "Nonsense," she grunted behind the tape. Some part of her was still holding out for a rational explanation for the seemingly intelligent behavior of the cicadas.

She rolled her eyes downward, surveying her immobilized body. Her silk blouse was crusty with lactation and spilled Mother's Milk; her bare legs scratched and hairy; her knee cocked open, groin exposed, the bulge on her inner thigh rimmed with dried pus and blood. A loud sob broke from her chest, inciting another wail of cicada song. When the insects quieted, the rumble of a vehicle could be heard, disappearing into the distance.

Girl reappeared in the backyard, flesh bouncing as she ran, surprisingly swift. "She said we could keep 'em, Ms. Mary! They belong to Her . . ." She froze when she saw the man, still spinning like a holy fool in the backyard.

Girl staggered backward, beyond the frame of the root cellar door, so that Mary now only saw half of her. "Dale! What are you doing here?" Girl squeaked, her voice reaching Mary through the advancing dusk.

The man reached inside one of the many pockets sewn into his vest. "I came to show you this!" he bellowed, his voice bright with affection. Mary was unable to make out the object in his outstretched palm.

Girl's thick fingers appeared, brushing Dale's hand before disappearing from Mary's view. "Never seen a cicada with a tail all powder white like that. Poor li'l thing."

"What are you looking for? Expecting guests?" Dale asked.

Mary knew. Real Mother. She'd return any minute. Mary howled against the dam of her sealed mouth and slammed her body repeatedly against the pallet. The cicadas responded with maddening precision, matching the timing and volume of her screams.

During the few peaceful hours when she'd pretended to be Girl's mother, Girl had shown her the source of the insects' relentless drone. Two hateful little accordion-like structures on each side of the male's abdomen, evolved expressly for the earsplitting reproductive serenade. Now, with rage burning through her, she imagined pressing her fingernails into the ribbed membranes, silencing each of the multitude of tiny beasts, one by one.

A fit of coughing replaced her screams. Her lungs faltered. She fell silent, exhausted, her throat raw. The cicada song petered out, and Girl's voice drifted through the door. Her hunched back slid into Mary's line of sight as she examined the insect in Dale's outstretched hand.

"What's wrong with her?" Girl asked.

"She's been infected with a fungus," he said. "*Massospora levispora.* That's the white stuff. Though she doesn't know it. In fact, she probably feels great. I'm developing a theory that the fungus accomplishes this by releasing powerful chemicals, including psilocybin, a hallucinogenic. An academic acquaintance deems the idea far fetched. But I have a hunch!" He chuckled. "Are you familiar with psilocybin?"

Girl shook her head.

"Oh, it's a wonderful plant medicine. Some even hypothesize that psilocybin catalyzed human consciousness."

"Huh. I use chamomile for my gut," Girl said.

"Excellent." Dale smiled and brought his hand closer, seeming to sniff the cicada. "She probably has no idea a fungal mass has replaced her lower body. Including her marvelous ovipositor, the most extraordinary feature of cicada anatomy. Don't you agree?"

Girl remained silent. One eyebrow wormed upward.

"The tubular apparatus she extends from her abdomen? To slice into the tree branch, then deposit her eggs?"

Girl's face lit up. "Saw-layer. That's what we call it."

"Of course! A much more descriptive term. And the saw component, a true stroke of evolutionary genius. Serrated! And, I'll wager, enhanced with metals like the saw-layers of some other insects!" He gingerly tipped his palm toward Girl. "Yet no match for the fungus. *Massospora* destroyed both the saw-layer and"—he cleared his throat and glanced around the yard—"sex organs."

Girl bowed her head, eyes locked on her huge mud-caked boots.

Dale's avoidant gaze bounced around the yard, then landed on the root cellar. He donned his hat, turned up the brim, and cocked his head. "A shed! You know the dirt floors of such structures often feature excellent examples of the mud emergence turrets constructed by our cicada friends. May I?" He grinned at Girl, then strode toward the cellar.

Again, the shimmering insectile hum buried Mary's shrieks. She shook her body, as if in the grips of a grand mal seizure, hoping the movement would draw Dale's attention. She arched her spine to the ceiling and slammed her outstretched knee up and down, exhausting the limits of her range of motion.

"Wait!" Girl's hand clamped down on Dale's shoulder, abruptly breaking his stride. "This cicada you got," she stuttered. "It ain't ours. Our Brood ain't never fallen sick with a rot like that. And her color's different." She herded him toward the center of the yard, and the two of them disappeared from view. Mary's heart sank.

"Yes. She's a different species, *Okanagana rimosa.*" To Mary's relief, Dale's voice, with its perfect elocution and strange formality, was still within hearing range. Her eyes jerked across the cobwebbed ceiling and along the sides of the pallet, seeking some means of creating a disturbance.

"Feel bad for her, though," Girl said. "But nothing we can do now, Mr. Dale. You better git. Come back another time."

"Alas, you're correct. She's too far gone." Dale ambled into view again, his thin neck elongated as he gazed at the sky, reverent and ungainly all at once. Girl followed, her hand timidly reaching for his bony shoulder, then withdrawing as he began pacing. "But her affliction may serve some higher purpose," he said.

Mary's eyes landed on the pallet, just below the leg Real Mother had bent and taped in preparation for Girl's primitive surgery. The carved wooden figurine lay on the pallet's edge. The metal pail rested on the floor directly below.

Could she somehow create enough motion to tip the wooden figurine into the metal pail, resulting in a clang loud enough to cut through the cicada noise? Not a chance in hell. But what was the alternative? Continuing to lie here, bearing witness to the mating dance of the wackadoos until Real Mother returned, machine gun blazing.

She began rocking her body, directing her force diagonally. The pallet creaked, triggering susurrations from the cicadas, then jerked to and fro. The motion seesawed the figurine on its rounded belly.

But the figurine failed to launch over the edge. She rocked harder, sweat flooding her armpits, lungs heaving.

Outside, Dale paced the yard, his words booming with messianic intensity. "There's another species of the fungus, *Massospora cicadina*. Induces the same behavior and symptoms. It affects periodical cicadas, including the seventeen years, like yours." The lopsided grin returned to his face. He toyed with the cord of his wide-brimmed hat, then spun around to face Girl. "And it's widespread. The fact that you've never seen any evidence of *M. cicadina* in your brood is highly unusual. Pointing to what you've been trying to tell me all along. These *are* indeed special cicadas."

Girl slumped forward. Her forehead twitched with confusion. Cicada song rippled around the yard, as if responding to her inner turmoil. Dale squeezed her thick fingers. "What if another undiscovered species of *Massospora* exists?" he asked. "Hyperlocalized to your property? Yet unique in that it evolved in a symbiotic relationship with your brood, rather than a parasitic one. What if, instead of *destroying* the cicada, the fungus *gifts* it with psychoactive, or even psychedelic, chemicals? Most importantly . . ." Girl started as Dale pressed his forehead against hers. His chest heaved. "Girl, what if this *Massospora* variant bestowed a kind of sentience or intelligence to your brood? My God!"

Dale released Girl's hand and whirled dervish-like across the lawn, his ecstatic cries echoing through the evening air.

Soaked in sweat, her body shaking, her muscles spent, Mary drew another great breath. Again and again, she thrust herself diagonally. The pallet swung forward in small motions, groaning and creaking. The wooden figurine bobbled and bounced.

Through the gap in the door, she caught sight of Dale performing his ridiculous gyrations, flitting in and out of view with Girl in pursuit, attempting to steer him away, toward the woods.

Mary rocked harder, her muscles cramping, her breath failing her.

"Tomorrow it is," Dale bellowed through the dusk. "We'll examine the Brood together!"

Mary roared into the hollow of her own mouth. Her iron will forced her depleted body into a final tremendous thrust. The figurine seesawed forward and, remarkably, torpedoed into the pail with a dull clang.

Dale paused. He glanced over his shoulder toward the root cellar. His eyes seemed to make contact with Mary's; then he shrugged before continuing on to the woods.

Mary's body turned to jelly. Her unseeing eyes wandered to the cobwebbed ceiling. Her mind sank into a fog of surrender.

The pallet groaned. Mary's body jerked forward as the front legs snapped in two and collapsed onto the ground. With a sharp, grinding report, the back legs followed.

Dale swung around. The rays of the setting sun pierced the root cellar, spotlighting the capsized pallet and Mary's duct-taped body. The cicadas drowned her screams in an explosion of song.

But it was too late. Dale's mouth hung open. His joyful expression had twisted into horror.

Chapter 14

Dale stood frozen in the backyard, eyes unblinking, fingers hidden within his multipocketed vest.

From the dirt floor of the root cellar, Mary shrieked at him, begging for help, her mouth foaming behind the duct tape, her bound body flailing amid the ruins of the collapsed pallet.

A few feet from Dale, Girl gnawed her fists, her eyes ricocheting from the root cellar to the man, her hulking form shrinking into itself. Suddenly she leaped into motion, brushing past Dale, whose mouth seemed stuck on a loop, opening and closing unceasingly.

"She don't want 'em, Mr. Dale," Girl babbled while hurrying to the root cellar. At the sound of her voice, the harsh keening of the cicadas died down. Girl filled the doorway, drenching Mary in darkness. "You gotta hush, Ms. Mary. Please. Else Dale will think something bad. About me and you." She moved toward the pallet and wrenched off the snapped legs so it lay flush with the ground. Mary redoubled her efforts, thrashing and screaming, her eyes never leaving Dale's waxen face.

Girl waved Dale forward. "Look here, Mr. Dale. Special! Our Brood! You are right," she gibbered. Her voice boomed out into the yard, amplified by distress.

Dale staggered closer, zombielike, his movements devoid of the joyful careening he'd displayed only moments ago. When he was close enough for Mary to discern the ghastly shade of gray that had stolen over his face, he halted.

Girl angled the pallet toward the doorway, then presented Mary's seeping clutch, a contorted smile plastering her face. "The miracle of the Brood. The babies." She then lifted her own shirt. "We are blessed to carry 'em. For Her In The Cave."

The setting sun was now closer to the horizon, its rays angled directly upon the thin membrane of Girl's clutches, illuminating the shuddering life within. A host of albino bodies, translucent and writhing, now articulated into forms resembling tiny translucent crustaceans with hair-thin legs, each tipped with the two red dots that would develop into bulbous crimson adult eyes.

"You see, Mr. Dale? Special," Girl repeated, her voice trembling. "I can show you more tomorrow. Like we planned. Please."

Again, Dale staggered forward, as if drawn by a great magnet. His mouth had ceased opening and closing, and now hung wide, as if unhinged. Spittle glazed his chin.

Abruptly, his mouth snapped shut. His lips twitched with mumbled words. "Isolated coevolutionary event. Human host. But mutualistic? Or commensalistic?"

Mary thumped her body, emptied her lungs with howling. Dale's eyes crept to her face, then to Girl's. "But why is she bound and gagged?" he asked.

"It's just until the babies come!" Girl wailed.

"You are a predator. Given the evidence, that's the only possible conclusion." Like a drunken man, he stumbled from the root cellar. Halfway across the yard, his clumsy ambulation morphed to spasmodic jerks. The explosive stutter of ammunition cut through the evening air. He collapsed to the ground, the cord of his wide-brimmed hat twisted around his neck, his body riddled with bullets.

A shadow fell across Dale's lifeless body. "What the fuck have you done now, Girl?" Real Mother appeared, the rifle draped across one shoulder. The tattoos on her ropy forearms seemed to writhe and slither. A machete dangled from her belt, a new addition to her arsenal.

Her usual swagger was gone. Instead, her lips gathered in a dour knot. Her glittering eyes darted from Dale's body to Girl's. "You useless twat! You think I got time to deal with this shit?"

"You killed him!" Girl said. Her eyes were wild. Her mounded fists pressed into her thighs, poised to strike.

Mary's heart leaped. Here was the anger that had so terrified her when Girl still imagined Mary was her abusive mother. Real Mother would soon find out what Girl was capable of when the switch flipped from adoration to rage.

"What?" Real Mother slapped the machete against her thigh. "You mad at me? That's a fucking crock. You better be thanking me! *You see, Mr. Dale? Special*," she mimicked, expertly capturing Girl's pleading tone. "Flapping your goddamn gums to a spy!"

"He wasn't no spy," Girl roared. Tears gushed down her cheeks. "He was a nice man. Loved the Brood. More than you!"

"Shame on you!" Real Mother's voice echoed across the mountainside. "You brought trouble. To me. To Her In The Cave. First with that old slut, and now with him."

"You don't know nothin' about a good man." Girl's shoulders shuddered, her teeth flashed. "Only bad ones. Like the ones you let hurt me."

"Listen up, you little brat." Real Mother lunged toward Girl. Her thick braid whipped and recoiled. "I never asked to be a mother. But I did the best I could. And I fucked up. Plenty. But what you did here today? Spilling your guts to a spy? Showing him your clutch? It's worse. By a mile. You're damn lucky I offed him before he escaped."

"Was not a spy!" Girl broke from the root cellar, her thunderous footfalls headed for Real Mother.

Real Mother brandished the machete, slicing the blade through the space surrounding her. Girl halted, her complexion a red tide, her bosom a heaving slab of armor, her arms cocked at her sides.

"Use your thick skull, Girl. You seriously think he wanted to be friends? Or get in your pussy?"

Girl bellowed something unintelligible. She threw her chest forward. But her broad shoulders began to slump.

"You're too ugly. And fat," Real Mother continued. "Ain't your fault. Her In The Cave probably wants it that way."

Girl's fingers uncurled into sodden mitts. Her great buttocks tilted to one side. From the root cellar floor, Mary railed and grunted, hoping somehow to shore up Girl's flagging fury and goad her into battle with her mother.

"No man will ever want you, Girl. And for good reason. Your duty is to Her In The Cave. To the Brood." Slowly, Real Mother lowered the machete. She nudged Dale's still-bleeding corpse with her boot. "You betrayed all that today. I'll do my best to help clean up your mess. But first we gotta find out who this sad-sack spy really was."

Mary silently cursed. Real Mother had worked her manipulative magic. Girl's whole bearing morphed, the meek posture returning as the tidal rage drained from her body.

Suddenly, Real Mother fixed her gaze on the root cellar. In a few long strides, she'd swooped into the dank, shadowy room. Mary tensed, struggling against her wrist and ankle restraints. Without warning, the tape was ripped from her lips.

"She's lying, Girl!" Mary roared with her first liberated breath.

Real Mother coldcocked Mary. "Shut your face, hag!" She deftly slit through the duct tape wrapped around Mary's body, yanked her from the pallet, and tossed her into the backyard. Mary panted, face in the grass, squeezing eyes shut as blood rushed to her numbed limbs. Her eyes fluttered open to Dale's blood-soaked shoulder, inches from her face.

"Now, Mary Whelton. Big-shot lawyer. Tell my daughter the truth. This man was a trespassing spy. Just like you." Real Mother kicked Mary in the ribs, then nodded at Girl.

Clutching her torso, Mary wobbled to her feet and faced Girl. "I never saw him before he came here. I swear. And he seemed truly fond of you."

"Will you listen to the lying Silver Tongue?" Real Mother slapped the broadside of the machete across the back of Mary's thighs, forcing her to her knees. "I'll tell you who this is, Girl." She aimed the machete at Dale's leaking body. "He's with them men who've been bugging you about the land."

"No!" Girl said.

"Oh yeah." Real Mother harrumphed. "That's probably why the crusty old bitch came snooping 'round here in the first place. All this other stuff has been a trick."

"But she's going to help. Make the papers so we can keep the land."

"Lies, you dum-dum. Think about it. Them men show up. Few days pass, she shows up. Week later, old Knobby Knees comes a-callin'. You think that's a coincidence?"

Girl's eyes dulled into brittle brown leaves.

"Oh yeah. She got you good, Girl. The car wreck. Pretending to be me so she could case the quarry and the cave. She's in cahoots with them men."

"But the car was messed up. And she was knocked out. And bleeding."

"People know how to do that, Girl. Wreck on purpose. Get hurt. Insurance pays money for that. Done it myself a time or two." Real Mother snorted. "Only she don't want insurance money. She wants the land. Hell, from what he said"—she delivered a violent kick to Dale's body—"she probably wants to steal the power of the Brood. Turn it into something she can put in those fancy little bottles and creams like the ones in her purse. Not to mention destroying Her In The Cave."

"It's not true, Girl," Mary said, shuffling closer to Girl. "She's lying to you as she's always done."

Girl remained silent, then backed away from Mary. Her hands curled into fists once again.

◆ ◆ ◆

Clad only in her silk blouse and underwear, Mary trudged behind Girl up the path to the cave, mosquitoes feasting on her bare legs and ankles. Cicada song raged through the gathering dusk. With each step, the swelling on Mary's inner thigh brushed her other leg, a constant reminder of the creatures incubating beneath her skin. Real Mother brought up the rear, her rifle muzzle jabbing rhythmically into Mary's back. Each step was met with the crunch of molted shells, shattering underfoot like dry autumn leaves.

The quarry yawned to Mary's left, its milky waters a curdled gray in the dying daylight. The trail veered onto the short, grassy plateau, and soon the trio began the winding ascent up the mountainside. High above, the cave hunkered at the trail terminus, an impenetrable darkness filling its mouth. The lowest limb of the ancient oak dipped and rebounded, as if tugged by an unseen hand.

Mary shivered, her gaze falling on the horrid burden slung between her and Girl—Dale's lifeless body. Girl gripped him at the shoulders while Mary clutched beneath his knees. His head lolled to one side. The wide-brimmed hat trailed in the long grass, catching repeatedly. His deadweight was heavy and unwieldy. Mary stumbled often and was prodded back to her bare feet with the gun muzzle.

All around, the earth seethed with cicada life. Mary was numb to the plump winged bodies spiraling past. Nor did she remove the squirming creature trapped in her mop of hair. Fight off one bug and it would only be replaced by another.

The trail entered the first of the three switchbacks. "Where are you taking me?" Mary called over her shoulder. She cursed as tiny bits of garnet needled the soles of her feet.

"Where the fuck do you think I'm taking you? Trail ain't got but one destination."

Mary recalled Real Mother's colorful description of draping Mary's body parts around the cavern as an offering to Her In The Cave. Their procession was unmistakably a death march, with Mary pitching in to transport the ill-fated cicada fanatic to his final resting place. And her own.

Large chunks of rock appeared, dark sentinels marking the trail every few feet, their ash- and rust-colored hues lost in the deepening dusk. Mary swept her gaze down the mountainside to where Real Mother's truck was parked outside the cabin. Her mind raced to find an angle that would buy her time.

"You're still vulnerable," Mary blurted, "until you file an adverse possession claim for this land. I advise you to let me file on your behalf. Regardless of your ultimate plans for me." Real Mother delivered a kick to Mary's rump. She stumbled forward, nearly dropping the corpse.

"I once watched a man choke on his own tongue," Real Mother remarked. "Cut out, then stuffed down his throat. Never done it myself. But I'm a visual learner."

Mary sucked in a lungful of air and adjusted her grip on the man's knees. His multipocketed vest was now a bib of dried blood. "The police will track him here," she said, pursuing a different tack. "He was clearly an important researcher, probably for the state. Or even the Feds."

Real Mother guffawed. "You just put my mind at ease about your buddy, the spy. Nobody gives a rat's ass about some piddly government egghead. Now shut your hole before I plug it with lead." Gunfire exploded from her weapon. Both Mary and Girl dropped to their knees. The body plopped to the ground.

"Up!" Real Mother barked.

Legs quivering, Mary took up her gruesome load once again, this time hooking her elbows beneath the man's knees. Girl knelt like an Amazonian runner on the block, then slid her palms beneath

Dale's shoulders, his head pillowed on her buttocks. They regained their footing and continued trudging up the trail, soon rounding the second switchback.

"How you doing up there, Girl?" Real Mother's hoarse caw rang out. A pair of bats swooped across the path, then skimmed the ground, feasting on the cicada banquet.

"Making my way," Girl replied.

"Good thing I showed up, huh, my sweet dingleberry? 'Fore the weasel took over the henhouse."

"Yes, Mama. You saved me from this stinkin' liar." The silhouette of Girl's hunched back swelled, a sea monster plunging into deep waters.

"Not to mention," Real Mother continued, "I brought the Brood of a lifetime with me. The biggest ever."

"Mama!" Girl stopped short and spun around. Mary rammed the grisly remains into Girl's haunches. "Brood comes for Her In The Cave," Girl said. In the descending darkness, her eyes seemed disembodied. Twin moons radiating distress. "Not us. We're part of it. But we don't call 'em . . ." A muscular swallow, a stone plopping in water. Then silence.

Real Mother's shriek sliced the air. "You telling me my place?" She raced around Mary to intercept Girl. "And in front of this trash outsider!" She punched Girl in the head. "Wasn't enough that you disrespected me? Too stupid to recognize your own mama? And too dumb to sniff out spies?" Again, her fist lashed out, pounding Girl's cheek.

As Girl raised her hands to protect herself, the man's torso slid to the ground. Mary dropped the leaden limbs and bolted down the mountainside.

"Goddammit, Girl!" Real Mother screeched. "See what you did!"

Mary charged off the trail, dodging patches of scrub and half-buried boulders. Scrambling down the steep slope, she prayed the dusk would drape her in shadows. The earth beneath her bare feet was alive with cicadas, their writhing regiments flowing upward toward the cave. The ground behind her echoed with the huffing and grunting of Girl's clumsy pursuit.

The night lit up with staccato flashes. A deafening stream of bullets flew past Mary. She threw herself to the ground, tumbling several feet. Dirt and rocks scraped her face, hands, and knees until she skidded to a stop.

Mary was yanked to her feet, blood streaming from her nose. Girl shook her like a rag doll, then crushed her in a powerful embrace. She dragged Mary back to the trail, a slavish hunting dog delivering prey to its master.

Real Mother's face glowed with renewed sadistic confidence. In that sneering countenance, Mary saw the inevitability of her own death. Her mighty successes, her escape from squalor, her accumulated wealth, it would all end in one brutal, meaningless act, at the hands of a vile creature who Mary, in her real life, would have stepped over to hail a cab.

"You're pitiful," Mary hissed.

Her skull vibrated with a blow from the gun butt. "Pick up the meat, bitch," Real Mother said.

Starbursts clouded Mary's vision while she groped for the man's knees and hefted his body from the ground. She spat a mouthful of blood and waited for Girl to scoop up the man's shoulders. Once they were moving, Real Mother wound a hank of Mary's hair around her fist and drove her the remaining short distance to the cave.

As they completed the final switchback, the peculiar strain of cicada song blared forth.

Oweee-oooo. Oweee-oooo.

Real Mother tightened her grip on Mary's hair, steering her by the skull into the cave. Once inside, a sweet fungal mist engulfed Mary, coating her skin, her face, even her tongue. The river of cicadas flowed through the entrance and swept past, radiating a faint glow, translucent wings flicking, jointed legs creeping, eyes winking like garnets.

Mary halted, horrified. Last time she and Girl visited the cave, there had been swarms of the creatures, yes. They were an omnipresent nightmare on Girl's property. But nothing like this. The fact that neither Girl nor Real Mother reacted to the ballooning population was of little comfort.

A flashlight switched on. Girl lumbered into the pool of light. Behind her, pale roots spiraled from the cave ceiling. "There," Real Mother ordered, aiming the light toward the rough-hewn arch that led to the stone stairway.

As Mary peered through the archway, her legs buckled. Her eyes darted around the cave, beyond the flashlight's glow, in search of the chute through which she'd plummeted to the lower cavern. She'd rather risk cracking her body open on stalagmites than walk into whatever horrendous fate awaited her at Real Mother's hands. Then there was the thought of millions of cicadas sharpening their proboscises, or whatever they used for "nursing," preparing to suck her dry. Warmth suddenly spurted from her breasts. She emitted a rageful sob.

"Shut it!" Real Mother shoved her toward the archway.

The chill air grew thicker, sweeter, as they descended the narrow stairs. At several points, Mary and Girl were forced to engage in an unseemly push-pull with Dale's leaden body. The beam of Real Mother's flashlight bounced crazily along the blasted walls. Girl scraped her arms and hips against the fractured surfaces of the tight passageway. All the while, cicadas streamed past, the walls a shifting mosaic of their dark bodies.

When she finally emerged into the lower cavern, Mary dropped her end of the body and heaved up the Mother's Milk she'd ingested hours before.

"Pantywaist," Real Mother said, glancing at Mary.

After gently placing Dale's body on the ground, Girl retrieved a propane lantern from a nook in the rock. The warm light pushed back the darkness, revealing the Pure Pond. A golden skin stretched across the still water. Stalagmites broke the surface, impassive and ancient. Girl hefted Dale's body back up on her own and shuffled forward. She glanced back, indicating that Mary should follow her into the water.

"You're dumping him in a shallow pond?" Mary asked. Every fiber in her body screamed not to enter the dark, unguent waters. A rock slammed into her back.

Real Mother growled, "Shut your face and move."

Girl remained quiet, but her eyes caught Mary's. Mary searched for some glimmer of warmth. But Girl's eyes remained dull, purposeful. Girl jutted her chin toward the crude altar on the far side of the pond, then entered the water. She glided to the center, the water bleeding into her corduroys and dampening her work shirt. Dale's body remained buoyant, bobbing in her roiling wake.

A thrust from the rifle propelled Mary into the pond. Her splashing echoed throughout the chamber, which had grown strangely quiet. The relentless droning and clicking of the cicadas had abruptly ceased, though every surface seemed encrusted with the insects.

Chill water slid past Mary's legs. Girl paused, waiting until Mary was close enough to take up Dale's ankles. Several times, Mary slipped on the pond bottom and pulled Dale's body taut to regain her balance. She was exhausted. Her muscles were drained. Yet she was also aware of the strange vitality emanating from her thigh that had enabled her to heft Dale's gangly body up the mountain.

When Girl was directly in front of the altar, she became still and quietly mumbled an incantation.

"That's enough, Girl," Real Mother yelled. "Ain't got all night."

Girl's body stiffened at the gruff words. She glanced back at Real Mother, who slouched against the wall, her gun trained on Mary.

"Thought you was following us." Girl's brows knitted, caterpillars colliding. "You got to purify too."

"Only reason I'm getting in that water is to beat you if you don't get a move on. Now clean yourself. Let's see if Her In The Cave sees fit to make an appearance."

Girl squeezed her eyes shut. Her nostrils flared. She released the man's shoulders and began splashing her face.

"I'm shocked, Girl," Mary murmured, "to hear anyone speak about Her In The Cave with such disrespect."

"Shut your lying face," Girl hissed. She turned her eyes upward to where the cave ceiling flowed into the chimney. Flecks of garnet and crystal sparkled along the walls. The first stars of evening shone faintly through the chimney's oval opening. Girl continued chanting while splashing her face with the waters of the Pure Pond.

"Oweee-oooo. Oweee-oooo." Girl's repetition of the haunting sound grew in force and volume. Somehow the sound seemed to escape her body rather than be created by it. On all sides of the cavern, the wings of the silent cicadas flashed with fiery iridescence.

Girl cracked open an eye and glanced at Mary's hands, indicating that Mary should perform her own cleansing in the Pure Pond. Mary hesitated, recoiling at the idea of bathing her face in water flowing past a dead body. A trio of gunshots exploded the pond surface. Wildly, she shoveled handfuls of water against her skin.

"Get the meat on the altar," Real Mother barked as soon as Girl completed her ablutions.

"Got to wash him, too, Mama. Don't you remember? That's how we did the other one."

A chill crept up Mary's spine. So the mother-daughter duo had teamed up to murder at least once before. And the pond where she was now standing, defenseless and under armed guard, was the place where they'd disposed of the body.

"That's right!" Real Mother's voice boomed across the water. "Almost forgot about that. Good old Ray. Fucker. No one gets rough with my baby girl."

Girl's thick fingers were suddenly pressing into Mary's skull. Her other hand fell heavily on Mary's shoulder. "Pure Pond takes us all," she said, forcing Mary down.

Chapter 15

Mary braced against the force of Girl's powerful hands, but still she felt the fetid waters of the Pure Pond rising, licking at her skin and bleeding into her clothes.

"Wait!" Mary said. "The body you and your mother dumped in this pond. Ray. Was he one of the men she forced you to have sex with?"

Girl's iron grip tightened.

Mary's knees buckled. Her whisper rose to a shriek. "You never should have been in that position in the first place, Girl. Do you understand—" The oily waters rushed up, filling Mary's nose and mouth, then swallowing her completely. She writhed helplessly, aiming spastic kicks at Girl's thick ankles.

"Be clean," Girl's voice sounded as Mary was jerked from the water.

Mary sputtered, "Mothers don't pimp out their daughters."

"Be clean," Girl repeated. Again water choked Mary's airways.

"It was wrong," she coughed when Girl hauled her up. "What she did to you was wrong."

Mary's butt hit the slimy pond bottom. A dark curtain of muddy particulate swirled around her, blocking out light and air, a deadly reminder that she was utterly alone, with no one to help.

◆ ◆ ◆

Mary padded across the pure white sand, riveted by the blue expanse sparkling against the horizon. She was a second-year law student, and this was her first trip to Florida, her first experience of the ocean. That such a thing existed seemed miraculous. The photos she'd seen of the Atlantic, and the images in TV and film, were pale facsimiles of this glorious phenomenon.

She halted, mesmerized, the wind caressing her legs and transforming her silk kimono into a shimmering wing. She'd splurged on the luxurious wrap to cover a tenacious patch of psoriasis on her outer elbow.

Gentle fingers clasped her wrist. "I called you like three times! You'd think you'd never seen the ocean." Ellie laughed. She was one of the five female law students, members of Mary's study group, who'd decided to vacation together. "You walked right past us." Ellie's bob, a wavier version of Mary's own, swayed with pleasing symmetry as she indicated a spot nearby. The others reclined on a huge beach blanket amid Tupperware containers of fruit, a bottle of suntan oil, two novels, and a dense textbook entitled *Trusts & Estates: Defining Cases.*

This group of women was the closest Mary had come to camaraderie in her twenty-three years of life. There were moments when she was sure she felt the reciprocal flow of friendship; when she unclenched and found herself grinning spontaneously; when something nameless and golden filled her chest, knocked at her heart.

But are you sure that's friendship? she continually grilled herself. *How would you know?*

She'd accepted the invitation for the beach getaway to put the question to rest. Surely spending a weekend together in constant company would settle the matter.

Well, perhaps not constant company. She would not be swimming. Through discipline, lessons, and the surprising discovery that she was a natural athlete, Mary had developed formidable skills in golf and tennis. But she could not swim. Teaching the children even basic survival skills in water had not been on the list of priorities at Saint Agnes.

After Mary settled onto the beach blanket, one of the women, Therese, plunked the textbook at her feet. Therese's elfin face clouded with anxiety. "Please. God. Explain asset protection trusts and look-through trusts."

"Jeez. Let the woman relax for two seconds," Ellie said.

But Mary had already launched into an informal lecture, drawing her dazzling understanding of the law from its sheath, happily entering into the only realm where she felt powerful and in control.

At some point, a tequila sunrise appeared in her hand. The talk turned to internships, then men, the dearth of women in law school, the veracity of reports that President Carter had been attacked by a rabbit. The waves sounded a sultry rhythm, the ocean rippled with shades of blue Mary didn't know existed. The nameless golden thing hung between them. Mary declared to herself, *This is friendship. I am certain.*

Ellie jumped to her feet, grabbed Mary by the arm, and dragged her from the blanket onto the fine-grained sand. "Let's get in!"

Mary gazed beyond Ellie to where two young boys in matching swim trunks romped in the gentle waves, the water only reaching their thighs. Behind them, a thickset woman glided toward the horizon, away from the shore, the bottom of her gold lamé bathing suit barely skimming the surface.

"Okay. But I'm not getting my hair wet," Mary said.

"I probably won't either," Ellie said. "My perm is still fresh."

Mary nodded, then braced herself. For the entire afternoon, she'd worn the kimono. Now it slid from her arms to the beach blanket, revealing the red, crusted plaque.

Ellie gulped a huge inhale of breath, and Mary braced herself for the insults. But she only lunged toward Therese. "Don't move!" Her hand smacked lightly against Therese's thigh, then pulled away. A tiny winged body haloed in blood clung to Therese's skin. "Possibly the biggest mosquito I've ever seen," Ellie said.

The women ambled across a stretch of beach to the ocean, then splashed past the point where small waves broke and raced toward the shore. The clean-swept sky seemed endless. Mary filled her lungs. Felt her shoulders drop. Her psoriasis was clearly visible, but the other women didn't seem to care.

The crystalline water felt like a second skin, gliding past her shins and then her thighs as she followed the others farther out. After five minutes, the water lapped at her ribcage. She glanced back at the shore and felt a nervous thrill. The beach seemed a quarter mile away. And yet the water was still so shallow. She considered discussing the phenomenon with Ellie, but decided not to, afraid that she would reveal her ignorance.

When she turned around, the others had drifted farther out. Everyone sported slick, wet heads except for Ellie, who paddled upright, her bob safely above water. Therese leaped into the air and dove, dolphin-like, into a rolling wave.

A harsh drone broke through the dancing wind and lapping waves. A trio of Jet Skis appeared. The grinning male operators, sporting tropical swim trunks and Ray-Bans, closed in on the group of women.

Abruptly, Mary's feet shot from under her, and she plunged beneath the shimmering waves. When she popped up again, the distance between her and the women had doubled. She thrust her leg downward, searching for the sandy bottom. But her toes met only cold, thick water, as if an abyss had opened beneath her.

Paddling frantically, she managed to swivel around to face the women. "Help me!" she screamed.

A Jet Ski shot past, circling the women and momentarily blocking them from view. "Ellie!" Mary called, taking in a mouthful of water.

Ellie failed to respond to Mary's cries. Instead she turned her attention to one of the Jet Skis, now parked and bobbing on the waves.

Panic detonated in Mary's gut. She paddled her legs and arms, but her body was out of sync with itself, and she quickly tired. The water seemed to grow thicker. Her muscles burned and spasmed. When she tried to suck in more air, water filled her mouth. Her eyes, wide with terror, rolled toward the women, toward Ellie.

Ellie seemed to meet Mary's gaze. Mary marshaled all her remaining breath and raised a final cry for help.

Ellie turned her back.

The undertow dragged Mary under, slamming her against the ocean floor. Her limbs were leaden, yet she fought her way to the surface. Now she was farther from the women. When she was pulled under a final time, her depleted body could no longer struggle.

The ocean swept her into its churn, tumbling her again and again, before finally spitting her out on the beach. She climbed, sputtering, to her feet, bikini bottoms weighted with sand. She ignored the concerned beachgoers who approached her and staggered back to the hotel. The golden thing flew from her chest, disappeared into the unending sky.

But what if she'd misjudged Ellie and the others? The question assailed Mary as she was ripped from the murky waters of the Pure Pond. What if her mind had only seen what it had been conditioned to see? Rejection. Neglect. Betrayal. The same warped perspective Girl now had about Mary thanks to Real Mother's manipulation.

Girl's ripe, honeyed breath clouded her face. "Oweee-oooo. Oweee-oooo," she intoned. She trickled drops of water on Mary's head, then her own.

Mary leaned closer, whispering, "You have this idea about me. About who I am. But it's wrong. I know what it's like to think you don't matter. That you're worthless." Her hand clutched Girl's. "You and I are the same."

Girl held Mary's gaze. Something seemed to flicker between them, some understanding. Then Girl dropped her eyes to the half-submerged corpse. "Bring Mr. Dale to the altar stone," she said. Mary tried to engage her again, but Girl barked, "Now."

Mary obeyed, gliding Dale's body across the pond to the altar, then working with Girl to lug it from the water onto the flat stone. Girl knelt alongside his body and straightened his blood-caked vest. She fitted his wide-brimmed hat on his head and tightened the drawstring.

"Go back to Mama," she said, without turning from her grim work.

"That's right, Mary Whelton," Real Mother bellowed, summoning Mary with the machete. "Get your big-time lawyering ass over here. 'Fore I shoot you to ribbons."

Mary sloshed across the pond, her legs moving woodenly, her mind racing. She assessed the conditions for escape, the dimensions of the cave, the shadow-filled niches, the location of the adjacent cavern where the Mercedes had once been stashed and through which she might flee on foot. She considered ducking underwater. Whatever course she took, a rain of bullets was sure to follow. Her chances of survival were slim, but greater than if she delivered herself directly into Real Mother's clutches.

"Move! Your! Ass!" Real Mother hollered, cutting figure eights through the air with the machete.

Then Real Mother froze. Her gaze jerked to the cavern ceiling. Her mouth twitched with silent words. She hugged the machete to her chest and stood swaying, eyes locked on the space above and behind Mary.

Mary followed Real Mother's gaze, even as she quietly slid underwater. Girl had planted herself at the head of the altar. Her habitual slump was gone. Her shoulders formed a broad, solid ledge. Cicadas clustered on her head in a writhing crown and flowed from her shoulders in a mantle of iridescent orange.

A swarm of cicadas spiraled above Girl, quickly growing in size. Insects poured down the chimney and flew from all corners of the cavern to merge into a great mass. The multitude of winged beasts twirled and softened, melted and curved, finally shaping itself into a mushroom cap that sheltered the altar and Girl.

Mary was transfixed, her face half-submerged, unable to move or even breathe. Even still, she registered the sudden, strange hyperacuity of her eyesight, enabling her to discern each monstrous detail down to a trembling antennae or tiny jointed tarsus. Another gift of the babies, like the accelerated healing of her wounds? Or a hallucination? Or a dormant capability triggered by stress, like mothers who lifted vehicles off their trapped children?

A maniacal whooping swept aside her thoughts. Real Mother screamed, "Saw the meat, sisters!"

The swarm bifurcated, one half hovering above the altar, the other slowly descending on Dale's corpse. The swarm settled, and soon his body was only discernible as a seething man-shaped lump, orange glints flashing from thousands of trembling gossamer wings.

All at once, as if prompted by a signal undetectable to Mary, the army of insects covering Dale's body pivoted in unison to face outward. A legion of hideous crimson eyes now stared into the cavern, tails thrust downward into the human remains beneath them.

The cicadas had maintained their strange silence throughout their shapeshifting above the altar. But now, the mass atop Dale burst into a stream of mad, earsplitting clicks that ricocheted throughout the chamber. As the sound intensified to a razor pitch, the shape that once was Dale grew smaller and smaller, shuddering and quivering at each stage of diminishment.

With sudden, horrible clarity, Mary realized the sisters were sawing Dale's tissues with what she now knew, thanks to Dale, were their serrated ovipositors, the saw-layers. The very feature he'd so loved about them was now whittling his body to dust.

With a final shudder, the mass of cicadas flattened, sending a puff of hot air, gamey and faintly sweet, across the altar rock and along the water's surface. Dale's body was no more.

Mary shoved her fist in her mouth, stuffing down a shriek. The unctuous waters of the Pure Pond lapped at her paralyzed limbs. Her mind screamed at her body to move, to find the tunnel to the adjacent cavern where she could escape into the surrounding woods. But she could not tear her eyes from the altar, now devoid of any trace of Dale. Flesh, bone, and blood had been reduced to tiny particles by the seething mass of cicadas. Only tatters of his many-pocketed vest remained.

The sister cicadas now rose from the stone to rejoin the males in a mushroom-shaped swarm hovering above. Girl presided over the altar, head bowed, the crown of dark winged bodies writhing on her skull. The iridescent mantle rippled along her shoulders and back. The booming insectile chorus pounded the cave walls, seething waves of sound punctuated by abrasive clicking.

While Mary struggled to jolt herself into motion, Girl's head snapped up. Her eyes flew open, pure white globes tinged with crimson. The wreath on her skull shifted and resettled, but the mantle of cicadas rose from her shoulders to merge with the mass above. She tore open her shirt, freeing her great, gleaming breasts.

Radiant flesh cradled Girl's three pus-filled clutches. A golden mist drifted from the hovering mass, gilding each of the swellings in a crystalline shimmer. The bruise-colored tissue rippled with inner movement. A scream erupted from Girl, ecstatic and pain filled. Real Mother's whooping blasted above Mary's head, mingling with Girl's wild shrieks.

The hatching of Girl's long-awaited babies was underway.

Mary's vision clouded. Her body began to shake. Her leg muscles hardened to stone. An ancient memory shook loose, of herself as an infant, stewing in a filthy diaper, drug paraphernalia and empty bottles crowding a nearby table. Grief washed over her as she regarded the incredible fragility of that small creature, herself.

An explosive howl pulled Mary back to the present. On the altar, Girl spasmed and moaned, her head thrown back at an impossible angle.

Mary goaded her body into motion, one foot in front of the other, her toes raking across the slimy pond bottom. She eyed the chute in the ceiling from which she'd dangled above the Pure Pond. Her gaze then dropped to the glowing white stone of the stalagmites. From there, she mentally traced a line to the opposite end of the chamber. The opening to the adjacent cavern was there, she assured herself. It had to be.

Mary glided to the water's edge. Girl roared once again, a visceral utterance that rattled Mary's bones and caused her to stumble.

Scalding liquid seemed to flood her thighs. Her vision blurred, then returned with crystal clarity. Only now she saw with the eyes of the Brood, hovering above and around Girl.

The first clutch swelled and pulsed. Soon the thin outer membrane ruptured and pus surged forth. From across the Pure Pond, Real Mother raised a thunderous cry.

Mary staggered. She felt sluggish, almost drugged. She had trouble discerning the source of the eerie drone pulsing all around her. At times it seemed to originate from within her own body. She tried to climb out of the water but couldn't straighten her leg. Her thigh muscle had contracted to a dense knot.

Two of Girl's clutches had erupted. The third and final was imminent. Watery pus leaked from the newly opened gashes until all that remained was raw pink tissue. The delicate substrate trembled and parted to reveal a legion of tiny cicada nymphs.

The creatures swarmed from the abyss of Girl's flesh, then wobbled across her body, barely visible on the white curd of her skin. They seemed to be metamorphosing at an accelerated pace. By the time they'd scaled the hillocks of fat and muscle, they'd already sprouted mandibles and their thoraxes had thickened. Having traversed the great plains of Girl, they leaped from her body, plunging to the earth to burrow into the ground for the next seventeen years.

Mary's thigh muscle clenched, tighter and tighter, as if soon it would tear to pieces beneath the skin. Gasping, she fell to her hands and knees. As the creatures crawled across Girl's body, Mary crawled in tandem, mirroring the awkward gyrations of the newborns as she struggled to the shore.

She dragged herself from the water, and her right adductor seized. Clutching her thigh in agony, she flopped on her back. Shrieks welled behind her sealed lips as she stifled her own screams. She gritted her teeth, drawing blood from her lips.

"Proud of you, baby girl!" Real Mother cried, one hand thrusting the rifle in the air, the other twirling the machete. She leaped into the Pure Pond and sloshed toward the altar. Mary crawled away from the pond's edge. They might have forgotten her for now, but if Real Mother caught sight of her, she'd level her with one pass of the semiautomatic weapon.

Mary crept into the shadows and steadied her breath. Sharp, wet rocks pressed into her palms and kneecaps. Her gaze remained on the altar, where hundreds of nymphs continued to migrate across Girl's torso. An ecstatic light suffused Girl's face as she gazed upon the still-hatching clutch.

When Real Mother reached the altar, she roared triumphantly. The sound sent a ripple through the spiraling mass of cicadas above Girl's head. Thousands of translucent, orange-veined wings winked and flashed like a portal to another universe.

"Mother-of-All," Real Mother cried. "I marked myself." She snatched the collar of her shirt and ripped the neckline to her belly button. The cicada tattoo burned brightly, crimson eyes blazing beneath the ridge of collarbone, orange-tinted wings overlaying her breasts.

A spasm ripped through Mary's body. Her vision untethered from the Brood's and retreated into the pain-filled darkness behind her eyelids. The throbbing cicada song swelled, sounding eerily like the voice of a woman. A chorus of women. Mary forced open her eyes.

All at once, the swarm collapsed to the size of a fist, then cast itself into a new form, one Mary recognized. She had seen it behind the outhouse, on the front porch, and in the wooden figurines Girl was so fond of carving.

The hovering silhouette quietly drifted behind Girl, pulsating and voluptuous, a shadow of Girl, but larger, more expansive.

"Bless this family!" Real Mother sang out, the shreds of her Metallica T-shirt flapping over her naked breasts.

Racked with pain, Mary gripped the wet rock and dragged herself forward. There was no way she'd make it out of the cavern in her debilitated condition. But there was a nook in the rock wall large enough to conceal her.

Her muscles contorted once more. She felt as if hot daggers were carving through her flesh. She collapsed, head slamming against a rock. As she thrashed, she fought to keep her gaze on her thigh, where a horrifying transformation had begun.

Chapter 16

Pain shot through Mary, stealing her breath, possessing her body. She clawed the pebbled mud surrounding the Pure Pond, dug her heels into the jagged surface of a nearby rock. Her inner thigh spasmed and roiled. A sob forced its way through her screams as the thin membrane enclosing the clutch expanded and ripened with tiny ripples from within. Violet blood vessels rose from the skin, an intricate, throbbing root system feeding the oval-shaped eruption.

Then the muscles within her thigh went slack. The pain subsided, leaving her limp and shivering. Above her own quiet panting, she listened for Real Mother's whereabouts and was relieved when a guttural cry of devotion echoed through the chamber. Real Mother must still be near the altar, groveling before Her In The Cave.

Shifting her weight forward, Mary prepared to drag herself to the niche in the rock where she hoped to hide. As she gathered her strength, her eyes drifted several feet upward to the large amber-hued mass she'd seen before, embedded in the cave wall. The translucent object glowed in the light of the kerosene lamp. The dark core, dense and irregular, hunkered within the resinous mantle, like an insect from the land of the giants, preserved in tree sap.

She edged forward through the muck, prodding her overtaxed mind to explore the memory and pinpoint her exact location. She knew she'd passed this strange rock when she'd escaped before.

Inches from the niche in the rock, her jaw snapped open. Her knees jerked upward, feet planting firmly in the mud, hip-width apart. The medial thigh muscles spiraled around the clutch, intensifying the pressure within. A soundless torrent of air rushed from her lungs, the physical agony overwhelming her screams. Like a tractor beam, her gaze was drawn inexorably toward her right inner thigh and the burgeoning clutch. Her vision became even sharper, with near-microscopic details sliding into focus.

The clutch ballooned, doubling, then tripling in size. The outer membrane stretched to transparency. Gradually the writhing inner world that had evolved within Mary's thigh was revealed, a microverse nurtured on the Mother's Milk Mary had delivered through her own blood and lymph.

Hundreds of tiny pale nymphs rushed upward through the swirling fluids. A multitude of eyes, like flecks of blood, pebbled the milky substrate.

The membrane stretched farther. The clutch was now extruded several inches above the skin.

Mary's roars crashed against the jagged cavern walls. Her body had been commandeered by a primal directive to release the hatchlings into the world. The nymphs writhed against the confines of the clutch. The tissue stretched to breaking.

Abruptly, the tidal force receded. Her muscles unwound. She whimpered, half-formed perceptions flickering through her broken mind as the pain drained away. She was vaguely aware of mucus trailing from her nose and spittle slicking her chin. Her hair hung in sweat-drenched hanks. She pitched her body forward, ready to claw open the clutch and scoop the unholy thing from her thigh.

But her body would not obey. Her elbows remained propped in the dirt, her legs bent and spread wide in a monstrous mimicry of human childbirth.

She drew in a ragged breath. Her right leg kicked spastically, then resettled. The tortuous tsunami was rebuilding, preparing to slam down. She sobbed, terrified.

Her thigh clenched and knotted. The muscles seemed to detach from the bone, fiber by fiber, the tendons to elongate and snap free, the skin and subcutaneous layer to burst and flay open. Her mind folded into itself beneath the weight of the pain, forming a series of chambers through which her consciousness wandered, encountering visions of her past.

She saw herself before the mirror, hundreds of times, thousands of times, squinting at the imperfections, tugging at the flesh, denying her corporeal self. She'd coldly edited the contours of her body, refining here, enlarging or reducing there, then communicated these revisions to the cosmetic surgeons who'd willingly demolished or reconstructed the targeted parts.

Continuing through the labyrinth of her mind, she revisited decades of rigid workouts, obsessive food plans, and costly supplements. Her entire adult life had been one long campaign to control and fortify the fortress of her body, dominate her feelings, deny her vulnerability, arrest time and decay. A thought arose, hazy at first, then gaining strength, terrifying in its implications. This control, this augmenting, it had seemed so important. Necessary for her survival. Her sanity. But what if she'd been wrong?

Her own screams jolted her back to the present.

At first she barely registered the rawboned figure looming nearby. But she forced her mind to focus.

Real Mother.

The machete.

"Why not me?" Real Mother's voice was soft with grief as she gazed toward Mary. Tears seeped through the rugged terrain of her face. The Metallica T-shirt hung in shreds, an open curtain to her naked torso.

"Didn't I burn my devotion into my hide?" Real Mother pressed the machete blade into her own bare breast. A streak of blood appeared on the golden wing of the cicada tattoo. "I'm kin. I'm in the sacred line." She swept the machete overhead, almost clipping the amber mass. Her eyes roved the shadowy recesses of the cavern ceiling.

"You see my heart, Mother-of-All! You know I'm not like Girl. I was born with a contrary nature. But I tried!" She fell to her knees, shoulders slumped, fingers loosely gripping the machete. Her thick braid trailed in the mud.

For a moment Mary thought Real Mother might plunge the blade into her own midriff. Then her lip curled. She turned hate-filled eyes on Mary.

"You," Real Mother growled, baring yellowed teeth. She seemed ready to devour Mary in a single violent feeding. "Doubts. Insults. Disrespect. That was your fucking offering."

In vain, Mary searched for a flicker of her own resistance. Her body was on the verge of collapse, her mind choked with exhaustion and shock. Soon, another wave of catastrophic pain would gather force and crush her.

"Now you'll be my offering," Real Mother hissed, climbing to her feet.

Mary felt herself sinking down, drowning in the darkest part of her psyche, the part that believed everyone at their core was as irredeemably selfish, brutal, and corrupt as the enraged creature now slinking toward her. The story Mary had repeatedly told herself, her personal mythology, described her heroic climb from a hellish childhood. Yet hadn't she passed on that same brutality in the protections she'd engineered for Teddy and her clients? Her path to success had been paved with the pain of others. Why should she not bow her head and die by Real Mother's machete?

Real Mother halted above Mary's prone and panting body. Mary squeezed her eyes shut, awaiting the burn of the blade in her pulsing thigh. *Let it end here. This monstrous birth. My sins.* She raised her hips, offering Real Mother a clear target.

A grunt sounded. The burn did not come.

Mary's eyes flew open. Girl had appeared, shirt hanging open, hair a sweat-streaked nest. "It's okay, Ms. Mary." The machete was now safely clutched in her hands. She turned her gaze to Real Mother.

Who had left the ground.

A cloud of cicadas cradled her body in midair, drifting toward the amber-hued mass in the cave wall. When Real Mother registered the trajectory of her flight, she shrieked, "No. Please! Mother-of-All!"

In that instant, Mary understood the nature of the dark irregular shape at the core of the mass—it was human remains, a body with head bowed, arms and legs gathered close.

Flailing on her back, Real Mother punched and kicked the swirling insects beneath her. But her struggles were useless. Her hands and feet failed to connect with anything but empty air, like a battle with the mist.

"Daughter! Call her off! Please!" Real Mother screamed.

Girl remained motionless. A single tear tracked the curve of her cheek. The humming cicada song grew louder, then sharpened into a piercing vibrato. Gradually, the swarm tilted Real Mother's body upright. She continued her useless struggles, striking out with hands and feet. Dark clumps of the insects nudged forcefully at her shoulders, waist, and legs to keep her standing.

Abruptly, her limbs stiffened and her struggles ceased. Her entire body appeared paralyzed, legs fully extended and locked together. Cicadas gathered beneath her arms, nudging upward, until the arms were fully outstretched and Real Mother levitated on a seething crucifix of cicadas.

Only her face retained muscular control. Her eyes roamed wildly. Her features twisted with the blunt terror of an animal ensnared.

The cicada song rose to a pitch so high that at times it became inaudible. Real Mother's skin flushed pink, then took on a darker hue. She began to move, though still not of her own volition. With a violent jerk, her arms and legs drew into her chest. Her body collapsed into a tight ball.

A second swarm of cicadas arrived, forming a flickering, spinning aureole around Real Mother. As the circling insects gained speed, they secreted an amber-colored effluvium, at first a few drops, then larger splashes. The sap-like substance plopped on Real Mother, then began rapidly spreading across her skin and body.

"Girl! I'm your mama. Please!" Real Mother shrieked. The effluvium swallowed both cheeks and flowed across her mouth, drowning her words and sealing her lips. The torn Metallica T-shirt and sinewy arms were engulfed, then her jeans and thick braid. The garish tattoos disappeared. Her anguished face, sputtering with curses and exhortations, was silenced behind a translucent amber veil. The secretion quickly hardened around her crouched figure, imprisoning her forever in a thick, chitinous shell.

A contraction tore through Mary's thigh. She screeched, a piercing note perfectly tuned to the eerie dirge of the swarm. The earth shook and dust sifted from the ceiling. High on the cavern wall, next to the human remains already embedded there, a large slab of rock sloughed away, leaving a hollow indentation. The swarm assembled beneath the new amber mass in which Real Mother was encased. Slowly, she was borne aloft, almost ceremoniously, and deposited into the hollow in the wall.

Mary bellowed. The clutch in her thigh bulged and shuddered. The membrane distended an inch above the skin, two inches, five. Every cell in her body felt ready to detonate. The swelling split open. Hot fluids gushed across her thigh.

She wailed, fighting to regain control of her body, even as the march of newly hatched nymphs began. As desperate as she was to be free of the gestating creatures, their emergence into the world from within her soft insides terrified her even more.

She cocked her open palm to squash the horrendous procession, but her wrist was stayed by unseen hands.

Girl's great form swam into view.

Howling, Mary tensed every muscle, every fiber, wresting back her power. This was her body. She would not surrender it.

Darkness gathered at the edges of her vision. She blacked out briefly as her blood pressure plummeted, then spiked, then plummeted again.

Still Mary held on. Her eyes rolled upward. The cavern's ceiling seemed to pulse and spin. She sensed Girl behind her, felt her head lifted into the wide cradle of Girl's lap.

Was it Girl? Mary's thoughts collided, splintered, reformed. Or was it the hovering silhouette? Her brain seemed to catch fire as this being, at once Girl and not Girl, held her gaze. Staring into Girl's eyes, on the verge of losing consciousness forever, Mary felt the presence of her young self, from her time at the orphanage—fat, surly, resourceful, strategic, a survivor. That kid deserved more than fifty-seven years of life.

"Help me, Girl." As the whispered words left Mary's mouth, the iron grip she'd maintained on every aspect of her body and life loosened.

She sighed a long exhalation, as if it had been trapped for decades, surrendering to the process her body had already begun, guided by the ancient, cosmic force that propelled all life forward.

And in that surrender, she stopped battling everyone and everything.

She surrendered her mortality and human imperfection.

The anxious need to prove and produce that had fueled her stellar career.

The betrayal and hurt that, brick by brick, had constructed her fortress of one.

She surrendered to being a woman, to the vulnerability and the power.

To the confusion.

To the mystery.

She surrendered to needing other human beings.

To desiring connection.

Three points of pressure warmed Mary's forehead. Once again, Girl had anointed her with the red markings of ocelli.

"That's right, Ms. Mary. Let your babies go."

Mary's body tingled. A strange euphoria overtook her. Her fingernails no longer clawed at the mud. Her heels softened against the jagged rock. The pain was still there, but somehow she accepted it, knew it belonged. She closed her eyes, wondering if some neurochemical cocktail was washing through her, designed by her own biology; or that of the creatures for which she was a host; or some combination of the two. Perhaps the paste with which Girl had anointed her was spiked. But this wondering dissipated as a new wave of creatures climbed from the fissure in her thigh.

Lifting her head from Girl's lap, Mary propped herself on her elbows, mesmerized by the minuscule life-forms emerging from her flesh. A half-dozen trails of ant-size nymphs were winding across her skin.

Some distant part of her mind shuddered with the familiar disgust. But that part drifted further away, grew quieter. She zeroed in on a single baby. It was opaline, in places almost transparent. The glistening body seemingly formed of light. Or water. Two delicate flecks of red hinted at the magnificent crimson compound eyes to come. She marveled at the six finely wrought legs, the glassy antennae trembling in the new air.

A deep ache pierced her heart as the tiny life-form, so vulnerable and exposed, shambled across her thigh. She wept for this innocent, seconds-old being, destined to dwell alone and in darkness for all but a few weeks of its life. What would the world be like when it was next above ground, in seventeen years? Perhaps a nuclear wasteland. A treeless stretch of asphalt. A reclaimed and protected wilderness.

The lone nymph dropped from Mary's body to burrow into the dark earth. Mary turned her attention to the remaining babies, tenderly regarding each one. Nearby, Girl sobbed quietly, her tears intermingled with murmurs of joy.

At least six hundred nymphs emerged into the world and journeyed to the edge of Mary's body. There they leaped, twirling, like leaves in miniature, before gently meeting the ground.

When the last nymph stirred the earth, preparing for its subterranean descent, a vibrant heat surged through Mary. Her vision blurred. Her surroundings melted into amorphous shapes and colors. She felt her *self* dissolve, shifting and reforming.

When next her gaze swept across her body, she perceived a pearlescent thorax, a delicate, segmented abdomen, a pair of neat, digging forelegs.

Mary was the nymph.

The nymph was Mary.

Ensconced in the earth, she methodically sculpted the underground tunnel, a curving chamber five feet in length, where she would spend the next seventeen years in isolation. In the darkness of her abode, she intercepted the flitting, dreamlike transmissions of surrounding mycelia, lullabies to comfort, encourage, and inspire during the passage of more than 6,200 days in darkness. When hungry, she suckled sweet xylem from hair-thin tree roots.

Slowly her body grew. She molted, once, twice, a third and fourth time.

Then the spring evening arrived, when the earth warmed, and a clarion call sounded from another universe, the above ground, summoning her to begin the final weeks of her life. She broke through the earth and froze. Blinded. Awed. On the threshold of a new world inhabited by throngs of winged creatures just like her. After seventeen years in solitude, the sheer number of her brood mates was joyous and terrifying, magnificent and humbling.

She was swept up by the raucous multitude and carried to a nearby tree where she scaled the rough, pungent bark. Her tender nymphal exterior hardened. Soon after, her progress slowed. She gripped the woody surface with all six legs.

All around, cicadas dipped and whirled. Males congregated in choruses, feverishly flexing sound organs to blast out love songs. Females flicked their wings, telegraphing an intimate code of seduction.

A deep joy overtook Mary as the Brood reunited, delighting in itself. Flickering between her human and cicada self, she suddenly understood what Girl and all her foremothers experienced each time they offered themselves to the Brood. A transcendent state of both sacrifice and freedom, of peaceful solitude and intimate communion.

And something she'd completely lost, if indeed she'd ever had it: trust in the wisdom of her body, muscle and bone, breath and blood.

Her forehead warmed. Her attention gathered in her ocelli and then joined with the ocelli of all periodical cicadas in a collective consciousness that spanned time and space. Mary flicked her wings and tuned into the energy triangulating between the three simple eyes. She understood that she was to be shown a vision.

A nursery. Inside, a teenage girl stoops over a crib, tenderly regarding a baby, Mary's infant self. The nursery door flies open and a terrifying, red-faced man shoves Mary's teenaged mother aside and rips Mary from the crib.

The vision shifted.

Mary's grandfather, the red-faced man, deposits Mary and a cash payment with a drug-addicted woman. Mary calls her "Mama," but she is really Mary's aunt. She sees the woman's yellowed skin, smells the odor of her failing body as she drinks and drugs herself to death. Bewildered and terrified, Mary is shunted to another relative, a man she'll remember as her foster father. She endures his humiliations until she turns five and the state of Virginia delivers her to Saint Agnes.

The vision shifted once more.

Present day. Charleston, West Virginia. The front porch of a stately home. An elderly woman rocks in a wicker chair, her strong cheekbones and hazel eyes the mirror image of Mary's.

The woman's soft gaze fixes on some distant point, even as her children and grandchildren chat and play all around her. The woman, Mary's mother, is engaged in a well-worn contemplation, the whereabouts of her lost daughter.

Her mother still lived and still loved her. The Brood had gifted her this knowledge. Mary's awareness returned to her cicada self, still housed within the hardened shell, clutching the tree bark.

A series of convulsions rippled through Mary's insect body. The ferocious bucking continued until the hard chitin at her thorax split open. She rose from the amber shell, headfirst, crimson eyes blazing. Her body followed, dense and white, like living marble. Finally, the surprise liberation of her wings, a graceful unfurling, shifting from ivory to gold and, finally, to the orange-tinted marvels that would spirit her away from the husk of her old self.

While she rested, her exoskeleton ripened from white to black, with shimmers of emerald. She tuned in to the riotous orchestra of cicada sound now swirling around her. One strain rose above the rest:

Oweee-oooo. Oweee-oooo.

Mary took flight and joined the fray.

Again her surroundings blurred, shapes and colors merging until she was back in the cave in the human body of Mary Whelton, fifty-seven-year-old attorney.

And yet she was not the same Mary Whelton. Not exactly.

Another tremor shook the cave. Dust plumed from the ceiling.

Mary glanced up at Girl. The side of Girl's body was visible through the tatters of her work shirt. The gashes from the three clutches had already reknit themselves into roseate scar tissue.

"You understand now, Ms. Mary? Why I stay here and serve Her In The Cave?"

"Yes," Mary replied.

"It's a whole world. Just as real as the skyscrapers and subways of New York City. And it needs me. I matter to it. Just like those clients and whatnot need you."

"Your mother," Mary said, gingerly drawing herself into a seated position. Mild muscle twitches shook her thigh. "Where did she go?"

"Back to the Brood. Nowhere," Girl said, her voice steady and clear, free of the bottomless need for mother's love that had so agitated Mary. Had that desperate yearning ever truly been there?

Girl turned her luminous face to a nearby rock formation. Which was not a rock formation, Mary realized. Through the thick amber mantle, Real Mother hunkered, eyes shut as if in peaceful sleep, hands clutched to her chest in a fetal self-embrace.

A groan sounded from deep in the earth, rising through the warren of mining tunnels below the cave. A final rumble shook the cavern. Then absolute stillness. Dust winked in the warm glow from the kerosene lamp.

"She is healed," Girl breathed from her lotus position on the rock. "The poking and prodding. The taking. It's done."

Girl turned to look at Mary. The oily sheen of Pure Pond was gone, the water now clear and clean. Slowly, Mary got to her feet, stepped into the water, glided toward the center. She dunked her head, washed her hair and face. Hesitantly, she brushed her inner thigh. Her fingers found warm skin, unbroken and textured with scar tissue.

"Girl," Mary said. "I'm ready to go home."

Chapter 17

From the deck of her concrete-and-glass island home, Mary gazed upon the sea, dark waves ignited by the glow of sunset. A lone sailboat glided along the horizon.

She ran her fingers through her still damp curls, quelling her annoyance as she spoke to her assistant on the phone. "No, Michael. I'm not joking. My car was stolen. And yes, I'm fine."

"Jesus. Do you need me to report the theft to the police?"

"All taken care of."

"You filled out a form?" he sounded incredulous. "But you hate dealing with bureaucracy."

She brushed her fingers along the ridged scar tissue of her inner thigh. "I rose to the occasion."

Actually, she had refrained from reporting the theft. Even a cursory police investigation had the potential to open a line of inquiry and personal exposure in which she had no desire to participate. She'd rather eat the loss than endure that ordeal.

"You're back day after tomorrow?" he asked.

"I'm going to extend. Take a leave of absence." She held off telling him that she had no idea when or if she'd be coming back. She needed time to better understand what the hell had happened, and who she was in its wake.

"But the MaxFauna case—"

"—will go on without me. Ian will be lead attorney. I'll be available for consult."

Which they will sorely need, Mary thought. Especially since she had funded an anonymous philanthropic grant that would be awarded to the star witness, the MaxFauna engineer with the chronically ill child. The witness would now be free from any pressure to bend or exaggerate the truth. The facts about MaxFauna's corporate culture and the accuser's claims would be brought to light. It would be up to the jury to decide.

"Next item, Michael. I want to file an adverse possession claim for a friend. A small plot in eastern New York."

"You have a friend who's a squatter?" Again, he sounded incredulous.

"Any other intrusive and inappropriate questions I can answer for you?"

"I'll get it taken care of."

"At the same time, she'll be processing a name change. To Kallie Dale Woods."

At Mary's suggestion, Girl had chosen her new name during the fifty-mile drive from the cabin to the Avis car rental.

Initially Girl had hemmed and hawed. "Already got a name. You use it plenty," she'd said, drumming the steering wheel.

"Girl is more of an omission than a name," Mary had replied. "We'll be pulling together paperwork for the deed for your land. Why not take the opportunity to give yourself a real name?"

By mile twenty-five, as the Adirondacks galumphed along the horizon, Girl had agreed.

"Kallie," Girl said, blushing profusely.

"Kallie," Mary repeated. "It's good." The name had a simple strength and guilelessness that perfectly suited Girl.

Kallie went on to describe a hazy memory of another Kallie, long ago. A kind woman, with a warm, worn complexion and calloused hands. "Maybe my grandmama."

She had also requested that Mary "put Mr. Dale in there too," in memory of the hapless insectophile who'd stumbled into his own death at Real Mother's hands.

"Woods," as far as Girl knew, was her actual surname. "Least it's what Mama used to give if somebody asked."

Michael had his work cut out for him. If there had ever been a birth certificate, it was long gone. And remarkably, Girl had driven her entire adult life without a driver's license, keeping to a small circuit that involved mostly rural back roads. If needed, Mary still had a few favors to call in.

Mary bid Kallie farewell in the car rental's near-empty parking lot. "I'll mail this back to you," she said, nodding at the work shirt billowing around her in the early summer breeze. Her filthy silk blouse and suit jacket were now ashes in Kallie's woodburning stove. The Fendi purse, however, was tucked beneath her arm, wallet and cell phone inside. Her laptop was with her as well, recovered from the cab of Real Mother's truck, though Mary's luggage was gone, either hauled off with the Mercedes or hocked.

"Keep it. Shirt's nothing compared with what I visited on you," Kallie said. "I'm sorry, Ms. Mary. Truly."

As Mary held Kallie's wide-eyed gaze, surreal images of the past two weeks flickered through her mind: Kallie's terrifying displays of hurt and anger; the dark confines of the root cellar; the swarming cicadas implanting eggs into her flesh; the fearsome apparition of the hovering silhouette.

And in that moment, Mary, holder of myriad lifelong grudges, forgave the woman who'd kidnapped and tortured her. The gesture was irrational and unwarranted. Even insane. And yet, as Mary gripped the rusted frame of the truck door, she felt a freedom unimaginable to the Mary Whelton of a few weeks ago. The memory arose of her cicada self, escaping the dead husk that no longer served, wet wings unfurling, the world made new; and the old Mary, a composite of hurts mortared with vengeance, falling away to reveal her true self, the Real Mary, capable of this extraordinary forgiveness.

"Take care of yourself, Kallie Dale Woods." Mary smiled, then moved to slam the door of the battered white truck.

"Wait!" Kallie said. She dug into her corduroys and withdrew a small object. "Mama never got around to pawning it."

Light glinted from Mary's emerald-cut diamond ring, the gift she'd given herself years ago after her first bonus. For a moment, she considered leaving the ring with Kallie. Then she extended her open palm.

"One last thing, Michael." Mary said. The Cape Cod sunset had cooled, leaving pale petals of light on the choppy waters. She cleared her throat. "I know I haven't been the easiest person to work for."

"Excuse me?"

"You've tolerated my rudeness and bullying for far too long. I'm sorry for that."

During the brief silence that followed, Mary lowered herself onto a lounge chair. Her bare feet remained planted on the deck, the wood still warm from the day's heat.

Michael's deep sigh drifted through the phone. "You're dying. Jesus. I'm so sorry. That's why you're removing yourself from the trial."

"No! I'm fine. I just had . . ." She paused, searching for the right words. Her gaze floated upward, where a delicate dusting of stars glimmered. "I had a moment of clarity. It happens."

"Okay," Michael cautiously replied. "Well. Yes, you can be . . . challenging. So thank you. Or rather, I accept your apology."

"I appreciate it. Appreciate you." She hurried on, coughing to mask an upwelling of emotion. "That's all for now. I'll email you the rest of the details."

After hanging up, she disappeared into her laptop, perusing the extensive materials she'd need to hand over to Ian for the MaxFauna case. After a few minutes, she paused to compose a text:

> Forgot one thing, Michael. Next week I'll be out of pocket. Traveling to visit family.

Three dots appeared beneath her text message. Then disappeared. A second later, the dots returned, then faded for good.

A ding sounded as Michael liked her text.

"Impressive show of restraint," she murmured to herself. Her soft laughter rose into the starlit evening.

She turned off her phone and placed the laptop on a small glass table, exchanging it for an object she'd placed there earlier. Smooth wood, exaggerated breasts and behind, feet tapering to a point. Kallie had surreptitiously slipped the figurine into the Fendi handbag. Mary traced the cool contours with one finger. She had forgiven Kallie, but didn't she herself need to be forgiven? To make some kind of amends for a lifetime misshapen by her dogged refusal to face her past?

Perhaps she should be the one to write the tell-all memoir, confessions of Teddy's fixer, how she'd convinced herself that neglect and abuse made her stronger because it was too painful to think otherwise; how that belief required that she diminish or deny the suffering of others, including the women Teddy harassed, pushed out of promising careers, or otherwise hurt; how this emotional and psychological Ponzi scheme had finally collapsed.

Or maybe it would be best to start with a single conversation and let that inform whatever might come next. She picked up her laptop again, navigating to an open tab, the LinkedIn profile for the woman she'd seen at the funeral, the congressman's wife. Forgiveness. Amends. Atonement. Mary's experience practicing these was severely limited. She'd have to ask him, but her apology to Michael was likely a first for their relationship. Instead of barreling forward with a plan, pieced together using her old weapons of reason and intellect, maybe she should just listen, notice what was needed, hear what was wanted—if the woman was open to speaking. She had a name too. Leila.

Rising from the lounge chair, Mary padded to the edge of the deck. She drew the figurine to her chest, then rocked back and threw with all her might. The goddess traced a graceful arc through the dusk, then fell into the sea's shimmering embrace.

The Kanawha River gleamed as Mary drove alongside it through Charleston, West Virginia. She checked her lipstick in the rental car's rearview mirror, wondering for the millionth time if her cosmetic enhancements, the lip plumping and the nose job, had greatly diminished her resemblance to her mother. She ran her fingers through her hair, arranging the silver streak alongside her left cheek.

At 498 Slip Drive, she slowed, veering right to park in front of a three-story Victorian with a turret and wraparound porch. She killed the engine and lowered the passenger-side window. July heat blasted the car's interior, even though it was only 10:00 a.m.

She guessed her mother's home was at least a century old. The house could have used a fresh coat of paint. But the garden surrounding the front porch was impeccably maintained, bursting with dahlias in vivid shades of tangerine, fuchsia, and gold, the largest blossoms Mary had ever seen. In contrast to the lively family scene of her vision, the yard and porch were deserted, as were the cracked driveway and ivy-covered carriage house. Inside the carriage house, a vintage pickup truck was visible, hood propped open, a greasy cloth folded neatly on the bumper.

After Mary had located her mother's address and phone number, she'd briefly considered calling. But she'd decided not to, drawn to the idea of first encountering her mother in person. Now, after climbing the front porch and ringing the bell several times, the idea seemed romantic and impractical.

She returned to the car, deciding to wait. If no one showed up in the next half hour, she'd try calling. As she slammed the car door, a horn blasted from behind. She whipped around to find a Jeep edging slowly toward her back bumper. The driver looked to be in her midseventies. She wore sunglasses and a tennis visor. She laid on the horn once more, pointing to the river side of the street, where a dozen or so cars were parked.

After an apologetic wave, Mary reparked the rental across the road. She wiped her palms on her thighs, locked up the car, and started toward her mother's house. She expected to see the Jeep parked out front, but it was now in the driveway. The woman climbed from the driver's seat, a tennis bag and racket slung from one shoulder, and made her way up the walkway to the porch.

"Excuse me," Mary called from the sidewalk.

The woman paused, one tennis shoe perched on the bottom step. Beneath her short white skirt, her legs were still lean and muscular, the result, Mary guessed, of a lifetime of tennis. The woman gave a cursory wave toward the river and the rows of cars. "Ferry tour office is over there. No idea what time the next one leaves."

The woman continued up the steps. Mary raised her voice, almost shouting in her desperation to bypass the lost decades and reestablish some connection, any connection, even one initiated by annoyance. "I'm looking for Elizabeth Ashby."

The woman froze. Slowly, she turned to face Mary, raising her sunglasses to rest atop her bobbed gray curls. "I'm Liz," she said, unshouldering the tennis bag and dropping it to the porch. Her eyes met Mary's, hazel to hazel.

"I'm your daughter. Mary Whelton."

The woman was quiet, her eyes never leaving Mary's. Then, her face lit up with such an unguarded display of relief and joy that Mary couldn't help but smile. When Mary reached the porch, the two women clasped each other's shoulders.

"Spot of bourbon?" her mother asked.

Liz's kitchen was cozy and well appointed. She buzzed across the creaking wooden floor, cabinets banging, as she assembled cheese, black walnuts, apple butter, and warm toast. Mary sipped coffee spiked with bourbon from bone china while peering through a wall of windows overlooking a sprawling backyard. Purple and white petunias bordered a brick-paved patio with the largest wooden picnic table Mary had ever seen. A Big Wheel and bicycle with training wheels lay haphazardly in the grass.

"I'll be just a minute," Liz said, sliding the platter of food to the center of the table before heading upstairs.

Mary stared at the beadboard ceiling, tuning in to her mother's footfalls moving from room to room. An irrational fear arose that all at once she'd hear silence, that this woman who shared her hazel eyes, long gait, and brusqueness might dissolve into the ether. When the footfalls reversed, descending the carpeted stairs, she unclenched her coffee cup, suddenly aware of her overzealous grip.

Liz reentered the kitchen, a faded pink shoebox under one arm. The cardboard was stamped with a department store name in gold cursive. She tucked into the chair opposite Mary and placed the box between them.

Earlier in the front hall, when Liz had asked how Mary found her, Mary had concocted a story of recently recovered orphanage records aided by her own extensive network. How could she even begin to describe the vision she'd seen in the cave? Even Mary found herself questioning its reality.

But the reality was right in front of her, stirring honey and bourbon into hot black coffee. As the pendulum of a dark-paneled wall clock marked time, Liz withdrew a black-and-white photograph from the shoebox. A young man in greasy overalls smiled at the camera, his arms plunged to the elbows beneath the hood of a fifties convertible.

"Your father. I was a sucker for a pretty face. Still am," Liz said. "I'd just turned sixteen." She tapped the car in the photo. "My birthday present. A Ford Thunderbird. Daddy had fallen out with his usual mechanic and so brought the car across town for a final inspection before buying it. Your father, Joseph, worked in his father's auto-repair shop. He also gave driving lessons on the side. Two driving lessons and one splendor in the back seat later, you were in my belly."

Liz ran a neatly trimmed fingernail along the rim of her cup. "I was five months into the pregnancy before I knew what was happening. Can you believe that? I was clueless about human reproduction. For a while, I managed to conceal the pregnancy as weight gain, with the help of Mama. My older brother, your uncle, had already left for college. But the time came when we had to tell Daddy."

Her hand fell from the crisply ironed tablecloth. Mary imagined her absently rubbing her belly.

"God bless Mama. She convinced Daddy to keep you. Drummed up a cover story for the town noseys. A faraway cousin died in childbirth. Left behind an infant who my parents would adopt. That sort of thing. But shortly after your birth, Daddy found out who your father was and the deal was off."

Liz went on to describe the exact sequence of events revealed in Mary's vision, with all its traumatic details, ending with Liz's father absconding with infant Mary into the night.

"All these years on your own. No family. No mother," Liz said. A tear budded, full and bright, then spilled down her cheek. "It must have been so hard for you."

"I made it through," Mary said. "I did okay." She slid her untouched napkin across the table and waited as her mother dabbed her eyes.

"I suppose Joseph was from the wrong side of the tracks?" Mary asked.

Liz shook her head. "Wrong side of the cross. Your father was Catholic. We were Protestant. The country was moving on from anti-Catholic attitudes. But Daddy wasn't ready to move with it."

Tentatively, Liz reached out to Mary, her warm, dry hand cupping Mary's own. "Daddy grew to regret it," she said. "It was the great sorrow of his life. I forgave him. Eventually. But I never let him forget it."

Mary caught the shadow of anger in Liz's voice.

"He spent years looking for you. We both did. Hired a PI. Everything. But after social services got hold of you, a flood destroyed the offices and all of the files. It was as if you vanished."

Mary drained the last of the spiked coffee, then waited while Liz refilled her cup. "No bourbon this time. I'm a bit of a lightweight."

After Liz topped off her own cup and refitted the cap on the whiskey bottle, her eyes darted up Mary's arms and across her linen blouse. Mary could feel her mother's curiosity, the urge to let her gaze linger, a yearning to familiarize a stranger who was yet her closest living blood relative.

Mary felt the same longing.

"Daddy tried to make it up to me," Liz continued. "Offered to send me abroad. Pay for an Ivy League education or set me up in business any place I liked. But in the end, I decided to stay in Charleston."

"And raise your family." Mary nodded, picturing the adult children and grandchildren from her vision.

"Oh no. You were the first and the last."

"But your grandkids." Mary gestured to the bikes in the backyard. A long-haired calico had appeared and was now sniffing the handlebars of the Big Wheel.

"Grandnieces and nephews. Eight of them. And in some ways their parents do feel like my own children. But you are an only child, Mary. I could never bring myself to have another."

Liz fell silent. The wall clock's soft peal sounded eleven times.

The depth of their shared loss washed through Mary, unanswerable, irreconcilable, never to be regained or amended. And yet, this same loss bound them.

"No children. So then why did you stay in Charleston?" Mary asked.

"Just in case you ever made your way back." Again Mary felt the gentle squeeze of her mother's hand. A knot rose to her throat as she took in this extraordinary piece of information. All these years, someone had been considering her, keeping her in mind, holding her in their heart. It was breathtaking and shocking all at once.

Liz fell back against the delicately carved antique chair. Her arms circled her narrow ribcage. The sleeves of her tennis shirt hitched up, revealing a patch of mottled skin. Mary's studied glance quickly found another small eruption winding from the back of Liz's neck.

"Psoriasis," her mother said, following Mary's gaze.

Mary lifted her sleeve to reveal a new bloom on the pale skin of her inner arm. Whatever curative effect she'd experienced while playing host to the gestating cicadas had worn off.

"Me too." Mary replied, surprised to find herself smiling.

Later that night, Mary awoke, startled by a bright light. A faint sound—a gentle, pulsing drone—seemed to surround her. But when she removed her earplugs, she detected only silence.

Bleary-eyed, she glanced around the unfamiliar space. Then she remembered—she was in Charleston, in Liz's guest room.

The bed was within arm's reach of the window. Moonlight streamed through the glass, spilling across the white quilt. Liz had advised her to draw the blinds, since a full moon was forecast. But she'd forgotten, falling into bed and dropping immediately into an exhausted sleep. She reached for the pull cord, catching sight of the yard below with its patio, long picnic table, and children's toys. Earlier in the evening, Liz had offered to bring the rest of the family together over the coming weekend, Mary's uncle and cousins, maybe even the grandnieces and nephews.

"Something simple. But only if you're up for it. There's no rush." Liz had smiled.

Mary had hesitated, both intrigued and terrified. What if she didn't like this group of strangers with whom she shared genetic material? Or vice versa? Would sticky-fingered children crawl into her lap? She imagined herself conversationally adrift amid the familial chitchat that took years of close connection to develop. What would she contribute—her roster of past sexual harassment cases? The details of her Paleo diet? In the end, she'd thanked Liz and asked for time to think it over.

Lifting herself to her elbows, she worked the blind's cord back and forth, trying to hide the bright light. "Come on," she muttered, then froze. In the center of the quilt, perched on her thigh, was a perfectly preserved cicada shell. Though instead of the usual translucent amber, it was rendered cool and silvery by the moonlight. Where had it come from? Kallie might have smuggled another memento into her belongings, but it was hard to believe the fragile husk could have survived the jostle of Mary's journey intact.

She plucked the shell from the bedspread and cradled it in her palm. A split ran down the upper portion, the escape hatch where the creature had burst forth from its wingless armor before joining the wild and woolly tumult of its brood mates. The vision from the cave returned, the experience of inhabiting the body and life of a cicada. How bold her cicada self had been, plunging into the lawless communion of teeming insects—a dynamic, messy, unpredictable chaos. Yet somehow she'd known what to do, instinctively partaking in the joyful fray. Astonishing.

She placed the shell on her bedside table and wrenched the cord once more, this time successfully. In the darkened room, she drifted into an easy sleep, but not before deciding to borrow a pair of jeans from Liz for the coming weekend. Denim was a durable material, perfect for wooden picnic benches and any small, sticky hands she might encounter.

Acknowledgments

I have many people to thank for the metamorphosis of *The Brood* from germinal idea to full-winged publication. Thank you to my husband, Gary Rabinowitz, for your never-ending belief in me and for keeping me laughing and hopeful at every stage of my writing journey. To my amazing mom, Linda, and my siblings, John, Will, Lily, and Lance, for your love and encouragement. To my dear departed cousin, Perch, to whom this book is dedicated. You were right about Mary.

Thank you to my agent and friend, Jeff Ourvan, for your excellent suggestions on the manuscript (especially Mary's final experience in the cave) and for getting *The Brood* into the right hands. To Alexandra Torrealba of Thomas & Mercer for being haunted by this story, and to Ali Castleman, Miranda Gardner, Katherine Kirk, Jenna Justice, Heather Buzila, and the rest of the team for your enthusiasm and diligence—and to Caroline Johnson for the incredible cover art! Special thanks to my developmental editor, Audra Figgins. Your thoughtfulness, insight, and expertise polished *The Brood* into a gem of a scary story. I am a better writer for having worked with you.

Much gratitude to Heather Siegel for our two-person writing workshop that led to the first draft of this book and kept my mind and spirit afloat during the pandemic. To Nitza Wilon and Dawn Rebecky, who got my wheels turning with discussions of women filmmakers and the effectiveness of the horror genre for exploring uniquely female experiences and anxieties. Thanks also for being early readers. To artist and friend Jamin London Tinsel for laughter and commiseration on the sometimes strange experience of being in a body and the many transformations we undergo as women. Our shared sensibility influenced this story. To Mary Minges, for being an early reader, for sharing your psychological expertise as I developed my characters, and for your fierce belief in this book. To Brenda Mehl, for inspiring me with your sense of wonder and curiosity.

My heartfelt appreciation for my early readers: Sallie Sanborn, Josh Tyson, Lara Tyson, Sarah Key, Jeremy Goldstein, Carinn Jade, and Judy Karp. Your willingness to navigate early versions of this story guided me toward the final draft. To Jay Rosner, for sharing your wealth of automobile knowledge so the car crashes rang true. To Paul and Heidi Leventhal, for hosting us in Pennsylvania during the emergence of Brood X, my one and only real-life encounter with periodical cicadas.

Thank you to the periodical cicada enthusiasts and scholars who keep the rest of us informed about these charming creatures. I consulted their work when creating the "special" brood for my story. Any mistakes with the nonfantastical characteristics of the cicadas are my own.

I found the below sources especially helpful:

Books by Gene Kritsky: *Periodical Cicadas: The Plague and the Puzzle* (2004) and *Periodical Cicadas: The Brood X Edition* (2021).

Samuel Orr's beautiful short film (viewable on YouTube), *Return of the Cicadas*.

The excellent info-rich website cicadamania.com, created by Dan Mozgai.

The scientific article "An Augmented Wood-Penetrating Structure: Cicada Ovipositors Enhanced with Metals and Other Inorganic Elements," (Lehnert et al. 2019).

I am supremely grateful to researcher Matt Kasson, who was kind and generous in replying to a total stranger's email inquiries about fungal masses, ruptured cicada abdomens, and the amazing scientific article by him and his colleagues, "Psychoactive Plant- and Mushroom-Associated Alkaloids from Two Behavior Modifying Cicada Pathogens," (Boyce et al. 2019). I took the liberty of having my character Dale speculate about one of the article's research findings, the discovery of psilocybin in cicadas infected with *Massospora levispora*, though the novel's timeline is six years before the article was published and the presence of psilocybin was not considered a possibility prior to the groundbreaking research of Matt and his colleagues.

Lastly, to the red-eyed, winged wonders themselves. Forgive me for the creative license I took with your already extraordinary behavior and biology. You are marvelous creatures just as you are.

About the Author

Rebecca Baum is a novelist, ghostwriter, and content marketer. While her ghostwriting has served founders of global nonprofits and mission-driven businesses, Baum wades into the wonderfully troubled waters of horror with her novel *The Brood*. Her prior book, *Lifelike Creatures*, was longlisted for the Crook's Corner Book Prize Foundation's 2021 best debut novel set in the American South. A native of rural Louisiana, Baum feels she has almost earned the right to call herself a New Yorker after more than twenty-five years in the city. She lives in Greenwich Village with her husband and favorite karaoke partner, Gary.